STORM CRAZY

Destiny Paramortals #1

LIVIA QUINN

The Livia Quinn Writes blog *is a no-drama place where you can get book links, comment on posts and read excerpts. Do come by.*

Praise for Destiny Paramortals

"My new favorite series!" "Okay, I'm hooked, Give me, give me some more!!!" "A bit of magic, a lot of fun and a budding romance!" "Tempest Pomeroy is the best new paranormal heroine of the year!" "Walk don't run to the buy button." "Destiny. . .is like a mini-vacation from the real world."

Books by Livia Quinn

Author Note

You never know when inspiration will hit. When we moved to the south from D.C., I experienced some of the worst weather of my life with tornados walking the Interstate in the middle of the night. Then came Katrina and Gustav. Is it any wonder I gave my heroine, a Tempestaerie, control over weather forces? Though the series is paranormal it embodies some of elements I love in my own life, the rich settings of Louisiana, my experiences as a rural carrier, quirky people and events. There are always themes of family, love and community. I hope you enjoy the series. Jack and Tempe have a lot to learn. Enjoy the ride. . .

The Livia Quinn Writes blog *is a no-drama place where you can get book links, comment on posts and read excerpts. Please come by.* Sign up for my newsletter to receive updates and deals or follow me on Bookbub

As they say in my favorite escape. . .
Caide Mile Failte', A hundred thousand welcomes. *Livia*

liviaquinn.com

Welcome to Destiny, or should I say Middle Earth...

I'm Sheriff Jack Lang. After an exciting career as a Navy pilot, Destiny seemed like the perfect place to settle down - safe, sane and secure, but that ship sailed when I met Tempest Pomeroy - sexy redheaded mail lady and trouble magnet. Tempe never fails to test the limits of my patience or the law. Every time I think it's the last straw, up pops another haystack.

My name is Tempest Pomeroy, and my human job is delivering the mail. I'm also a Paramortal like my family, or I'm supposed to be. If I didn't have a few little talents, I'd think I was adopted. To say I was having a bad day would be like saying Katrina dropped a little rain on New Orleans. My brother's genie bottle is missing, my mother's AWOL, and the sheriff and my ex-lover are squaring off like yard dogs staking a claim over a poodle. I am no one's poodle. I've denied my heritage for most of my life but all this chaos is a sign of my quickening Tempestaerie power.

Oh, and the sheriff? He thinks he's settled in a normal, quaint small town—like Mayberry?! We'll see how that turns out... Things better settle down soon, 'cause I'm about to go...*Storm Crazy*.

Chapter 1

There's wisdom on the wind, and power.
Think about it.
The same breeze that ruffled your hair
this morning
whipped the soccer player's shorts
in Spain yesterday
and guided the lightning bolt
from Zeus' fist
millennia ago.
Aurora Boreal

TEMPESTAERIES ARE OFTEN DESCRIBED WITH WORDS LIKE *"quirky, erratic... dysfunctional."*

TEMPE

Zeus' holey boxers! I'd known this would happen, but why now?

Why today of all days? I leaned against the heavy oak mantle, shoulders sagging suddenly, and studied the clearly delineated blank space in the dust, the exact shape of my brother's amphora—that's "genie bottle" to you mere-mortals.

My baby brother hadn't come home last night—for the first time since our little *chat*.

A month ago I'd have been calling his cell, taking a detour from my mail route to locate him, or if worse came to the *very* worst, calling our mother, Phoebe, to find out if she'd seen him. But that was before River and I had a *discussion* about what he called my "embarrassing over-protectiveness". As a result, I promised not to leap to dire conclusions when I didn't hear from him for a day or, he insisted, two. Since then I'd been hands-off, and spectacularly "un-protective".

Okay, so he's not my *baby* brother. He's only six years younger than me, and he runs his own contracting business, but I've practically raised him since he was four.

Was he testing me, I wondered, as I took the stairs to the slave quarters of our antebellum home, each one hundred and fifty year old step creaking under my weight. River and I are in the process of remodeling the old house, but each project has to take a back seat to my delivery job for Universal Mail and River's construction jobs, not to mention our shortage of funds.

I rapped firmly on his door as I have nearly every morning of his life.

"River! You up?"

Before I turned the knob to his apartment I sensed the lack of his Djinni force. The tidy bed confirmed he hadn't slept here last night. I was tempted to break our agreement right then and call his cell, but I'd heard him loud and clear, "What am I supposed to do, carry you with me when I decide to have sex with a woman?"

I sooo didn't want to go there. Of course, *that* had been his intention.

I couldn't afford to be late for work on EVAL Monday, so I scratched out a benign note, *Call me when you get in*, had second thoughts, grabbed another piece of paper and wrote, *Pizza tonight?* I sped down the stairs, plucked my keys from the counter and stepped through the front door onto the veranda.

Thunder gave a long low grumble in the South. As soon as I heard it I stopped, turned my face up to the sky. My heart rate slowed. My feet itched to sink into the wet grass, to plug into the fresh energy of the approaching storm. I stood for a moment feeling the wind's intimate caress, inhaling the sweet fragrance of the rain as it drizzled down my cheek. The cool wind lifted my hair with loving fingers. If my nature were feline, I'd have been purring.

But duty called, so I plucked the soggy newspaper from the driveway, got in my truck, and headed to the postal center. The temperature was starting to drop as the cold front advanced. There were sure to be weather consequences.

Hot, cold; moist, dry; calm, blustery. These seasonal disputes create a smorgasbord of ionic imbalances. For a Tempestaerie like me, wind is *menori*, the Breath of Life, and that smorgasbord—the fuel. It can manifest as a mild zephyr, or a full on weather disaster, like Katrina.

I'm also a Paramortal, a consequence of the ancient bond forged between the supernatural species to ensure peace and defend the weak.

At least, that's how it's supposed to be. If I didn't have a few little *talents*, I'd think I was adopted. You've heard that old song, "Cry Me a River"? Well, my emotions need to be running pretty high to produce even a trickle from a spigot.

If you look in the Paramortal dictionary, Tempestaeries are often described with words like "quirky, erratic... dysfunctional." No kidding, there might even be a picture of my family— if you could capture a Djinni on camera.

"Functional" would have described my family *before* Daddy died, before Mother became too preoccupied with her lifestyle to care for her children. Before I was left to raise my baby brother.

My name is Tempest Pomeroy. Yeah, Tempest and River. Bless mother's cliché lovin' heart. I'm just grateful we didn't wind up as Thunderclap and Snowflake, Black Cloud and Little Sprinkle, or Flash and Flood. With my hair—a bright copper streaked with rainbow hues—I'd have been Flash.

Back in the day, Paramortals intentionally mingled with human society, so it would be less traumatic for humans to accept our existence on those rare occasions when one of us is exposed inadvertently. Imagine how an unsuspecting meremortal would react if he knew the local bartender was a vamp, or the popular ambulance tech, a Dinnchensha. That's how a budding storm "witch" like me became a mail carrier.

A few humans suspect we live in their midst, but we try to keep the magical weirdness to a minimum—let them think of it as "quirkiness."". We don't just slap them upside the head with the truth, unless the human in question needs an attitude adjustment, or we're having a particularly bad day.

Like today—*EVAL* Monday, the first of seven days when the mail service re-certifies each carrier through an intense pressure cooker of counts, inspections and evaluations. We call it EVIL week because of the harsh, sometimes unfair scrutiny involved. If you fail to re-cert, one of the hovering substitutes could take your job quicker than you can say, "You've got mail".

The day was already looking like a seven on the EVIL crapola meter. My supervisor, Calvin Beck stood in the middle of the parking lot, scanning each carrier's progress and timing us with a stopwatch. "Do not spend company time organizing your packages," he yelled at the top of his lungs. "Get loaded and get out of here." Of course, if we didn't organize our loads, we'd find ourselves written up for not returning to the dock on time. And Beck knew it. The upcoming Mardi Gras holiday meant the mail was especially heavy.

"You just want to skew the results in management's favor, Beck," I said, already thinking ahead to my first deliveries, and hoping I wouldn't be chosen for a driver observation.

He ignored me and directed his next command at the new carrier who was applying the magnetic warning signs to the sides of her truck. "Barbara, move it. *Good God*, look at the time. You should have already had those signs on your truck. Nine minutes..."

"Ignore him, Barbara," I called. Beck aimed another glare in my direction. *Enough of this*. When he looked off I held my tattooed fingertip aloft, tapped into the moisture-laden atmosphere, and used *menori* to aim those molecules in his direction. Ten seconds later he was banging his stopwatch against his palm. That should do it.

But as usual, he got the last word.

"Time," he called—before I'd finished throwing the last few packages into the truck from my buggy. "Nine minutes, twenty-seven seconds." He scowled at me. "Next time make it eight, flat."

He stepped onto the bumper of Barbara's truck and yelled, "Listen up, people. There will be a back door inspection today when you return at 4:30. Make sure you're compliant with regulations and have no, I repeat, *no* undeliverables. Your scans *will be* monitored."

"Great." We also might be followed on our route, which meant no speeding, no talking on the cell phone, *no rule-breaking*. Too bad my brother wasn't handy. He was the only one who could grant my wish for things to go perfectly.

I secured the remaining packages and arranged the mail so I could climb in on the right side; stretch my left foot over the console and onto the pedal. I cranked the truck, flipped on my flashing light, and beeped the horn. With my left hand on the steering wheel, I looked over my shoulder and backed out of my space. And felt immediate relief.

The first two hours of the job, the part with all the BS—that part—I hate. Being on my own, driving the route, connecting with my customers—most days, it's like being self-employed.

A squeal of brakes interrupted my reverie and the "Toad" stopped his mail truck just short of my right bumper. With a blast of his horn, he leered out the window. "*Ze—Shootfire,* Fritz. You saw me pulling out."

He just leered and blew his horn. "Get those buns out of my way, sweet cakes. I've got mail to deliver." Scanning the area for onlookers, he grabbed his crotch and gave it a tug, "I can always find time for you, though. How 'bout it, Tem*pest*?"

"The way I hear it, that package is too small to even be certified." I heard chuckles behind me as I peeled out of the parking lot, chastising myself for letting him get to me.

Smoothing the furrow between my eyebrows with my middle finger, I considered the unique pressure. It was odd, not *really* a headache, more a rumbling threat. I told myself it was the barometer, the Toad's four-thousandth sexual innuendo, and the worst mail day of the year. It was not because I have a bad temper.

Chapter 2

His tall broad-shouldered physique could have stopped a train.

Tempe

I was back in a good frame of mind by the time I drove up to the little green and white rambler with its meticulously manicured pansy beds, plush green grass, and brilliant white picket fence. One of my little talents is reading auras, and the glow around this house said, "I'm contented. My world is perfect." Newlyweds with a penchant for gardening?

I was half right—*I* was contented when Mr. Newlywed answered the door. His tall broad-shouldered physique could have stopped a train. That is, if the engineer was a woman and she'd been transfixed like me.

He was all lean sculpted muscles and tanned skin above and below the white cutoff sweats. His ripped calves and abs spoke of hours of conditioning. The tendon in his thigh twitched and my eyes jumped to his face—to a broad smile, framed by a thick layer of fragrant white shaving cream.

"Mornin'." His deep voice reverberated, and I expected the vibrations to send the cream on his face sloughing off like an avalanche.

I regrouped, reading the name off the package, "...um, Jordan Lang?"

His light silver eyes crinkled and the moist heated scent of his skin stormed through my blood like whitewater rushing through a narrow canyon. A glistening droplet escaped the snowy cream on his cheeks and glided gracefully down the tanned column of his throat. Zigging and zagging like an X-games snowboarder on the bronze diamond slope, it plunged off his chest gleefully, moguled over finely chiseled abs, and disappeared into the snowy white material at his waist.

Those little water elementals...they have all the fun.

"... sign something?"

Another dollop of white fluff landed on the package I was holding and brought me screeching back to the present.

"The package..." His lips quirked and the crinkled lines around his eyes deepened. He rubbed a white towel over his wet hair, and my eyes went to his biceps which bunched and enticed with each rub. My favorite part of a man's body. "Do I need to sign for it?" he asked once again.

Zeus' bolts! I'd felt a mysterious pull when I looked into his eyes, like nothing I'd felt before, and I'd probably been staring at him like some star struck fan-girl. My face heated, but since I couldn't do like my brother—make a wish and disappear—I relied on routine, handing him the E-pad. "Print your name on the top line, please, and sign underneath."

"Who is it?" a female voice called from the interior of the house. The Missus? A flush of embarrassment hit. I grit my teeth to keep from rolling my eyes. I'd been about to flirt with a man who was *taken. Get me out of here.*

"Just the mail, Sweetheart. I've got it."

He angled in by me, accepted the stylus, and signed in bold, totally unreadable strokes. Must be a doctor—a surgeon with those hands. I could see them performing surgery, stroking a woman's cheek, *moving across my skin, easing upward...* I reached for the stylus and *zap*, chain lightning crackled along my heated nerve endings.

He'd felt it, too; his eyes elongated and flashed silver, focusing on me like lasers. Reality receded and the present went from brilliant and alive to gray, muted. Spinning dizzily, I felt as if my body left the porch and spun off into the clouds...straight up, the dome of the sky sitting around me like a bubble.

I LOOK BACK AT THE CLOUDS AND THE CIRCLING EARTH. AHEAD I see the white line of the horizon; higher I go until everything in front of me is the deep blue of the stratosphere. Beautiful. The weight on my chest is... unbearable. My eyes widen as I flip over into a swan dive, plummeting back to earth, the spinning horizon on my left as mountains come into view. Mountains... in Louisiana... huh!

I endure another dizzying rotation through a massive thunderhead. I hear... I hear—Metallica? rocking in the background and see rooster tails of dark water flying beneath me. I blast skyward like a geyser straight up into an azure sky.

Oohhh... Vapor flares behind me, curling away into the sun. I tilt my head awkwardly. The sky... is upside down. Squinting, I remember, "Don't look at the Sun." Suddenly, The heaviness on my chest is lifted and I stagger, dropping through a cottony carpet of clouds, descending toward black waves, blue flames, and silver green eyes...

"Hey." A hand encircled my wrist.

The green trim of the small porch materialized in front of me. I gripped the rail avoiding his eyes. *What* was *that?*

"Are you okay?" Hunky Doctor asked.

I beat the scanner with my palm to cover my discombobulation. "Uh, sure," I said, clearing my throat. "My... scanner quit," I said, keeping my eyes down on the instrument as I restarted it. I tapped my foot staring at the screen...waiting, waiting...feeling his steamy heat next to me. Finally, it came back online. I scanned the barcode and pushed the package into his hands.

"Have a good day," I called as I dashed down the steps to my truck.

What was with the hallucination? Another one of those symptoms Aurora kept warning me about? I gave myself a mental shake. No time to think about it right now. I had to get to the route, make up some time.

As I backed out of the driveway, I looked over my shoulder. Dr. Jordan made one arresting figure, but the female he had his arm around didn't look much older than seventeen. I sighed. *What a waste.*

I floored the accelerator, my tires squealing sharply as they hit the curb and found purchase on the asphalt.

There are a lot of things I love about my job—the rhythms of it, driving the streets, interacting with my customers. Well, most of them. My customers are like family, and you know how that is—sometimes you wanna kill 'em. If things didn't turn around soon, today might be one of those days.

JACK

"Where did *she* come from?"

Something about my new mail carrier appealed to me, despite the feistiness I sensed below the surface. She was damned sexy, *and* normal. She had a government job. Hell, part of what I found sexy about her was her normal-ness. Normal was great.

It made my decision to put up a mailbox rather than continue to get our mail at work a win-win. Jordie had been responsible for that. She didn't want everyone at the office knowing she was on acne meds, or speculating about her Victoria Secret packages. I was on board with that. So I bought the new mailbox and requested mail delivery, thinking we'd get one of those scruffy old mailmen like the one we had in Memphis.

I groaned as a few sprinkles hit the porch in front of me. Better get my act together and get dressed. Jordie's appointment was in twenty minutes.

As lightning flashed toward town, I pictured the mail lady with the bizarre rainbow hair, the only indication of a possible adjustment in my opinion. What was up with that? We didn't need another weirdo in our life for sure. I'd sworn off women after my first experience with Jordie's mother. It would have been nice to have a date, or a woman, now and then, but it was safer to be cautious.

Even as the image of T. Pomeroy flashed across my mind

again, I affirmed that it was better this way. Right now my job and Jordie were my top priorities.

I'd probably never see her again anyway.

Chapter 3

I sounded like a bad vamp movie.

Tempe

The mailbox at 5 Casino Drive was decorated in cheery green foil with a new red flag standing straight up. Odd, since this customer never put mail in their box. As soon as I slid to a stop the lid flew open.

"Happy St. Paddy's Day!"

An eight inch Leprechaun unfolded himself out of the mailbox and leaned against the opening, one ankle crossed over the other.

I aimed a look heavenward as I held my hand out. He slapped a green painted coin into it with a flourish. It read *Good for a Guinness at Bons Amis*.

He winked, "Dunnae' tell Liam." Liam is the half Churichaun-half vamp bartender at a popular local bar.

Marty's an Imp, *not* a Leprechaun, but he can shift into a variety of forms depending on his agenda. And he always has an agenda. Usually it's to create havoc whenever, wherever and however...thus the term "imp." Marty's *costume* consisted only of a red wig, shiny black shoes and a quivering four-leaf clover positioned squarely over his frisky Imp-hood.

"I don't get it," I said. "I thought imps and four leaf clovers couldn't—"

"It's just polyester," Marty grinned, stroking the clover and waggling his eyebrows, gauging my reaction. The show was about to begin.

"'Ahh, Colleen, where is your green?' "

He placed his hand over his heart and gushed Thomas Daly's poem in his best stage voice,

"'The whole blue vault of heaven is wan grand triumphal arch...

...Fur the whole world is Irish, on the Seventeenth o' March!'"

"Yeah, well, you've just *exposed* yourself as an IMPoster and certainly not Irish. Today is *February* seventeenth. You're a month early." I laughed.

"Wh—" The delight on his face vanished.

Uh-oh, he was miffed. Marty was a might unpredictable. Better smooth things over. "But, Marty, m' lad. You cut a fine Leprechau'ish figure, if I do say so m'self."

He sketched a solemn bow.

"Now, tell me what you're doing here—" A prickle of disquiet sizzled down my neck. Marty was often found in River's company. Did his appearance have something to do with

River? I shouldn't have ignored the feeling I'd had this morning that something was wrong. Sure, River had told me to back off, but he usually let me know when he had something planned.

"River." The name slipped from my lips, and Marty flinched, nearly dropping his cover to expose more than I wanted to see. True to his Imp nature, he ignored me, looking around and straightening the edges of the poly clover.

Sniffing, he said, "I just stopped by to wish you a Happy St. Paddy's Day, Tempest. But as ye pointed out me lack of proper timing, I'll be leavin'."

"Wait—" but the sulky little Imp had poofed.

"Damn. If only Marty were a cooperative sidekick—one that played by Paramortal rules. But then, maybe he did, and I didn't know the secret. If I saw him again, I'd have to figure out a way to make him cooperate.

"...Nothing but a bunch of high paid idiots."

Mr. Jackson's hands shook as he beat the envelope against the hood of my mail truck. The eighty-year old grouch stood around five-three, his body withered from arthritis and bad habits, cigarette stench wafting around him. He'd dyed his comb-over hair black, what there was of it, and his beady eyes looked just about that color. It was pretty creepy.

I sighed and watched him stomp—well, in his case—gimp with attitude in my direction. He attempted to plant his feet firmly in the thick grass, but rocked back and forth on his heels. He lifted his cane, and aimed it at me. It *did* make more impact than his wrinkly index finger.

Glaring he said, "It's not like it was when I worked for the Postal Service, the *real* one. We cared about our job. Now they put it all in order for you and all you do is ride around in an air-conditioned truck and poke it in the box."

I resent that. The last time I had air-conditioning was just before the Chevy turned over her second hundred thousand.

"Yet, here I am again getting mail that's *not even addressed to me*! Like this." He gripped an envelope in his gnarled fingers, shaking it in my face. While I waited for his rant to end, I looked up at the fast moving clouds. Then the sharp corner of an envelope hit my cheek. The old fart had thrown his mail at me.

I scrubbed my face with my hands trying to keep a lid on my temper. I overlook a lot of what Mr. Jackson does out of respect for his age and because he was a carrier for over forty years. "Mr. Jackson, I realize you're frustrated, but you need to calm down."

"Then stop giving me mail that isn't mine!" he screamed. If his purple complexion and the rigid veins in his neck were any indication, he was about to blow a gasket. He started trembling violently as if he were about to have a seizure, and drifted forward over his cane.

Uh-oh.

I slammed the lever into park, kicking packages and mail out of my way, and shoved the door open with my foot. I didn't remember grabbing my cell from over the visor, but as I knelt next to Mr. Jackson, I heard, "911" in my headset and realized I'd pushed the emergency button.

I leaned over to check his airway and listened to his chest. He wasn't breathing.

I tilted the old man's head back and began fast, brief compressions, the way my friend Montana, an EMT, had instructed me.

"911. What is your emergency?" the voice requested in a monotone.

"One, two, three, four...Phineas T. Jackson, 26 Stony Drive. One, two, three, four... Blackwell subdivision...doing CPR."

"I'm sending a unit. Stay on the line."

I sped up the compressions on his frail chest praying I wouldn't break anything.

The dispatcher said in her calm, almost bored voice, "ETA is eight minutes. Can you give me any information for the EMTs?"

Eight...friggin'... minutes. "Mid-eighties...he had some kind of seizure and he's not breathing." Seconds ticked off as I continued to pump his chest. I stopped, put my fingers to his mouth. *Nothing*.

"Oomph," I sat back. He wasn't going to make it. Unless... Maybe there *was* something I could do, but then I'd never actually attempted it. Usually it just happened when things got out of control. Well, not things—me.

Part of the problem was I'd be in clear sight of anyone looking this way from their front yard or driving down the street, but if I didn't try something before the EMTs arrived, he was going to die. I looked around. It had to be now. I wondered if my little zapper would have enough zip.

Mr. Jackson's tirade had miraculously not drawn any attention. The street was deserted. A squirrel bounded onto the road nearby, swished his tail madly and took off toward a large oak. At least he couldn't tell.

Extending my hand out in front of me, palm up, I concentrated, willing the power inside me to obey. Again, nothing. I squeezed my eyes shut tight, grit my teeth, and whispered hopefully, "Come to me."

Blast! I sounded like a bad vamp movie. Separating my index finger, the one with the tiny tattoo-like image on the tip, away from my other fingers, I turned it up toward the darkening sky.

The cells in my body began to vibrate. Like an energy solar panel, *menori* tapped the unstable air and focused it like a laser through the tattoo, accumulating until my head felt like it would explode.

The rumble beneath my feet was the only notice I had of the electric strike that rode straight up my legs, curling in my midsection and crawling swiftly along my right arm to produce my own version... of a 4th of July sparkler, emanating out of that fingertip. Then the sparks changed. Brilliant bolts of crackling white light spit and sizzled in my palm, sending jagged streamers of hot blue fire ten feet into the air. I just gawked.

A car entering a nearby street freed me from the mesmerizing light display. This was different from any of the charging I'd previously experienced. Bigger. Usually it just sort of replenished on its own. Panicked, I looked over my shoulder, and exhaled. So far so good.

Now what? I needed to command the fire in my hand to... what? Before I could say, "Be gone," or "Go thither," the light subsided to a small crackly glow. That was it then.

Instinct took over. I knelt beside Mr. Jackson, placing my glowing index finger against his chest. With a single *szzwaattt*, I zapped him, right in the heart. His chest arched up only the barest of seconds as it met my magical defibrillator, then his body relaxed.

Momentarily deafened and somewhat addled as my faculties came back online, I groped for the pulse in his neck. For a second I thought I'd failed. But then, his tired, smoke glutted organ started beating.

Thank the gods.

Only the slight whiff of burnt flesh remained on the wind. Drained of energy, I swiped the back of my hand across my forehead. That's when I noticed the mark.

"Zeus' rechargeable bolts! That better be temporary."

Centered on the spot where I'd zapped him, a pale image was forming. It looked like a pale, mini version of... well... me.

Chapter 4

Don't let the mere-mortals see you use your magic.

TEMPE

I held Mr. Jackson's wrist while we waited for the ambulance and spoke softly to him, telling him he was going to be okay, until a shadow moved over us, and a hand dropped onto my shoulder. I looked up. Silhouetted against the glare of the intermittent clouds was the broad form of a man, in a cowboy hat.

"Sheriff—I'll take over."

I rose and stepped aside, wondering what he'd seen. In the immediacy of the moment I'd almost blown Paramortal rule number one, *Don't let the mere-mortals see you use your magic.*

His capable looking hands replaced mine on the old man's wrist. He leaned over him and checked his responses. "He's breathing. Go move your truck so the EMTs can pull in."

"Right."

I parked my truck in the driveway adjacent to Mr. Jackson's and ran back to the scene on the right of way. Perspiration was causing the sheriff's white shirt to adhere to his impressively broad shoulders. I heard the ambulance approaching. The driver cut the siren as they turned onto the gravel road, pulling up even with the driveway.

Montana, and her partner, Rafe, one of a few enlightened humans, started unloading equipment next to Mr. Jackson. "We've got it, Sheriff. Tempe," Rafe said.

I caught Montana's eye, tapped my chest with my index finger and pointed discreetly at the prone figure. "He started breathing just before the sheriff arrived."

Her eyebrows rose. "Good thing you were here, Tempe."

The sheriff stood and I saw now that what I'd mistaken for a cowboy hat was actually one of those flannel trooper style hats. He addressed me, pulling a small notebook from his jacket pocket. "Your name, ma'am?"

"Tempest Pomeroy. I'm Mr. Jackson's mail carrier. He was by the road waiting for me."

"Explain."

"As usual, Mr. Jackson wanted to complain about some misdelivered mail. He was out of control, I mean, worse than usual—slapping his letter against my antenna, pounding his cane on my hood. I realized it was over the top behavior even for him when he started screaming, then he threw a letter at me. Before I could get out of my truck, he went face first into the grass."

While the sheriff took notes, I asked Rafe about Mr. Jackson's condition.

"Looks like an MI—cardiac arrest—but he's stabilized. Good job, you two." Closing the back doors on the gurney with Montana and Jackson inside, he stepped up into the vehicle and took off, sirens blaring, lights pulsing once again.

"Okay, Ms. Pomeroy, I have your statement. Give me your address and phone number and you can get back to work." He handed me the notebook.

The bill of his hat shaded his eyes, but I felt him studying me. Suddenly I wished I was wearing something sexier than jeans and a sweatshirt; my hair brushed out, instead of in a ponytail out of necessity; and maybe a bit of makeup?

I sighed. I am what I am. If a guy's looking for a fashion plate, he won't be interested in a woman whose priorities include a delivery job and remodeling a hundred-fifty-year-old house.

He reached for his pen and for the second time that day, I felt a little *zing*, and that weird weightless feeling. Maybe my luck was changing. I really should talk to Aurora about the visions and hormonal blips.

Before things could get awkward, I said, "I'd better go. I'm running behind. Ever since my first delivery this morning, things have gone steadily down hill." I started toward my truck.

"See ya' around, Tempest Pomeroy," the sheriff said under his breath.

"Back 'atcha, Sheriff." I felt his gaze on me all the way to my truck. You gotta love those little pheromones.

I backed out of the driveway, the oscillating light on top of my cab reflecting off his spotless vehicle. As he got behind the wheel I watched the play of strong thigh muscles against khaki and tried to get my mind back on my progress. I had four hours to deliver five hours' worth of mail—without further interruptions.

I pushed the pedal down, my tires slinging gravel. From the look I got in my rear view mirror, a rock had struck the sheriff's brand new SUV.

"*Shootfire.*"

Chapter 5

Hey, Princess, you're a little uptight.

T<small>EMPE</small>

I turned onto Hawthorn Street, and tried River's cell again. On the sixth ring I heard my brother's voice, "You've reached Pomeroy Construction, leave your name, state your—" I bypassed it, threatening him with his life if he didn't call me UDWITM, which he knew as "you don't wanna ignore this message".

So far, it wasn't working. For the first time since I left Harmony, I wondered if I should call the authorities. Now that was an overreaction! I could just hear him, "Back off, 'Mommy'."

I called Montana and asked her how Mr. Jackson was doing. "He's still stable. I see you finally met the new sheriff," Montana said. "Hunky, huh?"

"Yeppers," I said noncommittally. "I met another guy this

morning on my route, new customer—a doctor, I think." I described the man in the green house to Montana, who subsequently dubbed him "Six packs and Shaving Cream."

I laughed. "He wasn't wearing a wedding ring, but you know what they say—when something seems too good to be true... It looked like he was more interested in women half his age."

"At least your radar is tuned in."

"Um...that's not why I called."

"What's up?"

"It's River. He didn't come home last night."

"So?"

I sighed, my hands gripping the mail bundle.

"You are the meddling sister whose brother told her just two weeks ago to back off, are you not?"

"Yes..."

"Tempe, you're having empty-nest-while-still-in-the-nest syndrome. I get that, but River is a man. And hey—Djinni, remember? He can take care of himself."

Grudgingly, I agreed. "Ok, you're right. I guess."

"I'm right, and you should be concentrating on some of what River's concentrating on. How long since you've been on a date?"

An image of Hunky Doctor in sweat shorts intruded and I considered maybe I'd been wrong about the situation. "I think I'm losing you. Yes, you're breaking up, krchh, krrcccchh."

"You're not fooling me, Tempe. See if you can't hook up with that sexy doctor. A roll in the hay wouldn't hurt you a damn bit. See you tomorrow."

I knew she had a point. I hadn't so much as looked at another man since Dylan, though after two years we'd settled into an imperfect kind of friendship.

A couple minutes later I heard, "Call from Freddie. Decline or accept?"

"Accept?" I said tentatively into my headset, and crossed my fingers.

Freddie Taylor was a local handyman—think bull, china shop. When he fixed things without supervision, he usually cost me more than I paid him. Today, he was supposed to be cleaning up the mess we'd made last weekend preparing to install a new tin roof.

An excited Freddie said, "Uh, Tempe...uh—"

Oh, no! Tension settled across my shoulders, and I gripped the steering wheel, as if that could make the news any better. Rubbing my temples where the earlier pounding was turning into a thunder bumper, I asked, "What is it, Fred?"

"Well, you said to wait on the window—"

I squeezed the phone, crossed every appendage I could while driving from my awkward position, and prayed. "I remember. What happened?" I pulled onto the shoulder.

The huge window had been a special order for the wall in the dining room that overlooked the Forge, named for the ancient power cooking beneath it—the locals only knew it as Lightning Bayou.

"Well," his country accent made it sound like *wowl*, "I k-kinda had an accident."

I felt like I'd been sucker punched. A groan escaped before I could stop it.

"I didn't try to put the window in, Miss Tempe. I was breaking up some of that concrete mix we spilled near the back porch and a chunk flew over and hit the window." There was a long pause on the line and what I thought might have been a sniffle. "I'm sorry, Tempe. Do you w-want me to go?" Freddie's voice was soft.

I wanted to wring his damn neck. I should try to find someone else. To say this wasn't the first time Freddie'd screwed up was like saying Katrina caused a bit of flooding in New Orleans. *This* window cost me a month's salary. The first one had met its end when Freddie accidentally hit it with a long piece of roofing tin he was carrying a month ago. He knew as well as I did that I couldn't keep absorbing these losses. But when I thought about letting him go, I imagined his hangdog expression, and remembered he used his handyman funds to provide for his elderly aunt and sister. I'd just have to suck it up... and make sure River was on hand to supervise next time.

You'd think putting a little fear into Freddie about consequences would make him more careful but it only makes it worse. I'd have to dig into River's contracting account this time because we had to have that window. There was a black plastic-covered hole in our dining room wall and I was tired of looking at it.

My headset beeped. I shook my head. It was turning into Grand Central. I searched the street for postal monitors. "Freddie, I have another call. Just clean up around there, and I'll see you this evening. Okay?"

"Yes, ma'am," he said dejectedly.

I pressed the button on my earpiece. "Hello?"

"Is this Tempest Pomeroy?" an angry man on the other end asked.

My first thought was that my check to the Window Store might have bounced. The guy on the other end was on the rude side of professional. "Who's this?"

"Max Rutledge. Your brother made me cancel another job to have my men here at six this morning. You can tell him I expect him to pay for our time. It's not my fault he can't keep his business straight."

Fear slithered through me. 11:50 and River hadn't made it to the site. "Have you tried his cell phone?"

He made an irritated huff. "Since seven-oh-five this morning; all I get is voicemail."

"And you left a message?" River would never ignore a call from one of his contractors.

"What do you take me for—"

What was it with the men in my world today?

"Mr. Rutledge, please...I've been trying to get a hold of him myself. You have to admit, it isn't like River not to show up. I'm truly sorry for the inconvenience; he wouldn't expect you to hang around indefinitely."

Max Rutledge sighed through the phone. His next words were lower, "Well, I just assumed." He cleared his throat. "One of the framers said, hmm, well, he saw him leavin' the Wasted Turtle with a woman last night, and they looked pretty... chummy, if you get my drift."

So he *had* been with a woman. "Do you think I could talk to that worker?"

If River had been at the Turtle last night, it would explain why he hadn't come home, but *not* why Mr. Responsible hadn't shown up for work and wasn't answering his cell phone. *Easy, Tempe.* Maybe he'd overslept. It was unusual for River to sleep in on a workday, but it happens to the best of us, especially after a night...*uhn, not going there...*

"I sent the crew to another job." Rutledge's tone sounded almost apologetic, "but here's his cell."

I wrote the number down and acknowledged the contractor's apology. "I completely understand, Max. I'll let you know when I hear from him."

As soon as I hung up, my phone rang *again*. If I hadn't been afraid it might be my brother, I would have ignored it. I pressed the button. "River?"

"Penelope. What's up?"

"Dylan." More mini-pheromones. Unwanted ones. What did he want?

Dylan is an independent investigator and my ex-lover. It had been over between us for two years. I was somewhat embarrassed that since we'd become friends again, I enjoyed a warm feeling whenever he called me one of those "P" names. I'm pathetic.

Before you ask, the "P" names are a mystery to me as well, but they remind me of the happy times between us. *And* also, the annoying ones. Honestly, it was hard to remember a time when he'd actually called me by my name. *Huh*.

"Where are you? Did you see me pull over to use my cell phone?"

"Hey, Princess, you're a little uptight. *Evil week getting you down?*"

"Yeah, that's it," I said. Add to that multiple strange encounters with alphas this morning—count 'em—two postal employees, a sexy doctor, a mad contractor, a hunky lawman, a wayward Imp, and the one on the other end of my phone, my ex-lover.

"What do you want, Dylan? I'm behind."

"Uh-huh, in a hurry. And yet you're sitting on the side of the road..."

I looked around.

"Your words," he reminded me.

"Dylan, can we do this later? I need to deliver a package." I drove the short distance to Inez Messer's driveway and blew my horn to announce my arrival, *and* so Dylan would get to the point.

"Sorry, babe. I need to ask you about the delivery for Mrs. Karrakas." My teeth ground together. "She's insisting there's a witness you didn't leave the package like you said."

That— "Dylan, we're talking about the Karrakases. It's common knowledge they paid for that villa on the golf course with lawsuits."

"Hey, Petunia, I'm on your side, remember? I just have to get to the bottom of it. Now, run it by me one more time."

It would do no good to argue with Dylan once he got the doggy bone in his teeth. I let out a long noisy, frustrated sigh and recited for the gazillionth time, "Wednesday, 1:05, I pulled up to the house, rang the bell, scanned the package with the *permission to leave* label and left it just inside the open garage. I even sat there rearranging bundles while I waited for her maid to answer."

"Did you see anyone on the street? Kids, services, anybody that might have seen you?"

"No." My interest was piqued. "Why is this such a big deal?"

"The club was worth almost a thousand."

I frowned and pictured that scene in my head again, searching for anything I'd missed, while I tapped my fingertips on the steering wheel. "That doesn't make sense. Why would anyone send something that valuable through the mail and not register it, or at the very least require a signature? Sounds fishy to me."

"Well, don't worry those rainbow tresses. I'm on a job, but I'll be in touch."

I'd heard that one before.

Chapter 6

He was cruisin' for a bruisin'. . .

Tempe

I'd lost thirty minutes on the phone calls from Freddie, Max and Dylan. If things kept up like this I wouldn't get back to the mail center before midnight.

As soon as I got caught up I'd call Phoebe. I dreaded conversations with my mother. Besides, if River had spent the night at her place he'd have shown up for work. And taken his bottle. Then again, he might have called her; they had a better relationship than Phoebe and I did.

I risked using my cell one last time to contact the worker who'd seen River. His service said he was unavailable. I resolved to call River every hour, whether it was against the rules or not.

Like many of my elderly customers, Inez Messer spent the

time between ten and one anticipating the arrival of her mail. Today her anticipation had paid off. I grabbed the registered package and walked up her driveway.

She stood hunched over near the edge of her porch, her eyes bright with child-like energy. Even in her eighties her hair was still mostly blonde. I had seen the photos of Inez on top of her TV. She'd been a Grace Kelly lookalike, with thick blonde hair and gorgeous skin. Her soft pink angora sweater matched the high color in her cheeks.

"Hi, Ms. Inez. How are you?"

"I'm so excited, Tempest. That package is from a girlfriend I went to nursing school with... sixty-seven years ago." Her eyes lit up, making her seem younger than her eighty-six years. She reached for the box and whispered, "We dated the same boy in college—the two-timing slug—both of us ending up old maids."

I hadn't heard that term in a while. "Men are such jerks."

It seemed like that, today at least, not to mention that I'd never had a relationship with a man that they didn't die or walk away. It was enough to give a girl a complex, not that I have one. I kept trying to tell myself that I'd been the one to end it with Dylan...

I stepped onto the porch. "Would you like to see what's inside, Tempest?" Inez asked nearly bouncing up and down on the lounge cushion.

What was another five minutes? "I sure would, Ms. Inez." I knelt down while she ripped into the box with the enthusiasm of a five-year-old birthday girl. *Oops.*

"Is it your birthday?"

"Oh, no, dear. Nancy and I celebrate our friendship each year with an anniversary gift. You see, our fiancée skipped out on both of us. I found out about Nancy when the jeweler had a mix up and we both showed up for the ring sizing. Apparently, that shuckster had paid for the ring already. So, Nancy and I decided to get him back. She broke up with him, then told him she'd lost the ring."

"Good for her. What did he say?"

"What could he say? I think he knew he was cruisin' for a bruisin' if he messed with us. I confronted that cad about the jeweler and bid him good riddance."

I smiled. Her words gave me a hint of what she'd been like back in the fifties. Or maybe the years following her broken engagement had given her that spunk along with the independent streak.

Inez placed the little box on her lap, turned it toward me, and flipped the lid open to reveal a stunning diamond and emerald ring. "It's our reminder that we didn't need a man to have a full life; it's my year to wear it."

She slid the ring onto her left thumb where it dangled like a bracelet. Her smile faltered, the bravado slipping.

I stood, placing my hand on her frail shoulder. "Well, I have to run. Maybe we could dress up one night and go show that stunner off."

"I'd like that."

I made a mental note to do just that. *Soon.*

Inez hugged me briefly. My throat tightened as I hugged her back.

"Tempe, honey," she paused, measuring her words. "Don't use me as confirmation of why your relationships with men haven't worked out. After all, it wasn't your fault your father died, nor his, and not *all* men cheat." She patted my hand. "Sometimes, shit just happens."

I nearly choked as she rose. "I'm going to go call Nancy and let her know I got the ring." She turned back suddenly. "Oh, Tempest, I almost forgot. Have you met that new Sheriff Lang? He is such a hottie."

I coughed. "The sheriff?" I could feel the flush rising on my neck, which belied my next words, "Uh, I hadn't noticed."

As I returned to my truck, I heard, "You will, honey. You will."

Traffic was bumpered up like rush hour in Baton Rouge when I pulled up to Flowers by Dick and snatched my ePad off the dash. Cars, police cruisers, telephone company service trucks, and a bus were packed into the parking lot for Gator's Grub, Destiny's hottest lunch spot.

The package I had for the flower shop was really too big for me to manage, though I'd never admit it to Dick Randall.

"What in the world could a florist need that is this heavy?" I grunted, setting my hip against the side of the truck and struggling to get my arms around the box so I could maneuver it.

"If you asked real nice, I'd help you with that."

Dick stood leaning casually against the front of his shop,

arms crossed, revealing his true intention, to do nothing, and enjoying my struggles. "You should grab a napkin, Dick; the sarcasm is dripping down your shirt," I said through clenched teeth.

Dragging the box off the edge of the pickup, I lugged it slowly up each step as he watched, a mean smirk on his face.

"Swing the door open wide, please."

He followed me into the shop, and I thought, *stay away from me*, just before I felt the pinch on my butt. I whirled. The corner of the box hit Dick in his considerable belly causing me to lose my grip. Ok, so maybe I uncurled my fingers a wee bit. The box upended, slamming down onto the floor.

"Yowww!"

Too bad, Dick's foot was between the package and the floor. Oh, well...

Dick struggled to pull his foot out from under the box. "You bitch! I'm calling the cops."

"Suit yourself," I said. "Meantime, hold it right there while I scan the confirmation." I aimed the scanner at the barcode and heard the bleep as it registered the delivery. "Allllrighty then. Have a good day." I smiled sweetly and started for the door, but it was blocked by a familiar figure.

Not now. Not *now*. I stomped my foot down and huffed out a breath.

"Ms. Pomeroy," Sheriff Lang tipped his hat with a lifted eyebrow that asked, *you again?*

My thoughts exactly. "Sheriff."

Behind me, Dick whined, "Sheriff, I want her arrested for assault."

The sheriff and I both turned like our heads were on swivels and looked at the hulking, red faced slob swaying on one foot at the other side of the four and a half foot package, trying to look mortally injured.

"I assaulted you? You creep!" My temper returned with a vengeance. And when I got mad... Come to think of it, my emotions seemed to be getting the best of me today.

"And you are?" the sheriff asked the flower shop owner, taking his trusty notebook from his pocket.

"Dick—"

"—Head," I finished.

Dick glowered at me. "Dick Randall. Mayor Randall is my brother." He flung those five words at the law officer as if to say, "you might as well haul her ass to jail right now." The sheriff's lip quivered as though struggling not to smile.

"How unfortunate for you," I said.

The sheriff turned to me, his face now carefully stern. "Miss Pomeroy, if you can't restrain yourself, I'll have to ask you to wait outside while I get Mr. Randall's statement."

I wasn't going anywhere while Dick gave his statement. I stomped to the front window and looked at the arrangements in the display.

Flowers by Dick. What kind of name was that for a flower shop anyway? The arrangements in the window were chinzy fabric or plastic, his stamp on each abomination as unique as a criminal's fingerprint. Come to think of it, his idea of art should be a crime. Everything looked like it'd been mass produced in a sweatshop and shipped by the container load. Cheap.

"I was trying to be a gentleman—"

"Oh, puleeze." I spun and caught the mean smile on Dick's face just as the sheriff spun toward me.

"That's it." He waved his hand in the direction of the door. "Out. I'll take your statement when I'm done with Mr. Randall's."

Fuming, I strode out onto the front porch, throwing myself onto the bench by the diner. What I really wanted to do was give ol' Dick a major zap with my Zeus juice. Unfortunately, I seemed to be zapped out. Too bad I didn't catch him elsewhere with the corner of that package.

I sat forward, my shaking hands hanging between my knees, and took two long breaths. It wasn't just my hands. I felt like all the forces of weather my kind influenced were clashing inside me.

Listening to Dick's whining voice from inside, I looked at my watch, and groaned. 12:15. Now, I was at least two hours behind schedule, and I had an Xpress delivery that had to be delivered on the other side of town before 3:00. I might have to ask someone, a supervisor someone, to deliver it. Ugh!

JACK

I went looking for Pomeroy and found her sitting on the bench checking her watch, her foot tapping the porch impatiently. She still hadn't recognized me and the jury was out on whether I wanted her to or not. She could certainly benefit from an Anger Management Class, though Dick Randall would try anyone's patience.

Then there was the call I'd received this morning from a councilman's wife about a missing golf club she claimed her mail carrier, Tempe, had stolen. Sure, I'd just met this carrier today but her being a thief didn't track for me.

"Miss Pomeroy."

She jerked up off the bench like a child's jack-in-the-box, her hand on a cocked hip. "He's lying, you know."

"You didn't drop the box on his foot?"

I almost laughed when she stammered, "Well, yes...er, no... but he wasn't trying to help me by pinching me on the as... butt. If I hadn't had my arms around that package, I'd have given him more to worry about than a dinged toe."

I chuckled. Randall had been goading her. Her emotions were so close to the surface that she was an easy mark for someone like him. "Just the facts, ma'am," I quipped, trying to give her a break but she wasn't helping her case.

"Surely you don't believe that lying—" She vibrated with frustration.

I held up my pad, "Let's start from the top. You got out of your truck..." I moved my pen in a circle.

Her shoulders rose as she looked up at the sky then blew out the rest of her mad. "Okay, but sheesh..." She ran her hands through the dyed strands of her hair. "I am getting so far behind," she said, sounding near tears.

She recounted her version of the events, her animation causing her hair to fly around her shoulders. It was close to how I'd assessed the situation, having seen Randall's type many times over the years, their M.O. being mean arrogance and casting blame like manure. "When it sticks, they win."

"What?" Tempe frowned up at me.

"Just going over my notes," I lied. "Come with me." I led the way back into the flower shop where Dick was sitting on a chair making a fuss over his reddened toe.

He glared at me. "She should have to pay for the doctor's charges—"

"Get over it, Randall. I'm leaving both statements in writing just in case any further incidents should call for a review. Understood?" I won the staring contest, though Randall grumbled under his breath.

"She should have to at least apologize—"

"Like hell," Tempe said. "This isn't the first time you've caused me grief, Dick."

"Oh, no." Dick rose and looked like he wanted to advance, but I was in the way. "We have a *his*tory," he said putting emphasis on the first syllable.

I turned to look at Tempe and met eyes the color of a derecho, the tumultuous teal colored clouds on the edge of a straight-line wind. I felt like the referee between a lightweight and a super heavyweight, and right now... I'd have bet on the storm.

I pointed at the floor between them, and delivered my best glare, the one that works on everyone—except my daughter. "Starting now, the history stops here."

Prolonged silence.

"Are we clear, people?" I pushed.

No answer, but Tempe turned and stomped to her truck. Dick shoved his foot into his shoe and limped around behind the counter.

I stared at the ceiling and counted to twenty. After Tempe spun out of the parking lot, I walked next door to finish my lunch.

Chapter 7

The carrier is the first line of defense.

TEMPE

For the next two hours I made headway. I delivered three certifieds, gave some tourists directions, documented undeliverable pieces, tried without success to run over Mrs. Wilson's crazy tire-biting cur dog, and left my route at two-thirty to catch the Xpress delivery so I could retain some Brownie points with my supervisor.

I still couldn't reach River or Phoebe.

"Perkins," the supervisor on duty answered when I called for permission to leave my route.

"Hey, Richard, just wanted to let you know I'm diverting to Newcastle for the Xpress, then I'll come back to Enchanted Glen."

"Having one of them days, huh, Temp?"

"You heard about Dick?"

"He called Bancroft and complained."

"Great!"

Ed Bancroft was the corporate man in charge of EVAL certifications, and he was looking for any opportunity to trim the budget.

"What did Bancroft say?" I rubbed at the tension creeping across my scalp.

"He told Randall he could always drive the twenty miles to pick up his packages but then he wouldn't get an opportunity to harass you."

"Sweet."

"Yeah well, then he said..." Richard huffed out a sigh, "tell you to be in his office no later than seven o'clock tomorrow morning."

"Blast."

BY THREE-FIFTEEN I'D MADE UP TIME. I TOOK THE CURVE out of Camelot Court and the familiar rhythms of my job became like a delivery dance as I guided the truck with my left hand on the wheel and feathered the fingers of my right through the sun warmed air out the open passenger window. I glided to a stop as something moved in my peripheral vision.

Lancelot, the twelve-foot alligator and Enchanted Glen's bona-fide water hazard, plodded across the fairway behind the Karrakas' house. Lancelot rarely appeared on the golf course during the day, but after living to such a ripe old age in the slew behind the clubhouse, he probably knew the course was closed on Monday.

I watched him slide into the swampy slough on the other side of the third green. I'd been fourteen when the parish decided to cart Lancelot to parts unknown (or supply someone with a gator tag) and fill in the slough prior to the development of the Enchanted Glen Country Club. Environmental activists and "Children for Lancelot" had come out of the woodwork to protest the plan. I thought my slogan was the best —*Without Lancelot there is NO enchantment.*

At the Gator Run stop sign, I looked down the cart path marked by white lines and considered not driving through the loop by the clubhouse since they were closed. Odds were they hadn't left any mail in the box, but I decided to play it safe in case I was being monitored. I drove between a stretch of live oaks toward the stately white building at the head of the circle drive.

Carts were backed up to the side of the building. The parking lot was bare except for the maintenance man's old pickup peeking out from behind a long dumpster, and as I'd expected, the mailbox was empty. I eased forward, glancing over at the front of the building out of habit, and braked.

The door to the clubhouse was partially open. The wind had probably blown it open when maintenance neglected to lock it. I looked at my watch. 3:22. It wouldn't take but a second to check it out.

The carrier is the first line of defense, was the training mantra that rang in all postal carriers' heads. I put the truck in park and cut the engine. Approaching the front door, I called out, "Yo, the clubhouse. Anyone here?"

Yo, the clubhouse? I huffed out a nervous breath.

I pushed the heavy door with one finger. It slid open smoothly, silently. The wind caught it, sucked it closed, then swung it open again exposing the darkness beyond like the hungry maw of some mythological serpent. Okay... no more *Titans* movies for you.

The foyer carried an aura of old money, which seemed amplified by the vacant atmosphere. Mahogany shelves ran the length of the entryway on one side topped by a display of clubs by some of the biggest names in golf. The white and black checkerboard floor gleamed from a fresh waxing. To my right was a glass counter stocked with golf balls, gloves and specialty tees, some of which were strewn across the floor behind the counter. I heard what sounded like maintenance moving chairs around.

"Hel*looo*, mail service." No answer. The banging in the other room continued. What was he doing back there?

I moved toward the noise but stopped as I was confronted with an invisible wall of odor, like rotten eggs and something dead, coming from the hallway. Gagging, I buried my nose in the crook of my elbow. That's when I saw the long line of shiny reddish black goo spoiling the checkerboard pattern.

"Zeus!" I leaped back a step.

My breath hitched and I felt my cheeks flush. With jerky motions I grabbed at the display of clubs. They clattered to the floor. A *snick* and *thump* came from the locker room. Now my aura thing was kicking in and the message I was receiving wasn't good. I bent down looking for the largest, longest, most dangerous looking club and hefted a Greg Norman wedge.

I backed toward the door but *Menori* urged me to fight. My

heart accelerated, and blood rushed through my veins like a flash flood. Fingers tingling, I prepared to defend myself.

A squeak of metal came from the locker room. Someone was trying to open the exit door.

On a whim, I yelled, "Police."

Chapter 8

I locked onto the remnant of River's force like a Star Trek tractor beam.

Tempe

Agh. I didn't just do that. *Now what, Stop or I'll shoot?* With the heavy wedge in my fist, and a rising press of power I didn't quite know how to control, what should I do next?

Well, duh. *Run like hell.*

I backed up to do just that, when the intruder in the locker room rammed the panic bar and escaped down the outside pathway.

Leaning on the wedge and gasping for breath, I cast *menori* out to search for any sign of life. Better late than never, right? I was alone, except for whoever was at the other end of that trail of blood.

Dread settled on me as I followed the putrid smell past the

bar toward the locker room, and nearly hurled the piece of fried chicken I'd grabbed at the UPak-It fifteen minutes earlier.

A nude body lay in the access hallway near the locker room. The man's face was so battered and bloody he was unrecognizable. I retched and spun toward the wall, pressing my jacket lining tight to my nose and mouth.

Zeus' dead bolts! Could this day get any worse?

There was something about that smell... The coiled elements of my heritage twisted, reassessing sensory data, analyzing cell degradation, moisture and blood into their individual components. I had a flash of insight prompted by this new ability.

The body on the floor looked human, but he wasn't a man at all. He was a variant—not a species you wanted to meet in a dark alley. I leaned over to get a better look at him and reached down to feel his neck, not relishing the idea of putting my hand on him.

The squish and slide of my foot in the dark blood threatened my equilibrium. I managed to regain my balance, when a familiar green object caught my eye, lying on the floor just inches from the man's outstretched hand.

"Is that what I think it is?" I looked closer.

The object looked like a small pointy witch's hat but was in fact, a lid—to my brother's amphora. What was it doing here, beside this dead fae? I focused, sending the tendrils of my force behind the malodorous wall. It twisted around the body and the nearly solid rankness, searching for an essence I now recognized. River's.

"Oh, no." Where was he? Why hadn't I recognized his presence immediately? "River!" I called. Nothing. My breath was coming in gasps as I rejected thoughts of bodily harm like *this* being done to my brother. "No," I cried. No. He must be okay. I faltered briefly, closing my eyes and concentrating.

I swallowed and cast *menori* forward, stepping over the body and around black congealing blood. The *Breath* curled around chair legs, over counters, behind appliances. It avoided an air conditioning vent and exited the kitchen. I followed.

In the members' lounge slash gym, I glanced over at the closed exit door and stopped in front of the flat screens and wet bar. No sign of River. Had my brother been here? If so, what had happened to him? Could the fae have fought with him? My mind was in turmoil. Too many questions. So much weirdness. I couldn't handle much more of this.

River. *Where are you?* I pressed my fingers to my jaws to release the tension settling there. My body quivered as if I was in a freezer but I don't get cold. Everything that had happened today came rushing at me: River's missing amphora, Marty's appearance, the contractor's call, the lunatics...was it all connected? *Get it together, Tempe.*

I looked at the expensive decanter of whiskey. Just a sip might help calm this raging sense of chaos inside me. I wavered. Tempestaeries and earth elements don't harmonize which is why I usually abstain, but in the end, I splashed a small amount of golden liquor into a glass with shaking hands and chugged it.

Fire burned like lightning down my esophagus and forged through my veins as I followed *menori's* progress. If River wasn't here, then it must be his amphora. Like a slender trail of smoke, *menori* drifted into the vent holes of one of the lockers, identifying my brother's essence. What was his amphora doing in that locker? Who was the variant out front and what did he have to do with River?

I should call 911, but they couldn't help the creature in the front room. And my cell phone was still in my truck. For only a second I vacillated—get my phone and wait for the authorities, or get my brother's genie bottle. No contest.

I turned back toward the locker. The room spun. *Probably shouldn't have had that little drinkie.* I did feel calmer however, the shaking subsiding.

I locked onto the remnant of River's force like a Star Trek tractor beam.

Forget 911. I had to find my brother.

The locker that held his bottle was secured with a hefty combination lock. It's a little more complicated to zap that kind of lock, or maybe I just wasn't thinking clearly. I had the solution, though, in my left hand—the heavy wedge.

I spread my legs like the golf pros I'd seen on TV, pulled the club back and swung *hard*, hitting the combination lock dead center—which accomplished nothing, except the lock seemed to taunt me with its imperviousness. I hit it with more force, over and over and over until finally it shattered into smithereens. Tossing the club aside, I opened the door to the locker and stared at my brother's amphora, lying on its side on the top shelf.

"Oh, River."

I reached inside for the elaborately decorated 11th century Chinese vase. Securing it with both hands, I lowered it gently—

"Freeze. Police."

Chapter 9

Murdering someone a little too much for you?

TEMPE

For a second I thought I'd repeated myself, but my *windsense* warned, *human male in the room.* I started to turn holding on tightly to my brother's bottle.

"I. Said. Freeze."

The menacing voice was familiar so naturally I ignored the command, and spun slowly on my heel to face Sheriff *What-shisname,* his gun aimed at my chest in a classic two-handed grip.

"Um, I know this looks bad." *Oh yeah, very bad.* "Don't you have something better to do than turn up everywhere I go, Sheriff," I asked, pulling my cheeks up into a half smile and pretending confidence I didn't feel.

He didn't return the smile. This man has no sense of humor.

So I appealed to his sense of duty. "How could you just walk past that dead..." *Careful...* "Aren't you goin' ta do somethin'?" I waved my free arm in the direction of the door, and landed against the lockers.

"Put down the vase," he said, pointing at it with his gun.

"Not—" I shook my head. "No." I said, gripping the amphora tighter.

"What happened here, Ms. Pomeroy?"

"Uh-oh, yer mad, huh?" One polyester clothed hunk blurred into two. I blinked quickly.

"Are you..." His eyebrows crashed together into downward dogs as he stepped closer to me, put his face next to mine and sniffed.

"Jesus, you're drunk."

He looked over at the wet bar, his eyes hardening to unfriendly gray steel. "What's the matter? Murdering someone a little too much for you?" He grabbed for the vase and got a hand on it.

I clasped it tighter as his words sank in. "What are you talking about?" I shrieked.

"Let. Go."

"No," but I dared not tug too hard. "It's mine—well, River's."

"Who's River?"

"My brother."

At the risk of damaging the irreplaceable vessel, I relinquished it. "Please, please, be careful with it. It's..." I shook my head. *Sober up, Tempe*. I willed clarity to return. It ignored me.

"Is this what you hit the guy with?"

"What guy?"

"You know, the nude dead guy in the other room? The one with his face smashed away? Ring any bells?"

"Oh, him." My head spun worse now that I'd given up the amphora. "I gotta siddown." I did—*hard*, on the bench in front of the lockers. I pressed my fingers to my temple and closed my eyes. *Bad move*. I grabbed the bench and opened them again. "I remember now... ", *the fae, the blood... the smell*. "I think I'm going to throw up." Gagging, I bent over and a plastic lined trashcan appeared in front of me.

Think of something else—River, on his first day as a Djinni, Phoebe on my ninth birthday, Dutch... I stifled a whimper. I would *not* lose it in front of this man. He'd already seen me in too many compromising situations today. It would be one embarrassment too many.

He placed his gun into its holster and reached for my elbow. "Come with me."

I rested my forehead in my palm as he pulled me up. My words kept getting tangled around my tongue. If I just concentrated harder, I could prom-pron- prolly...figure out what to say. I waved a hand toward the door. "Why don' you jus' go do what you have to do? I'll be here... when you get back." I looked up at his narrowed eyes and grim face. *Mad again*.

"Nope. You're coming with me." With one hand wrapped around the neck of the bottle and the other grasping my elbow, he pulled me along with him to the entryway, stopping by the man on the floor. This time the stench was more than my roiling stomach could handle.

"Ag—" I turned just far enough away from the body in front of me to let loose in the direction of the sheriff's trousers and shiny black work boots. *So much for pride*. Only his strong arm around mine kept me from collapsing on top of the body. Which was probably what he was trying to protect.

He looked at the ceiling for a good five seconds, then led me through the dining room toward the restrooms. He pushed me down in a chair and pulled a handkerchief from his pocket. "Here."

What a swell guy, I thought as I closed my eyes, the world spinning behind my lids.

The snick of metal caused me to look up but not before he'd handcuffed my wrist to the seat back and walked out the front door, taking River's amphora with him, leaving me sitting eye level with the long silver utility handle on a door marked, "MEN".

My sentiments exactly.

Chapter 10

This isn't a cozy TV mystery and you are not a nosy sleuth.

JACK

When I got back from changing and putting the weird vase in my cruiser, she was deep in thought—or on the verge of passing out. She shook her head, chuckling.

"What's so funny?" I asked.

She jumped. "You're very... stalky." She squeezed her eyes shut gave her head a shake trying again, "Stealthy."

I snapped on latex gloves and waited.

"I was just thinking what a bad mail day this's been. Get it? Bad M-A-L-E day?"

Hell, she was going to go hysterical on me any minute. "It hasn't been a piece of cake for me, either." I unlocked the cuff and rubbed her wrist.

"Yeah, but this's, this has been withoutta doubt, the wors' day of my entire life." Her eyes focused on the wall behind me so hard, I started to turn, then her face fell and a sob bubbled up from her throat. She turned those watery blue eyes up to mine. "Except..." she swallowed, "the day Phoebe told us Dutch was d-dead."

My voice was sharp. "Who's Dutch?" Two dead people in the life of a person Pomeroy's age was unusual and something to remember in the big scheme.

She ignored me, as usual. Then, her eyes filled with misery, her breath hitching. "I'm sorry." She breathed in unsteadily. "I'm worried about my brother."

"Who's Dutch?" I repeated. Lawmen are as tenacious as bird dogs.

"My father," she said quietly, a tear trailing down her cheek.

I felt an unfamiliar little bump in the vicinity of my heart, which I'd thought a granite wasteland. An honest to God heartfelt tear had never sprung from my ex's tear duct. As a matter of fact, I could have sworn that once, I smelled onion. She'd been a champion manipulator and a pathological liar.

You can imagine I'm more than a bit hardened toward a weak acting female. But I'd had more stimulating, bizarre, intriguing contact with this woman in one day than I'd had with any in the last three years; the word *weak* didn't fit.

Just to be sure, I looked down at her hands. No onion.

Maybe it was a sign. Of what? Besides the fact that I didn't believe in signs...in one day, we'd gone from mutual attraction to standing on opposite sides of a dead body. Tempest Pomeroy was turning out to be a trouble magnet of the first magnitude. I groaned inwardly. It was...problematic, and yet,

I couldn't help but feel a little sorry for her. She *had* had a hell of a day.

And I had a job to do. I walked over to the body and leaned across the pool of blood to feel the man's skin above his wrist; his muscles were in the beginning stages of rigor. The blood was drying in shiny layers on the tile and his skin temp was a couple degrees below normal. He'd been dead a while. "Did you know the dead man?" I asked, going for shock value.

She flinched at the word "dead" and shook her head. That meant nothing. I'd seen murderers cry at will and still pass a polygraph. "Did you kill him?" *Bad cop.*

"No!" She grabbed my arm, eyes wide. "No, I found him like that." One hand went to her head and the other pointed toward the door. "When I drove up out front to check their mailbox, I saw the door ajar. I figured the wind blew it open."

"What made you walk in? Didn't you figure that would be dangerous?"

She jerked her head back like a chicken, glaring at me. "I watch out for my customers. Besides, I heard what sounded like someone walk-working in the other room, and I thought it was the maintenance man. I-I was just going to check, then I smelled... " She pointed toward the body in the hallway and angled her head to peer around me.

"Why didn't you call 911?"

"I was going to but..." She licked her lips and looked down at her twisting fingers.

"Go on," I coached, wondering how much of what followed would be the truth.

"I heard a noise in the other room, a door squeaking," she squinted as she thought about it, "a click...and I shouted—"

She winced, looking up, "Where did you put my vase?"

"It's in my cruiser."

"Is it locked?" she asked urgently.

"Of course." I thought maybe she intended to steal it, but she looked relieved. "You shouted what?"

"I... mighta...um, 'Police?'"

"What?" I gaped at her. "Are you nuts?"

She winced and shrugged. "It just...you know how they tell you on those cop shows that if you just yell or fight or scream bloody murder—" She looked at the body on the floor, "Sorry —that the perpetrator will run, out of fear of being caught?"

"Perpetrator..." I shook my head. "Here's the problem with that. Those are TV shows, fiction. This isn't a cozy TV mystery and you're not a nosy sleuth." I hoped. She was definitely nosy. "What if the perpetrator had decided to attack instead of run?"

"I had a grgnrbwg..." her voice trailed off as she ducked her head.

"What?"

"A...golf club." She arched a brow. "A Greg Norman wedge."

I looked over at the dead man on the floor as a siren sounded outside. "The club you used on the locker?"

She nodded.

"I heard about you and a certain golf club," I said.

"Not you, too. Does everybody add two plus two and get... nine?" I watched, holding back a laugh, as she slowly added in her head. She huffed a breath and plopped her chin on her palm.

"The truth will come out eventually." I scratched my head. "All right, Ms. Pomeroy, this is what I'm going to do."

"I'm going to give you a while to think about what you're not telling me and I'll be back." I guided her head down, through the door, installing her in the back seat of my cruiser as if I were taking her to jail. I didn't know what I was going to do yet. Whoever had killed the man in the clubhouse would have had blood spatter all over him, and Tempest Pomeroy was clean except for that single step in the blood pool. I wanted to make her squirm for a bit and see if she 'remembered' anything. After all, I did catch her in the act of damaging private property. In the meantime, I needed to secure the crime scene and take some pictures.

"But—"

I started to shut the door, then remembered, "Where's your cellphone?"

"In my truck, why?"

"Evidence."

"Ooooh, what are you talking about? I told you, I didn't kill that man. Let me out. I need River's vase back. I have to find my brother. And I..." as if it were an afterthought, "... have a route to finish."

She shook her head from side to side, setting an aqua colored curl free of the scrunchie. "Today of all days."

"Don't sweat it. I'll get a deputy to lock up your packages and make sure the mail center gets someone to finish your route—"

"Ugh, that'll go over real well." Sobriety had returned, and so had her temper.

"Quit working yourself up into such a lather and let me do my job." I shrugged out of my jacket and tossed it on her lap. "Here. Wouldn't want you to get cold." I closed the door firmly in her pretty, agitated face.

As I walked toward the clubhouse, I heard her beating on the window, and the muffled sound of my name.

Chapter 11

I was finally, chillingly sure that my brother was in trouble.

<small>Tempe</small>

I shivered as I thought about the events of the last—I looked at my watch—fifty-five minutes! It seemed like hours since I'd driven up in front of the clubhouse. Lang had handed me his jacket before locking me in the prisoner section of his car —the prisoner section! I watched him march up the walkway, surveying the area around the building. The masculine scent wafting up from the warmth of his jacket triggered the memory of the rotted fish smell coming off the variant inside the clubhouse.

What was he? I'd have to ask Montana or Aurora or, as a last resort, Dylan. My mind was finally starting to operate normally again.

I wasn't under arrest, just locked in!

I smiled.

Peering through the grate, I looked for River's amphora. It was lying on its side in a clear bag on the front floorboard. For the first time I noticed the other seal was gone. No self-respecting Djinn would be caught without a back door. River's emergency exit was through the short spout. Had it been there when I pulled it from the locker? Everything had happened so fast.

I closed my eyes trying to remember exactly how it looked when I'd taken it off the top shelf. I had only sensed a remnant of River's essence. But if the lid was gone, where was it? More importantly, where was River's force? And how long could River last with his life source suspended out there somewhere in limbo?

I was finally, chillingly sure that my brother was in trouble. I slapped my palm against my forehead, twice. Stupid. Slap. Stupid.

Another cruiser drove up and a deputy got out. He looked my way briefly then walked toward the clubhouse. The sheriff had already gone inside. When the deputy walked through the door, I decided on a plan. I couldn't let them take my cell phone. It was the only way my brother could get in touch with me. And right now, River was my main priority. It was about time, I chided myself. I mean, I'm sorry about the man in the clubhouse, but I didn't kill him. And I was sure there would be no evidence pointing to me, so I closed my eyes and went to work.

~

JACK

I checked the front door. There was no evidence of forced entry. Who had tripped the silent alarm—the victim or

Pomeroy? What set it off? According to her version, the alarm had been going when she arrived. That coincided with dispatch receiving notice of it from the monitoring agency.

I'd called the lab techs after putting the mail lady in my vehicle. I wanted to get a look around before they started tearing into the scene. I bent down to study the victim's proximity to the counters and locker room. He reeked for sure.

While I waited for the coroner and my deputy, I shot a few pictures.

He looked African-American, though his face was mangled and bloody from the force of what looked to be repeated blows to his head. Judging by the grey in his hair, the beard and the fleshy skin beneath his neck, I figured he was in his late fifties, early sixties.

Why wasn't he wearing clothes? And where were they? I searched the other rooms and found no discarded clothing in the men's room or behind any of the counters.

An upturned bar stool and a spread of gold plastic tees indicated a short struggle. I did a 360 looking for a weapon but nothing else clicked. I'd found Tempe in the locker room so I stepped over the victim and slowly worked my way to the threshold. There was a spray of blood on the wall and door, which suggested it had been closed when the man was struck. But lying just inside the door to the gym on the right was a wedge.

"Greg Norman, I presume." I inspected it for trace material but didn't see any with the naked eye. I walked over to the locker and used my gloved finger on the corner of the door to swing it open. The inside was empty except for a package of golf balls. Until I knew what I was looking for, I'd just sweep the locker and bag the contents. I opened the door to the outside and looked for footprints. The grass was crushed near the sidewalk. I marked one area for pictures and saw more apparent indentations in the grass.

I turned as Deputy Basile came through the door. "Sir? The lab techs will be here any minute."

"Fine. I need you to cordon off the clubhouse and grounds. You might as well call your wife and tell her you won't be home tonight. We have to set up a grid and search outside before the rain gets worse or curiosity seekers mess up our crime scene."

Basile vacillated.

"What are you waiting for?"

"Yes, sir. Uh, sir, what's that smell?"

"Very observant, Basile. I intend to find out."

He nodded. I thought about Pomeroy. "First, though, I need you to go outside to that mail truck. Put any packages from the bed into the front seat, lock it up; bring me the cell phone and keys. Oh, and check on the woman in the back seat of my cruiser."

"Yes, sir."

I reached for a slide from my pack and tried not to inhale. The odor emanating from the victim was unlike anything I'd ever experienced. Separating each of the man's stiff fingers, I pressed them to the slides and carefully stored them in my evidence case. I moved to the cart path on the side of the building.

"Uh, boss." Basile again, from the doorway.

"Yes, Basile." I was wrapping a piece of pink flagging on the end of a holly bush when I realized he was waiting for me to look up. Impatiently I asked, "What, Basile?"

"I didn't see a mail truck. And there ain't nobody in your car."

"Shit!"

The deputy and I loped around the building to the parking lot. Sure enough, Tempe Pomeroy and her truck were gone.

Chapter 12

❧❧❧

If you keep this up I won't be able to dig you out with a backhoe.

J<small>ACK</small>

"Basile, keep everybody away from the lawn, greens, fairway —and everything else around here. I'll get Peggy to call the police department and see if they have any personnel they can loan us."

"Gotcha, boss."

I flipped him the yellow crime scene tape. Walking back to my cruiser, I peered inside. I could have sworn I'd locked it but I guess I'd screwed up. Tempest Pomeroy had flown the coop and taken the possible murder weapon with her. In my experience those actions translated into an admission of guilt.

There was something very odd about this whole scene. I just couldn't put my finger on it. Something to do with that damned antique vase. Figuring it out would have to wait. Right now, I had to secure the crime scene and make sure the collection of evidence was handled expertly—quite a challenge with Destiny's small town resources, part-time lab techs, and borrowed coroner.

I released the radio from the dash and called dispatch. "Peggy, put out an all points on Tempest Pomeroy. Call the Mail Center and get her tag. The Feds will track her down. If they find her before I do, I need that fancy vase in her possession. It's evidence, and not that it'll do any good, but tell them not to handle it."

"I'm on it, Sheriff," Peggy said.

We had a word for a day like this in the Navy—FUBAR. "Oh, and call DPD and the Citizen Patrol and see if they have anyone who can volunteer for about twelve hours at this location."

I disconnected and immediately my cell phone started playing "Call Me Baby" instead of my choice—"Ride the Lightning" by Metallica. Jordie had struck again. "Hey, baby, I know, I'm late. I'm on a case. Can you catch a ride?"

"I'm fifteen, Dad, not eight. I'll see you at Grandad's later," she said, and hung up. Why did she always get the last word?

I sighed and punched more numbers.

"Kirkwood," said the voice on the other end, a SAR specialist friend of mine who I'd talked into making his leave from the Navy permanent.

"Ryan, I need you on a crime scene PDQ..."

"Roger that. Where?"

Fifteen minutes after calling Peggy, I had two men from the police department down in Amity and Ryan Kirkwood helping to secure and search the area. I assumed Peggy's call to the Universal Mail facility would get some results.

Even when I'd caught Pomeroy in the act she hadn't been forthcoming with her reasons for breaking into the locker except to say the vase belonged to her brother. She never said how she knew it was there.

I dialed the office. Peggy picked up immediately.

In the six months I'd been sheriff Peggy had never not answered on the first ring. She was maneuvering for a promotion to investigations.

"Peggy, find out everything you can about Tempest Pomeroy and, her brother, River."

Without breaking stride, Peggy proceeded to give me some of River Pomeroy's background off the top of her head; one good thing about having a hometown desk Sergeant. I listened to her praise—self-made contractor, in business four years. His sister had practically raised him from elementary school through college.

"And paid for everything herself," Peggy said. "River's a sweetie, and Tempe's solid."

"Yeah, well, today wasn't one of her stellar days," I muttered. "I caught her breaking into a locker at the clubhouse just a short hop from our victim."

Peggy's voice lowered, "Jack, Tempe and River are well respected around here, a miracle considering their early years."

That caught my attention. "What does that mean?"

"Their mother is a flake. Take it from me."

I did. Peggy doesn't even criticize the prisoners in lockup. "So, Tempe's mother wouldn't get the Peggy Donovan Best Parent Seal of Approval, eh?"

"Let's just say, if it hadn't been for Tempe, she and her brother would have wound up in foster care. If she broke into that locker, she must have had a reason."

"If she does, she's hiding it from me."

I started to ask about the father but the lab techs arrived. "Get me addresses on all the Pomeroys, Peggy, and anything else you can think of. Leave it on my desk. I'll be late. You don't need to hang around."

I ended the call and thought about the information she'd given me on River Pomeroy. He lived at Harmony Plantation, near Lightning Bayou, with his sister.

I couldn't help but wonder why a successful contractor would be so attached to such an ugly vase?

TEMPE

"What kind of trouble are you in now?" Dylan's quiet voice grated over my cell, like he didn't want to be overheard.

"I thought you were out of pocket," I said.

"You'd better be glad I returned this call. Seems the local badge put a BOLO out on you. It won't be long before they find you."

I groaned.

"Damn, Te—if you keep this up I won't be able to dig you out with a backhoe."

All morning my emotions had been close to the surface, affecting my ability to hold my Tempestaerie-ness in check, like a tropical storm on the verge of earning an official name. But two blocks away from the clubhouse I started thinking more clearly and a plan formed. I could make two stops and stay out of serious trouble with UM; one to deliver my last big package and the second to deliver on a promise I'd made this morning. Then I'd drop my mail in the first collection box—not the preferred method—and arrange for Tuesday off so I could look for River. I'd run Phoebe down tonight and see what she knew.

"I'm aware I'm not the most popular employee right now with the new agency, Dylan, but I've got to find River. I can't do that locked in the back of a police car. I'm going to drop all the mail in the closest collection box before 4:30. It'll be close, but I think I can make it."

I counted to six while colorful curses flooded my ears. "That's against procedure, and you'll miss your return inspection." Irritated, he asked, "The sheriff's dispatcher mentioned stolen evidence?"

"River's amphora. I'm not giving it back."

He was silent.

"Yeah. I found it in that locker in the clubhouse. Now I *know* there's something wrong." My voice caught. "I didn't worry when he didn't come home last night—okay I did, but not overly—then one of his subcontractors called me this morning, irate, when River didn't show for their meeting."

My phone beeped, the caller ID read *Beck*. I ignored it.

"Look, Dylan, if you want to help, just sit on all this for a couple hours. Gotta go." I snapped the phone shut and knew wherever he was, his blood pressure had just gone up.

I intended to pass up the rest of the boxes but a familiar figure in his premature St. Patrick's Day getup was seated on the end of the last one, legs crossed, all gray Impy skin and green clover. "Hear ye've had a bad day, eh, Colleen?"

"Get in, Marty. I'm in a hurry. And can the Colleen crap."

Eyes wide, he backed up, one hand holding his polyester clover, the other palm out. "No, I can't get in that old truck. Too much iron, 'ya know."

"You're not a faerie or a Leprechaun so it doesn't matter. I don't have time for this, Marty. Get in, now!" I ordered, tears dangerously close. Why was he being so uncooperative?

He gave up the charade. Carefully picking his way down onto the lid of the mailbox, he leaped across the two-inch distance between lid and window, then pulled out my cup holder and plopped his butt into it. "There, now, lassie. Let's calm down." The little sycophant.

I tossed the mail in the box and slammed it shut. My hands shook. Whether from adrenaline or fear, I didn't know. Then there was that quickening thing everybody kept talking about.

We drove in silence for a few seconds.

"What do you know about River?" I asked.

"River? Nothing, I swear. Why are you asking *me*?" he squeaked.

What an odd reaction—guilty? "When was the last time you saw him?" Marty was kind of a family familiar but he is an Imp after all which means he's selfish, caring more about *his* schemes than doing familiar kind of stuff, you know, tagging along with or being a support to his holder, handler, owner —whatever.

He made a show of trying to remember, propping his chin on his index finger and squeezing his eyes shut. "I *believe* it was Saturday."

"Marty, could you change into something less... clothing minimalist. I need you to do some undercover work, see what you can find out."

Many of the fae and supernaturals resented clothing; they claimed it interfered with their natural abilities. I could relate, in fact, but I'd grown up more human than supernatural and I'd absorbed their social mores for the most part to fit in with the community and at work.

"Okay." Marty transformed into a black unitard, like a mini cat burglar. "Perfect for playing spook," he said.

He *was* perfect for it. Marty could go anywhere, be anything —anything small. He was inquisitive and resourceful, and, all that aside—I was desperate. He was officially my brother's familiar, but I never saw them together.

"So, what seems to be the problem?" Marty asked in a tell-the-doctor-everything voice.

"River's missing," I said. Marty frowned, looking genuinely concerned. "I just found River's amphora at the scene of a murder." I pointed to the bottle on the floor by my feet. Marty peered down at the bottle and paled, diving head first over the back seat into a mail tub.

"Let me out of here," he whined.

What in the world? Iron wouldn't affect Marty. "There's

nothing in it, Marty." I picked the vase up and tried to coax him back into the front seat. "See?"

His eyebrows disappeared up under his hairline, and he squeezed himself up into the corner behind me, flattened against my backside glass. He screamed, "Keep that thing away from me. I promise, I'll see what I can find, but let me out. Please, Tempest," he begged.

I banged my head against the headrest. What was his problem? More Impish-ness? "Fine. Get out." When the next mailbox drew even with my window I eased it open. He scrambled out from behind my seat and dropped out through the open window.

"Tempe." He hung from the window edge briefly. "Be careful."

The expression on his face, oddly one of compassion, triggered a memory long buried. Marty had appeared for the first time to River and me, the day Dutch died.

Chapter 13

I didn't mention the being a fugitive part.

TEMPE

I drove up to the high school entrance five minutes later to fulfill the promise I'd made to the school secretary. The clock on the radio read 4:21. In less than ten minutes, I was going to add another sin to the list I'd already amassed today.

A teenager sat on a bench out front as I pulled up to the double doors at St. Mary's. Face turned toward a young male leaning down over her, she turned as I drove up into the driveway. The young man trudged off, head bent; worn athletic shoes scraping the pavement. He glanced back at me once before turning the corner of the building. Something didn't seem quite right there.

I got out and skipped up to the double doors, finding them locked. "*Shootfire*," I said, glancing over as the girl walked toward me, hands extended.

"I think you're looking for this." She handed me a rubber banded flat of large envelopes. "Miss Madge said to give them to the mail carrier."

"Thanks." I took the letters and started to get in on the passenger side of my truck but something about her tugged at me. Her air was confident, her posture erect, unlike so many kids that slouched around the high school games. But there was a lonesome independence about her, as if she didn't have, no, it was more than that, didn't *need* friends. "Was that boy bothering you?"

Her eyebrows sank a bit as she looked off in the direction the boy had taken. "Not...really."

Hmm, that didn't sound good. "Are you waiting for someone to pick you up?" There weren't any cars in the parking lot and no one milling around but her, and that boy.

"No, Ma'am. My dad has to work and I couldn't get in touch with my grandparents. So, I'm going to hang around until the guys' practice starts and catch a ride with somebody, or wait on my dad."

"Where do you need to go?"

"My grandparents live over on Ledgerton, off Oakland Drive?"

Add another sin—riding a passenger. "I'm going near there. Jump in. I'll give you a lift."

"Uhh... I don't know. I'm not supposed—"

I stuck my hand out. "My name's Tempe. I'm safe." I held out my ID badge. "See, mail carrier, Federal background check, picture ID and everything." (I didn't mention the being a fugitive part.)

She leaned over to look at it cautiously. "Well..."

"What's your name?" I prompted, because we had to G-O-Go.

"Jordie," she said after a pause.

"Nice to meet you, Jordie." I looked toward the corner of the building. "Somehow I think your family would feel better about you being with me than sitting at a locked up school building after hours."

"I guess, but..." she peeked in the window, "where am I going to sit? Aren't you driving from the passenger side?"

"Oh, that. Just get in and we'll take care of this stuff on the way. I have to drop this mail in the collection box near the Donut Shop by 4:29."

I ran around to the driver's side, looking at my watch. 4:26. She buckled her seatbelt and we peeled out of the driveway.

"Okay, if you don't mind, collect those packages on the floor at your feet and this bundle." I handed her the mis-sorts from my dash.

"Now, put these in that tub with the other letters and that batch of mail Madge gave you, and when I pull up to the collection box, shove it through the slot."

I looked in my rear view mirrors as she stuffed the mail into the box. *Very efficient.* I pulled forward when she was done and asked, "So, where am I dropping you?"

"My grandparents' house," she said and gave me the address, which was two blocks from my favorite malt shop. My stomach growled.

*UN*believable.

"How about a malt? It's on the way and we can drive thru."

The smile she gave me was perfect and completely unself-conscious. "Sounds great."

≈

JACK

"Jack," Kirkwood ran up the walkway to the clubhouse, "that Pomeroy woman—" his voice lowered ominously, "She's got Jordie."

Fear sliced into my gut. A red haze glided over my vision. I blinked it away, grabbing his shoulders. "What did you say? Never mind. Where? Hurry, man." He filled me in as we ran toward my cruiser.

Jordie had been seen in Tempe's truck at the malt shop. I threw myself into my vehicle, flipped on the siren and raced through the subdivision toward town. "The friggin' malt shop?" I yelled in disbelief, pounding the steering wheel.

I called Peggy. "Forget what I said, Peggy. No one goes home until I find my daughter. Tempest Pomeroy was seen with her at the malt shop. Get the head guy from the mail center on the phone. And report a kidnapping to the DPD. I want her found ASAP!" I shut the phone and pounded it on the seat.

What did she need a hostage for? Was this personal some-how? No. I tried to think like a lawman, but as a father, all I could think of was losing my little girl to yet another crazy ass woman; another woman my instincts had mistakenly convinced me I could trust.

I tried Jordie's phone on the way to my parents' but all I got was *not available*. "Damn it." I slapped the dash in frustration.

I pulled up to my parents' one story brick rambler and ran to the door. No one responded as I let myself in. I made a quick sweep of the rooms to verify Jordie wasn't there, and got back on the highway.

My blood pressure rose, making my head pound. I took three breaths, but I was too stressed to manage anything more than shallow attempts. I was reacting like a father when I needed to think like the Memphis detective I'd been a year ago; get my mental and ultimately physical reactions in line with the training I'd practiced as a fighter pilot. A simple exercise in centering like I'd exercised while flying brought me to a place of calculated calm.

Where would Tempe go? I turned on the visor light to look at my notes. I had her address, the old Harmony plantation near Lightning Bayou.

So the bottle—what did she call that thing—ann fora? belonged to her brother. He lived with her. Maybe she was covering for him. Or, maybe they were in on it together. I could be there in three minutes.

TEMPE

I parked in the driveway of the brick home and waited until Jordie gathered her stuff. She swept her long brown hair behind her ear.

"Are your grandparents home?" I asked. It didn't look like it but some folks were on the reclusive side and didn't make a lot of noise.

"They're over at the mall doing their five mile run." So much for them being recluses. "But I have a key." She held it up and shook it. "Thanks for the lift—and the malt, Tempe."

"No, problem, Jordie. You were the best part of my day."

She tilted her head, "Must have been a pretty bad day then."

I smiled, "Oh, I don't know, maybe you're just selling yourself short, girlfriend."

She started to turn away, then turned back, biting her lip. "Would you like to come to my basketball game Saturday?"

"I'd love to. Night game?"

She grinned, flashing that beautiful smile. Probably had more than one boy trailing after her. "Six-thirty sharp. But there will be stuff going on all afternoon, if you want to come early."

"I'll be there." *If I'm not in jail.*

"Great. See ya. Thanks again for the ride."

I couldn't get past the feeling that I'd seen her before.

TEMPE

The closer I got to the Voracious Monster—the nickname for my money pit of a house—the darker it got. Moss hanging heavy from live oaks obscured the view of the stars. Crickets, hoot owls, cicadas, and tree frogs ceased their chatter as I shut my car door and locked it—without the use of my hands.

I heard a quiet click of metal behind me, spun around and swallowed a startled gasp. I was staring into the barrel of a mean looking gun, and at the other end of that rigid grip was an even meaner looking Jack Lang, the one I hadn't met until now, a cold-as-ice predator. His knuckles were white but his arm was steady as a granite mountain.

"Where's...my...daughter?" he growled. One eye actually twitched as silver eyes whitened into pure frost. If he was trying to scare me, he'd succeeded.

A sound rumbled up from his chest like that of an animal. "What have you done with Jordie?"

Recognition came in a flash. I smacked my hand against my forehead. "I knew I recognized her."

His eyes seemed to take on an angular appearance, brows winging up, but the gun never wavered. "Woman, you'd better start talking or you're not going to like my next move."

Not an animal—*a papa-bear*.

"I'm sorry."

He gave a snarl of pain and grabbed me. "What do you mean you're sorry?"

"I mean..." I squirmed in his bruising grip... "I'm sorry I didn't put it together."

He roared, "What the hell are you talking about? Where is Jor—"

"She's at your parents'." It finally dawned on me. He thought I'd kidnapped his daughter. *Zeus' newborn godling!*

"You're lying. I was just there." He recoiled when I put my hand on his arm, but thankfully, he was professional enough not to pull the trigger. My guess: he was probably tempted.

"Call her," I suggested.

He pointed his finger at me and glared. "You. Don't. Move."

This time, I obeyed.

He eyed the amphora I clutched to my chest but said nothing. Pulling out his cell, he spoke into it, "Call. Dad." He didn't put his gun down right away, but I could tell when Jordie came on the line. His shoulders relaxed and even in the dark his eyes shone with relief.

He spoke deliberately, like he was afraid of losing his disposition. "We're going to have a talk when I get there about getting into vehicles with strangers."

The word *strangers* was more of a snarl than a word. Then, "I know. Still goes. I lov—."

His lids lowered briefly as a frustrated sound escaped his throat and he squeezed the phone. Then he lowered the gun, and I watched his shoulders rise as he took one long shaky breath. He strode off toward his car. I thought he was leaving. Just like that, but he spun around toward the house, his face in profile, planted his hands on his hips and looked up at the sky like he was waiting for some kind of divine intervention. The whole time, I watched his aura change and vent, like colored steam pouring from a boiling teakettle.

I drummed my fingers together under my chin, understanding that now was not the time to push things. (I'm not always so erratic. Really.) I saw the minute he'd made his decision, his shoulders relaxed, his aura turning a cool Caribbean blue. He stroked his chin as he walked back over to me, still holding his gun at his side. Now that I knew he was Jordie's father, I wasn't as intimidated as I'd been at the end of that icy glare, looking down the barrel of his gun.

"You've done a wonderful job with Jordie, Sheriff. She's a great kid."

He holstered the gun with more force than necessary. "And you're an expert on parenting, I suppose."

Low blow. I should have expected that I guess. So much for a truce.

"I know a bit. Now, if you've come to arrest me, do it. Otherwise, I've had a horrible day. I want a long hot bath and a cold glass of sweet tea."

"You think you can just walk away after what you did? I ought to haul you off to jail."

Anger flared, "I gave a teenager a ride—your teenager, an act of kindness that may put the nail in my employment coffin in the morning."

That serpentine glare returned. I seemed to bring out his inner dragon. "You...escaped custody," he gritted.

"Hello..." I waved my hand. "I don't remember being arrested, just illegally detained." I punctuated that with a poke to his chest.

Big mistake. Memories flooded in of my first customer in nothing but sweat shorts and shaving cream.

"*Zeus' perfect pecs!* You're..."

Hunky doctor.

Chapter 14

I knew when you delivered that package this morning, you'd be trouble.

TEMPE

I laughed at how wrong I'd been and felt my face color.

"Yeah," he said with an unfriendly smile. "I knew when you delivered that package this morning, you'd be trouble." He rubbed his forehead. His hands were strong and perfectly shaped, like the rest of him. Uh-huh, the skin on my arms pebbled as I remembered the rest of him.

"You could try trusting the authorities—me. I'm not trying to railroad you, or your brother. If you aren't guilty, you have nothing to worry about."

Maybe in his world. But when it came to Destiny's version of the real world—our im-mere-para-mortal realm—what would a human sheriff be able to do?

"I've learned that trust is easily misplaced, so I'll wait until it's earned, if you don't mind."

He looked pensive, then nodded beyond me toward my truck. "What's the deal with the door locks?"

Oh, you saw that did you? "*Uhnn.* It's a little trick my father taught me." Not exactly a lie, my abilities *are* inherited.

"Handy skill, that. Most people I know who can do it are in jail."

"Make up your mind, Sheriff. Arrest me. Or Leave."

He held out a plastic bag. "Drop that thing in the bag, or I will take you into custody."

I was tempted to let him take me to jail so I could keep tabs on River's amphora. How could I turn loose of it knowing River's life depended on the fragile porcelain container? But I needed to be free to look for River, and even the amphora wouldn't do River much good if I didn't find the other lid.

"Drop isn't a word I want to hear regarding my brother's twelve hundred year old bottle."

That shut him up.

I took advantage of it. "Could I ask a favor of you?"

He grunted. "You can ask, but I'm not feeling real charitable toward you right now."

"If I run into an emergency and, um, need the bottle back, temporarily..."

"Tell me what kind of emergency could involve you needing an ugly old vase? And why should I grant you any favors?"

I held my breath for a full three seconds before responding.

"Because you understand what it would mean to lose someone you love."

His eyes narrowed and I could feel the thrum of mental activity, like he was working a puzzle. A puzzle called *What's Her Angle?* but I couldn't exactly explain. I *could* tell my comment hit the mark, though. He didn't say anything, just pushed the bag toward me. I carefully placed the amphora inside.

The gears kept grinding behind that discerning gaze. Time stretched as we stood nose to nose sizing each other up; all right, more like forehead to Adam's apple. After a few moments of tension filled silence he said, "You know, I was this close," he held his fingers a quarter inch apart, "from blowing you away."

I thought maybe that made him uncomfortable.

He tweaked the brim of his hat a few too many times before setting it on his head. His eyes locked with mine. "I would have, if you'd hurt my daughter."

I was proud that my voice didn't reveal the hurt I felt, "Seems that *trust* you mentioned, doesn't run both ways."

He turned on his heel and left, taking the key to my brother's survival with him.

JACK

After placing the bag with the vase in my trunk, I left Harmony Plantation and called Ryan at the clubhouse. "What's goin' on?"

"Building's locked up and I'm stationed outside. Peggy said you cancelled backup. You get the Pomeroy woman?"

"Yeah. Believe it or not, she was just being a Good Samaritan and gave Jordie a lift home because I was busy. Crazy, huh?"

Ryan was quiet for a beat then asked, "So... you're not taking her in? What about the B&E?"

"Let's just say, at this point, I don't really have anything except the B&E to hold her on. She pointed out correctly that I didn't really place her under arrest. She wasn't thinking of the vase as a possible murder weapon.

"Hell, it's a mess, Ryan. She hasn't slipped through the noose yet, though. She'll have to deal with restitution to the golf club for the damage to the locker."

"You're the boss." Ryan sounded as if he was holding back; as if he thought I'd flipped. Maybe I had.

"We know where to find her if we have questions. Look, I'm whupped. I'm going to check on Jordie and get some shuteye. Call me at 0300."

"Roger that."

I called my parents' house. Jordie answered.

Love, relief, and leftover fear engulfed me. Tempe had hit a nerve. She wasn't telling me even a little of what was bothering her but it was a dead cinch it had something to do with her family, and how well I got that.

"Hi, sweetheart. Why aren't you in bed?"

"I heard about what happened over at the clubhouse..."

I smiled. My curious teenager. "Heard about it from who?"

"Whom, Daddy."

"Whom did you hear it from?" I chuckled when the exasperated sound came across the phone.

"Melissa's mom saw Tempe's truck there and the Sheriff's Department. She said a Medi-flight helicopter sat down in the golf club parking lot and somebody was put on the helicopter in a body bag. What happened...did somebody die... did Tempe see it...is she okay?"

"Wait, wait." I shook my head to clear it. "You know I can't tell you anything, especially anything that might get back to Melissa's mother."

Jane Fortune was Destiny's answer to 900-PSYCHIC and the local gossip columnist. She made a good living from her three jobs though she got most of her news as a cashier at the Cajun Market in Alliance, then passed it on to her customers on the 900 number as psychic transmissions, and finally to the other facet of curious humanity on Fortune's Telling, her local tabloid column for the Destiny Tribune.

"She's looking for gossip, honey, and I have a crime to solve. I can't have her involved." That was an understatement.

"Daddy, you can trust me. Melissa knows I don't gossip. I listen, but I don't tell. Please."

I sighed. "You want me to pick you up?" I might as well; I wasn't going to sleep until I saw her anyhow. The way I was feeling right now, she could skip school tomorrow and do a career day with her "daddy".

My new life—since the divorce and custody hearings revolved around Jordie, my brilliant, too mature little girl. My gut turned inside out when I thought about how close she was to being grown and on her own in a world that was getting more dangerous every day.

My initial opinion of Destiny as a cozy traditional small town had been skewed slightly today, but still, a few eccentricities were nothing compared to the violence and wackiness I'd seen in Memphis.

"I'll be waiting outside—"

"Oh, no you won't. Just watch for me. I'll be there in—"

"Gotta take this call, Daddy," and then nothing but dead air.

"Damn. Someone's got to teach that kid some phone etiquette."

TEMPE

I did not treat myself to tea as I'd said to Lang. I had more important things to do. Instead, I went searching among some old bottles for a replacement vessel for River's genie force. The one I found would embarrass him among the Djinn population but then, I didn't know of any other Djinn in our neck of the swamp, except a burgeoning newbie River had been mentoring. I picked a cheap glass model from over the kitchen stove, one that had probably served as a marijuana bong in an earlier life. Tomorrow I'd have to locate someone who could prepare it, or find a better one.

Running high on adrenaline, I decided to search again for the missing lid. I went through the trash, emptied drawers, swept under River's bed. "Whew, if you're not in trouble, little brother, you're going to face the music about eating in your bedroom."

I cleaned the entire house, marked bags for trash, including some *bedside* items, since I may never be interested in my own personal satisfaction ever again.

The radio on the nightstand read 1:00am. It hit me then, staring at the digital readout, something so obvious I nearly threw up. River had gone AWOL from the Pomeroy family radio frequency. Not so much as a blip since...when?

I sat on the bed, tugging on my hair, as if that could pull details out of my brain. I remembered conversations with Dylan and River and Aurora insisting that training was important for me to expand my awareness and connection to the environment, where my power lay. Aurora said my quickening was coming no matter what and my lack of control would just increase until I knew how to tap into it.

I'd ignored them, determined to live like a mere-mortal, refusing to allow River or my mother to speak to me through the intimate mindlink. Not to mention avoiding discussions or attempts at initiating me into the *valo*, the path. What if my stubbornness, my refusal to accept my heritage, had ruined any chance to find River? Worse, what if I'd caused it somehow?

What was I going to do?

JACK

Jordie and I sat outside in the car talking until her eyelids drooped and her head sank against my shoulder.

"I liked her, Daddy."

"Who's that, baby?"

"Tempe. And I thought you might like her, too." She tilted her head up and looked me square in the eye.

I remembered the first time she'd done that, during my first leave home from Afghanistan. She'd been three, all pink, chubby cheeks and blonde curls. I was underneath my old 4X4 changing the oil when she crawled in next to me and propped her chin on one oily, plump palm. She'd regarded me intently, waiting with patience beyond her years until I put my wrench down. "What's on your mind, Button?"

She reached out and put her hand on my cheek like she'd seen my mother do when she was serious about something. I frowned, watching as her expressive green eyes curved downward. "It's Mommy." I started, keeping myself from gripping her little hand too hard. After a pause, to make sure I was listening, her serious cherubic gaze met mine and she said, "Mommy doesn't yove me, Daddy. Wanna go 'ive with grandpa."

If I hadn't been on my back already, I'd have dropped to my knees. It had been a good thing I couldn't get to her mother at that moment. I'd swallowed the lump in my throat and the blinding rage and pulled her in close, silently promising myself, and my baby girl, that she would not stay one day longer than necessary in that woman's custody.

My stomach still gripped painfully when I remembered that day. Flying out two days later had been the hardest thing I'd ever done, but I'd put a few safeguards in place with my parents.

Now when she looked at me I recognized the same intuitive patience, so rare in a fifteen-year-old. I don't know why that surprised me. *Oh, yeah.* Half of her came from me, but the other half came from the crazy maniacal bitch I'd been married to. Not that I'm a saint, but I must be pretty close to balance out her influence.

"This morning, remember when she delivered—"

"I remember." Yeah, just thinking about the way Tempe had looked at me was making my pants uncomfortably tight, before she'd figured me for some kind of cradle robber. I chuckled. "You should have seen the look on her face when you came to the door this morning."

"Hmmm?"

"Come on, baby, time for bed. Want me to swing by and drop you at school so you can sleep through your study hall?"

Jordie looked at me through long golden lashes and tugged her coat closer as she pulled away. "No. I promised to tutor one of the girls from French class during study hall. So," she yawned, "I'll catch the bus."

"Okay, then, let's hit the sack." I looked at my watch. Barely two hours until I had to spell Ryan. I'd made it on a helluva lot less sleep. If sleepless nights were the price for spending these precious hours with my baby girl, well, bring 'em on.

"I'll call you and make sure you made your bus." When we walked through the back door, she turned and hugged me. "I love you, Daddy."

My eyes burned as I hugged her tightly. "I love you, too, sweetheart. More than you can possibly know." I kissed her on the forehead and turned her toward the hallway, "Now, to bed."

The last thing I thought about before falling asleep was the pain in Tempe Pomeroy's eyes when she'd said, "'I've learned trust is easily misplaced...'"

The ex-husband and sheriff in me might agree, but the man couldn't help but wonder who had destroyed her faith in men.

Chapter 15

Could this whole case be drug related?

JACK

I dragged myself out of bed when Kirkwood called and after a quick shower, headed over to the crime scene. On my way, I checked in with the medical examiner's office. The autopsy would be performed after their backlog of victims was processed. They estimated late afternoon.

"Got a cause of death?" I asked the ME's assistant.

"Cause isn't official, but my guess is blunt force trauma to the face—his nose cartilage has a new home. We'll know for sure after the autopsy."

I hung up. Smart ass. Maybe they would come up with an impression or fragment that would lead to the weapon.

I turned on the defroster and wiped at the fogged window with my sleeve. Through the smears I saw something huge dart across the road and into the tree line. A bear? Walking upright? I thought bears were rare around this part of Louisiana; for sure there were no grizzlies. I slowed, wiping faster, but Sasquatch was gone.

I rubbed my tired, burning eyes. Coffee. I needed coffee.

At the Easy Stop I purchased a large cup of Community coffee. One of the best things about living here was the rich, dark brew for which there was no comparison. I laced it with cream and three sugars and picked up the just delivered *Destiny Tribune*.

Emblazoned the front page, impossible to miss was

Mail carrier finds body in Enchanted Glen Clubhouse.

I spread it against my steering wheel and read:

> *Tempest Pomeroy, a mail courier for the ritzy golf club subdivision was discovered on the closed premises of the Enchanted Glen clubhouse, this reporter was told by a unanimous source.*

Rather than snicker as I usually did at the vocabulary gaffes of Melissa's mom, the gossip columnist, I had the urge to strangle a certain fifteen year old. She could keep a secret, huh? Which was why I'd only told her what I wanted to put out to the public. She must have sent a text to Melissa before she went to bed. I read on...

> *This is not the first time the Pomeroy name has gained public attention. Tempest Pomeroy's father died under suspicious circumstances when she was a child, but this reporter can't seem to remember—was a body ever found? Unnamed but pliable sources also claim that Ms. Pomeroy's brother, River, has not been seen since*

early Monday morning, the same day of the unfortunate incident at the golf club.

Whoa, who had the gossip been talking to? I really hated it when I was the last to find out about something significant. Funny how Tempest Pomeroy didn't tell me her brother was WUK, whereabouts unknown. Wait until I got my chance at her again. Had Fortune made this up? Somehow I didn't think so. I should have stopped there.

Destiny's new sheriff, Jack Lang, is on the job. He was seen interrogating Tempest Pomeroy at least three times Monday. That was an interrogation wasn't it, Sheriff Lang?

I threw the paper on the passenger seat and headed to Enchanted Glen. At the clubhouse, I broke Kirkwood from his shift and retrieved the vase from the back of my SUV. Sitting in the car beneath the light of the parking lamps, I studied the item in the evidence bag.

The raised design on the base was that of a warrior, the upper body massive and distinct with detail fading and narrowing toward the bottom. Above the widest part where a short spout was located, was a ringed five-inch neck. The lid Tempe had found next to the body looked like a 3 inch long upside down witch's hat.

The thing looked like a drug user's pipe. Could this whole case be drug related? I stuck the spout to my nose. No weed. No mildew. Absolutely pristine.

I locked it up in my trunk again and walked back into the clubhouse. Kirkwood had used my camera to take pictures of the body before the coroner's office picked it up.

If I hadn't been worried about Jordie, I never would have

turned that responsibility over to someone else, not even a conscientious observer like Kirkwood. I'm not a control freak, but contamination of the crime scene isn't something I like to take chances with.

In Memphis I'd developed a routine for working crime scenes, locking myself in with the dead guy to re-live his last moments. I had a portable kit that had some basics in it; tape measure, thermometer, liver temp checker, gloves, fingerprint kit, slides, body paint, and a stack of small notebooks. No one was allowed onto my crime scene until I'd completed my notes and taken photographs from every angle.

Having lost my chance to shut myself in with the victim and do the first part of my routine, I could only hope Kirkwood had gotten some decent shots and kept the helicopter crew limited in their access to other parts of the crime scene. Come dawn though, I'd be able to examine the unpolluted outlying area around the building without distraction or interruption.

I closed my eyes, imagining the scene as I'd found it—the blood, the victim...the smell. I flashed on an image of Tempe, that stolen vase gripped in her fists. In that moment she reminded me of a bird dog I had when I was a kid. I retired her from bird hunting the day I found her standing in the field, quivering, doe eyed with innocence as if to say, *Who me? With bird feathers stuck to her mouth and one ear*. That was Tempe.

My instincts said she'd been in the moment with no thought about consequences. What was so important about that vase that she risked her job and her freedom? I stood in the doorway to the lounge. No other lockers were disturbed; all but that one, locked.

I put myself in her place. She claimed that she'd seen the body, heard a noise in the locker room and, stupid woman, went to investigate. She said the attacker escaped when she entered.

I thought about Ryan's question the night before. He seemed to think I should put Tempest Pomeroy in lockup for principle alone. No, not just on principle. I thought through the explanations Tempe had given and asked myself, if I'd ever just given a suspect in her position the benefit of the doubt without requiring more proof of their innocence. In this case, I was giving Pomeroy a pass or at the very least, I was withholding judgment until I had more to go on. It was crazy and bad detecting, but there was something else I hadn't shared with Ryan that pointed to her innocence—in the murder at least.

I turned toward the lockers.

What did she do next? Use her x-ray vision to see that her vase, correction, her brother's vase—was sitting on the shelf behind door number three? Right. Had someone told her it was there? If it really was her brother's vase, what was it doing in the locker? How was it connected to the murder?

I wrote, *ID lockers of members, esp. broken.* Maybe her brother... I looked at my pad... River Pomeroy. "River, old boy, do you golf? Was that your locker?"

Damn, the more I looked at the evidence, the fishier her story sounded. I snapped my fingers. *Fish!*

I realized what had been bothering me earlier. The smell was off, not the normal decay of human flesh, more like fish and eggs left on the bank in the hot sun. Very distinctive. Most importantly, it was too soon for the body to have an odor, especially in the clubhouse where the thermostat had been set at 60 degrees.

If not for the extent of the spatter, I'd have doubted the location of the attack. My first thought after seeing the condition of the body was that the murder might have occurred somewhere else. Wouldn't it tie up nicely if he'd been killed in the swamp and beamed straight into the clubhouse foyer? Except for the blood, of course.

I shook my head. So many inconsistencies with this case—the timeline, the evidence, Pomeroy's story.

I went through it again. If the door was open like she said, who set off the silent alarm? And if she was there innocently, how did she know where to find her vase? Maybe she'd broken in to steal it and the victim interrupted her. But where was her weapon? Where was the brother? Maybe he'd been in the clubhouse when she got here. Did he have a confrontation with the dead man over the antique? I needed more answers from her. She was protecting someone, probably her brother.

I looked at my watch, daylight in another hour and a half. Then I could search outside specifically for footprints and the murder weapon because it couldn't be either the wedge or that vase. No blood. Whatever had been used to kill the victim had been wielded with a lot of force and would be imbedded with blood and tissue.

I doubted the tech team would get anything off the vase the way Tempe had handled it. I made note of some questions for the club manager regarding the victim.

A beam of light moved across the floor, its source outside the clubhouse. Pulling my Glock from its holster, I eased toward the French doors, quietly pushing them open. My eyes adjusted quickly as I edged along the back of the building toward the practice green. Coming around the corner I spotted a figure.

"What the—"

Ryan wasn't going to let me hear the end of this.

Chapter 16

Ever heard of the perp 'returning to the scene of the crime'?

TEMPE

After searching my house from top to bottom and finding nothing helpful, I drove to Alliance to find out if my mother had seen River, but her house was dark. Where could she be? Oh, any number of places, but as usual, not available when you needed her.

I was exhausted, but no one had called me to tell me I was fired, so I assumed I would be expected at the mail center by seven with my taboo bounty of mail and packages. With only a few hours until then, I decided to continue my search.

I parked in the maintenance lot near the fourth green and walked up the fairway to the clubhouse. If the killer...the killer—*Zeus*! It was as if I was someone else. That someone had found a dead body here yesterday. Was it *her* or me that made the decision to return to the... *just say it, Tempe*...

crime scene, and not return, so much as sneak past the yellow tape marked plainly, "DO NOT TRESPASS - CRIME SCENE" that surrounded the clubhouse and practice green.

The sheriff's SUV drove up. He sat there for ten minutes before he entered through the front door and his deputy drove away. All I needed was five minutes to find the other lid, before they started searching outside. I switched on the headlight I carry in my truck and flipped it on.

After the rain, the smell of fresh cut grass was strong and delighted my senses. My tennis shoes made squeaking noises against the wet blades, and I stopped on the sidewalk surrounding the clubhouse to scrape the grass off the bottoms. I didn't want to leave a trail of grass the sheriff could follow to find me.

It was dark and I fiddled with the headlight so it would shine on the fairway where I hoped I'd find the lid. If I was quiet and kept the light aimed away from the building, I might be able to search for fifteen minutes. The person who'd run out of the locker room exit had to have gone down the path and across the fairway. I pivoted toward the cart path—"Aiy."

"What the—"

"*Zeus' shrunken blue ball..oney!* You like to gave me a heart attack." It was true. My heart was pounding in my chest, my breath coming in gasps. On top of that, I'd just blown my chance to search for the lid. And from the look in the sheriff's eyes, I was in deep doo-doo.

Jack Lang grabbed me by my upper arms, cursed tautly, and let me go. More like *shoved* me away.

"What the hell are you doing here?"

"Um, I was looking for...clues?" Lightning flashed in the sky above Lang's head. Thunder followed. He didn't budge.

"So weather doesn't bother you? I know people who would duck at the first flash of..."

He just stared at me.

Hmm. I was in trouble. I tried again, "The way I have it figured the, uh, perp might have dropped something outside when he left."

I always know how to make matters worse.

"I was thinking the same thing myself," he said, with an inflection I didn't like one bit. "Since you've been reading up on crime scene vernacular, ever heard of the perp 'returning to the scene of the crime'?"

I gulped.

"Mm...hm. So, you know this is making you look even guiltier than you looked yesterday."

"But—"

"I should have arrested you, but it's not like I had to worry about you leaving town. I can't friggin' get rid of you."

It must seem like that to him, but still, I wasn't doing anything wrong. The hurt expression on my face didn't stop his tirade.

He paced. "I'm coming up with a lot more questions. Most of them come back to you and that ugly ass bottle." He used his index finger to accentuate his thoughts. "And then there's the little problem of you contaminating my crime scene. And I have to ask myself, 'Why?' What don't you want me to find? Maybe you did it after all."

"I didn't." Surely an experienced police officer could tell when someone was telling the truth. But I was only telling a half-truth, and he'd figured that out. My fists gripped the edges of my t-shirt and twisted. I caught myself and slowly released the fabric, pretended a calm I didn't feel.

He shrugged, jaw jutting out. "Maybe. And maybe it went like this. That Chinese piece of ugly art is worth a lot of money. And maybe that killer remodeling job is sucking more dough than your mail job can cover. You overheard about the vase on one of your visits to the clubhouse, or from a customer, met the victim here under the pretense of buying it from him, tricked him into telling you where it was, and then you killed him." He rubbed his chin, "Yeah, it's coming together for me now."

"What?" My eyes went wide and a night bug actually flew into my gaping mouth. Where was he getting all this baloney?

"Then, you went to the locker, busted the lock, grabbed the vase and were about to take off when your buddy the sheriff showed up. "Bet you thought that was convenient." His voice was etched with contempt.

I squirmed under his predatory gaze. Swallowing was impossible as my throat tightened around that night bug, and my mouth went dry.

"And here you are. Back at the scene of your crime."

Now I was scared. If I hadn't known I was innocent, he might have even convinced *me* I was guilty. What if he arrested me? Not only would this put a serious kink in my life, but if I was locked up, I couldn't look for my brother. And forget about my job.

"Sheriff—surely you don't believe that."

His smile was feral. "But you see, it's starting to make a lot of sense. I come back here after leaving you at your house, and in the middle of the night I find you scarfing around out here looking for 'clues'," he said, miming quotes with the fingers of both hands. "What are you looking for?"

"A second lid. I thought I might find it in the grass."

He didn't say anything for a long time, just studied me like a pinned frog on a biology class slide.

"What kind of vase has two lids?" he scoffed. "And what's so important about finding it at *four* in the morning?"

"The amphora is practically worthless without it. And..."

JACK

She was a terrible liar, telegraphing the next one with her whole body. I crossed my arms and went in for the kill, "When were you going to tell me about your brother?"

"Wha—um."

I watched the emotions cycle across her face like one of those time lapsed videos of brewing thunderclouds. Shock, surprise, worry, wariness and finally, *hmm,* relief.

"I—oh, crap."

The tension left her body at once, her shoulders slumping like a balloon depleted of helium.

"I've been so worried about him."

This she was not lying about—the fear. The trembling in her voice was genuine.

"Where is he?"

She shook her head and sighed, "I don't know. He didn't come home Sunday night. And," she blinked rapidly, placed a fist against her chest and looked off, "I should have known something was wrong."

"Why?"

She paused. "He never stays out all night. And yesterday morning one of his subcontractors called because he didn't show up on the job."

"See, two things bother me about this story. You think your brother is missing but you've been reluctant to tell me about it. And you haven't filed a Missing Persons report."

"Oh, come on, Sheriff. It hasn't been twenty-four hours. Don't you have to wait at least forty-eight? That's what they always say on those TV sh...um." She looked at the floor.

She had me there.

"Then there's the situation with his amphora."

Uh-huh. She'd hang herself if I gave her enough rope.

"You came in when I was taking it out of the locker so I knew you wouldn't believe me. The bottle was stolen. That's the truth."

Meaning the next thing that came out of her mouth...

She didn't meet my eyes and there was just the slightest pause before she said, "Someone called me... and said he had it."

"Ah," I said, watching the relief cross her face. That was a lie, or I hadn't just spent the last fifteen years reading the motives of junior officers and criminals. "So, the dead man stole it or knew who stole it; he was holding it for ransom.

You met him, refused to pay, killed him, and then retrieved it."

"No!" She actually stomped her foot. "No, no, no." She pressed her fingertips to her forehead. I could almost hear her teeth grinding.

"How'd you know it was there?"

She looked up, her eyebrows forming a deep crease above her nose.

"The vase. How'd you know it was there?" I asked again in a growly whisper.

"I..." Her voice came out thready, and she looked a little scared.

Wait for it. Wait...here it comes...

"I...sorta... smelled it."

Just once I'd like to be wrong. "*Right.* The place already stunk worse than any crime scene I've ever known, and you're telling me you smelled it? I have to hand it to you. If they gave out blue ribbons for fabrication, you'd win hands down."

I reached for my handcuffs.

"What are you doing?" She stepped back.

"I'm taking you in." I could hold her for a day or so. Maybe spending some time in our no-star resort lockup worrying about losing her job would get me some answers. But I had a big problem with arresting her. According to the ME the time of death was indeed noon-ish, which meant I knew who Tempest Pomeroy was with and who her alibi was.

Me.

Chapter 17

I wanted to have it out with Diablo...take it outside, so to speak.

JACK

I installed Pomeroy in the empty jail cell but didn't lock it, although I was tempted to see if she'd try her hand-me-down skills on one of my locks. Pulling a case file from the desk drawer I remembered I'd promised to call Jordie.

"Where's Tempe?"

The voice sounded like it belonged on a classic western, laced with tequila and cigarettes. I turned to face a tall man dressed in black. I could almost hear the cheesy "Good, Bad, and Ornery" music in the background. His name would have been *Diablo*.

I hadn't even heard the door open. I thought of the covert operatives I'd met while serving in the Mideast. Intimidating, with his wet slicked black hair, dark eyes and stubbled jaw—

this man would be hazardous to your health. His face held no expression, hands hanging loose at his sides, but I recognized a seasoned warrior when I saw one. Battle-ready.

"Who's asking?"

"Dylan McGuinness, Special Investigator." He pulled his black leather jacket aside to expose his badge.

What was he to Tempe? I wondered, as I pointed to the chair by the door. "Have a seat."

He hesitated for a minute then, moving mindfully, taking stock of his surroundings, lowered himself onto the chair. Spring-loaded... dangerous... and proprietary were my impressions.

"What is your relationship with Tempest Pomeroy?" I asked and was blindsided by an irrational stab of... jealousy?

His lip quirked in tandem with an eyebrow. "What's it to you? I'm here on official business, Sheriff..." he eyed the name plate on the desk, "...Lang." I didn't know the man but felt an instinctive dislike and distrust. What was his association with Tempe?

"State your business then—McGuinness, was it?"

I wasn't sure how it happened, but we seemed to be in some kind of pissing contest. "Ms. Pomeroy didn't have a phone call so how did you know she was here?"

"Why *didn't* she get a phone call, if you've arrested her?" His thumb and index finger rubbed his whiskered chin and it wasn't lost on me that he hadn't answered my question.

I felt a sudden perverse sense of non-cooperation. I didn't just *not* want to answer. I wanted to have it out with Diablo...

take it outside, so to speak. Where was that coming from? Talk about irrational. And I prided myself on my rationality. I regrouped.

"Well, she's not exactly arrested—yet. I'm still thinking on it."

McGuinness' narrowed eyes failed to conceal the workings of his quick lethal mind, and if I guessed correctly, a fondness for my prisoner.

Her comment about misplaced trust came to mind, and I felt myself bristle. I made fists under the table trying to push down the ugly green emotions roiling up inside me. Once again, I had nothing to go on, but my instincts were screaming in his presence.

"So, what do I have to do to spring her?"

"Depends. If you can keep her away from my crime scene, I'm tempted to let you have her," I said, with implied double meaning.

He nodded. "I might be able to handle that. She has a sit-down with her boss in less than an hour, and if she doesn't end up suspended, she'll be busy working all day. I have to get a couple statements from her this evening or tomorrow."

I winced as I remembered her comment about being fired over picking up Jordie. "How well do you know her?"

McGuinness' head tilted, and he hesitated before answering. One black eyebrow arched, he asked, "What's it to you?"

Ah, there it was.

"Just curious if you know her brother, River."

He nodded. Contemplating again. This guy wasn't one to run off at the mouth.

"I know River." He inhaled, his shoulders relaxing finally. "I talked to Tempe earlier; she was concerned about him."

Oh, she did, did she? "Why talk to you?"

"I guess she thought I might be able to help."

"Again, why you? Why not the cops, her mother?"

"I was a friend of the family."

"*Was* a friend?"

"Am a friend." McGuinness' head tilted again, and he placed his elbow on my desk. One big fist came up to casually prop up his chin. "Sheriff, is this going somewhere? Should I be calling a lawyer?" The man didn't rattle.

"You know about the body we found at the clubhouse." It wasn't a question. I got the feeling he knew a lot more about this whole situation than I did.

"I was in touch with her because of UM's involvement and an ongoing investigation that happened prior to this incident. When I talked to her, she was upset that River hadn't shown up on his job site, yesterday morning."

"So her concern about her brother has something to do with this stolen amphora?"

Oh, he was good. There was just the slightest flash of—alarm? Recognition? It was gone so quickly I wondered if I'd imagined it.

"His amphora probably went missing about the same time he was last seen."

I would come out better questioning the unskilled liar in my cell than this PI but even pros slip up now and then. He'd known when River was last seen.

"When was that?" I asked.

"The contractor said his man saw him Sunday night at the Wasted Turtle."

"Well, he's probably sleeping it off somewhere, then."

"Apparently you've never met River," he said.

There was another space in time where we marked our proverbial territories, then I asked, "Work undercover much, McGuinness?"

After a quick mental assessment in my direction, he said, "Every now and then."

I got up. "Before I release her, I should mention that I'm not done. I still have a case to solve and a lot of questions unanswered." I looked at him pointedly, "By everyone." It was hard to tell by his inscrutable expression if he heard me. Or cared.

"I have a couple more concerns to clear up with her and then she can go. Wait here."

TEMPE

The sheriff strolled in and leaned nonchalantly against the wall across from my cell. "Your boyfriend, McGuinness, corroborated your story about your brother."

"He's not my boyfriend."

"Yeah, that's what he said. Ex-boyfriend... whatever," he said sarcastically.

What was his problem? "What do you want, Sheriff?" I blew out a breath. He was exasperating. The weight of the last twenty-four hours sat on my shoulders like twin boulders; it would probably be another eighteen before I got any sleep. And I hadn't made *any* progress in finding River.

"When did you know your brother's vase had been stolen?"

I blinked. It didn't seem like a trick question. "It sits on the mantle. When I got ready to leave for work yesterday morning it was gone."

"Your brother lives with you?"

"Yes." My voice came out hoarse, and I cleared my throat. "Occasionally he stays with my mother."

"What's her name and address?"

"Phoebe Pomeroy." I recited her phone number but had to think about the address.

"Is there some reason why you don't want to give me her address?"

"Hold your shorts, Lang. Phoebe and I are not close. I'm trying to picture her mailbox." I closed my eyes and yawned. "Try 61479 Hwy 217 in Alliance. I drove over there last night —well, this morning—before I came to the golf course. She wasn't home."

He wrote the information on his pad and I was aware of the masculine beauty of his hands once again. Someone said he'd been a fighter pilot. I could picture those hands on the stick, working the controls.

Unbidden came an image of tanned dexterous fingers stroking my thigh, his darker skin contrasting with mine... I shook my head to banish the image. It was a waste of time to think about this man in those terms. Any attraction he might have felt twenty-four hours ago was surely dead and buried.

"Am I still a suspect?" I asked.

"There's the B&E at the clubhouse, and you're connected to the vase, but unless you can be in two places at once, you're clear of the murder. The same can't be said of your brother."

"What? You make me so mad." I wasn't volunteering another word. I paced the small cell.

"Your brother has been AWOL since Sunday night and, most likely, so has the vase. I haven't figured out the connection yet, but I will."

"Sheriff, you need to start thinking of my brother as a victim —before it's too late."

"There you go again, pinging my cop radar. You might want to consider that if something happens to your brother, and you haven't told me everything, you'll be partly to blame."

I closed my eyes, knowing it was true. "I already am."

When I leaned against the cell door it swung open. I glared at him. I'd remained captive in an unlocked cell. Bet he enjoyed that.

I shoved past him to the front room where Dylan waited. There was a rare look of sincere concern on his face. "You all right, Pumpkin?" For some reason the "P" name irritated me more than usual.

The endearment wasn't lost on Jack Lang as he leaned against the doorjamb watching us. "I need my cell phone."

He rummaged through a drawer and brought out my keys and cell. Before I could ask, he said, "The vase is locked up in the evidence room."

I was relieved that it was safe, but still furious with him for keeping it from me. "Don't let anything happen to it. I'll be checking with you this afternoon to see what progress you've made on finding my brother."

"I don't doubt it."

Dylan followed me through the door to his pickup. "Where to?"

"Drop me at the house. I've got to change and get to work." Maybe I should have thanked Dylan for springing me but it felt a bit too much like a rescue, something I could barely admit to myself, much less confess to my one time lover, especially after the way we'd split.

As soon as I walked through the employee entrance, several voices rang out.

"Tempe, Beck's been lookin' for you."

"Hey, boss, jailbird's back."

"Oh, lay off her, will 'ya, Charles," Janice said.

"I wouldn't want to be in your shoes," one of the clerks said.

James Allen slid in next to me as I walked the mail and packages to my case. "Temp, a postal investigator was at the back door yesterday evening looking for you."

"Who?" It couldn't have been Dylan. "Dark hair, dark everything?"

"Nah, this was a new black dude from New Orleans—a real hot shot, looking to make a name for himself. I'm thinkin' you made waves yesterday and he wants to ride them up the ladder. Look, if you need help today, with anything just—" He made the hand sign for a phone to his ear. "I'm serious."

James' route runs near mine and we often exchanged deliveries if we got in a bind. He was African-American with nearly white hair, even though he was only in his early forties. He had a friendly smile and a perpetually positive attitude I admired, while maintaining a realistic perspective about life, and the postal service.

"Thank you, friend. But you may want to steer clear of me for a couple days. You might catch the termination plague."

He grinned. "I've been inoculated." Meaning he'd been grandfathered in from the other system and they couldn't touch him. We rapped knuckles and he went back to casing his mail.

The intercom shrilled, "Pomeroy, come to the office."

I laid the undeliverable mail and packages from Monday down on the counter and crossed the floor to the office feeling twenty sets of eyes on my back.

Twenty-five minutes later, after an official warning, a yell fest by Bancroft pointing out that I'd picked a fine time to get official eyes turned on his little mail center, and some transparently self-serving questions from the New Orleans PI who definitely had me in his sights, I was told to get back to work and don't call any more attention to myself.

"Tell that to the dead guy at the clubhouse," I muttered, *which* I shouldn't have said to my boss before I asked for the day off to look for River.

He turned me down.

Chapter 18

Staying out of trouble hadn't been working for me so far, so why start now?

TEMPE

The rest of the day held no news about River, which kept me with a feeling of impending doom and in a bad mood pretty much all day. There were no appearances by law enforcement, recalcitrant Imps or ex-lovers—that was certainly a relief—but it didn't mean the day had no aggravations. The EVAL Cert continued, the mail was extraordinarily heavy, and then there were the usual odd customers.

Like Mrs. Abercrombie who stood waiting at her mailbox to instruct me in the care and maintenance of her ornamental mailbox flag, shaped like a hummingbird. An elegant lady in her sixties, she said, "I'll put my flag like this"...bird snout up..."when I have mail, but once you collect it I want you to put it here." Instead of returning the flag/snout to its horizontal position next to the mailbox per regulations, she placed her slender index finger at the tip of the humming-bird's beak and eased it to a forty-five degree angle. I may have been smiling and nodding, but inside I was doing a monster eye roll.

Less than ten houses later a retired accountant asked if it would be possible to put her mail in alphabetical order. Grrr... Customers like these were becoming the norm rather than the exception, since every mail service in the country was jumping through hoops to secure business. Unfortunately, these two women would continue to be disappointed with my service.

I did manage to get in touch with a man at The Tricked-Out Tarot on the south side of Destiny who said he could prepare the replacement bottle for River. I still had the same problem though. River's force was in limbo. Without River and the bottle in the same, say, twenty square foot area, I wouldn't be able to reconnect my brother with his life force.

And I figured it would be better if I had the original bottle with its 'soul recall'. That meant I had to find the other lid, and soon.

At 11:30 I called Peggy. I asked what she found out at the Wasted Turtle, but she just put me through to the sheriff. He'd gone home for a couple hours. If irritation could be transmitted through the phone, mine would have been a hot blue flame biting at his eardrum. He was the cause of my being in this tired, irritable state, and he was wasting time sleeping when he should be out looking for my brother.

"What!" the sleepy voice groused.

"My, aren't we the picture of voter appreciation. How do you expect to find my brother from your bedroom?"

"Get to the point." His voice was muffled, like he'd pulled his shirt over his head. Then I heard a zipper...

"What did Peggy find out at the Turtle?"

Another sound, water running. "She talked with Rutledge's man and got a description of the girl, though not much of one. Blonde, curvy, medium height, nice ass. His words. He either didn't see her from the front, or didn't look at her face."

Figures. "I want to know what you find out, *when* you find out," I said.

"Just get me that picture of River."

The only "picture" I had of my brother was a self-portrait River had made with a wish that I had scanned once upon a time to use for just such a purpose.

"And stay out of trouble."

I hung up. Staying out of trouble hadn't been working for me so far, so why start now?

I wracked my brain to come up with someone River might have gone out with Sunday. There was one girl from River's past, but she was a brunette. Paige Whyte. We'd never gotten along. She worked at the Red Carpet Inn. After work I drove by the motel, but it was Paige's day off and her boss wouldn't give me her address or phone number. Halfway between my house and the fairgrounds sat Joe's Crawfish. I pulled in hoping he hadn't already run out. He stopped scrubbing his ice chest when I got out of my truck.

"How 'bout you take some crawfish off my hands, Tempe? I have three pounds of crawfish and a bunch of potatoes and corn. You can have it all for five dollars."

"Are you sure, Mr. Joe? That's awfully cheap."

He opened a small chest and withdrew a bag, handing it to me. "I'm sure. Now I can close up and get outta here. Crawfish are dyin' on me. I shoulda known better than to open this early in the season. This cold front will just screw it up for another week." He pocketed the money, then picked up his hose and resumed his cleaning. Conversation over. My stomach growled as I put the truck in gear and headed home.

"Oh, man." I pulled up beside the porch. I'd forgotten the broken window. I stood there, taking in the jagged edged sheet of glass propped against the tree. There were beads of glass everywhere. I must do something about Freddie.

I set my crawfish down on a stack of leftover roofing tin, pulled my gloves on and moved the broken pieces next to the house, covering them with the cardboard box and a tarp. Then I carried my dinner to the edge of the swamp and sat down on a fallen cypress tree.

Dusk is my favorite time of the day here. Everything wild takes a siesta, and the bayou turns into a mirror. Once or twice a day, a flock of white egrets flies low across the water, like now, creating the illusion of two flocks. The rain clouds were gone and the increasing moon sat just above the trees.

We'd named it Harmony, and any other time, this spot by the Forge would restore my sense of equilibrium, but tonight it wasn't working. I couldn't even eat Joe's tasty crawfish. My stomach was queasy with worry.

I walked back to the house and looked in River's telephone book for Paige. No luck. I called the phone company, pleaded an emergency to try and get his cell phone bill. They refused, since I wasn't on his account. I copied his phone book for Peggy, printed the scanned portrait for the sheriff and printed

50 color copies because Sheriff Lang might be too cheap to print them in color.

I called Phoebe again, starting to wonder where the heck she was. But time moves slowly when you're worried and watching the clock, Besides it wasn't unusual for Phoebe be off on some tangent, or to shut me out.

I sat at my desk looking at my brother's picture. He'd been such a cute kid. He'd grown into a sweet hunk of a guy, too. Clear golden eyes, unruly tawny hair, muscular build that was inherent to Djinn—to my mind, a real catch. If I had my way, he wouldn't get involved with Paige again.

THIRTY MINUTES LATER, I PULLED INTO THE PARKING LOT at the community college and saw the SOAPs standing outside waiting for me. We met formally once a month, and February's activity had been selected by Bailey, a two-night workshop on social media at the local community college. I promised Montana I'd pretend enthusiasm even though learning how to Squawk or use Snapchat was way down on my list. Like holding up the bottom.

I felt better after a group hug and warm smiles from Aurora, Montana, Mariah, Shannon and Bailey, five of my six Paramortal sisters. SOAP stands for Sisters of the Astral Plane. We let the mere-mortals think we're daytime TV fans.

I knew I wouldn't be able to concentrate on a class when my world was nuts. Montana slipped in beside me and turned her computer on.

The florescent lights apparently did nothing for my complexion because Montana remarked on it, "Tempe, you should take tomorrow off. You look like you were the corpse instead of finding one."

"I'm starting to feel like it, too. I got a sub for tomorrow, which is just going to give my boss more ammunition against me." Six computers were set up around each of two large tables, but we had pulled some chairs close together taking advantage of the minutes before class started.

Montana said, "I filled the girls in yesterday evening about River, and Six Packs." She winked. "Anything new?"

"Now that you ask...is it my imagination or am I not having more trouble with the opposite sex?"

Montana held up her index finger and thumb an inch apart. "It did seem as if Mr. Jackson and Dick Randall were focused on you more than usual."

Bailey said, "Billy Huber was in the DMV today and he said he heard you were stealing the contents of your packages and selling them on eBay."

Bailey Duplessis sat on the other side of me. She was a petite blonde with green eyes who worked at the DMV during the day and after hours at Bons Amis as a waitress. If you met her on her night job you probably wouldn't realize you were talking to the same person you got your tag from. She's a chameleon. No, she's actually a chameleon. It's her supernatural nature. People describe her as quirky, but I think what they're really seeing is her dual personality.

Mariah said, "And I heard you broke into the golf club to get some of those expensive clubs to pawn because you're running short of money for the Voracious Monster."

I just stared. "Where do people get this stuff?"

Montana said, "Well, here's some good news. The guy with the coroner's office told me he stuck the body—"

"What?" Three voices sounded simultaneously.

Montana explained, "This is not for public consumption: SOAPs only. The sheriff called the coroner and asked him to get a body temperature on the victim so he could get an idea of TOD. That's 'time of death'," she clarified.

Aurora asked, "Why wouldn't he just wait for the autopsy?"

I sat back, thinking about that. "The sheriff was probably trying to get an idea if he should let me go, or arrest me."

"For what?" Bailey's eyes widened. "Killing that man?"

Montana tapped Bailey's hand. "Shush, Bailey." She turned back to me. "Well, if what Bobby, the coroner's man told me is correct, he was killed around noon. You were delivering the mail right?"

I nodded and couldn't help but smile. "If that's true, Sheriff Lang can't arrest me. He's my alibi."

We all laughed except Aurora, who just eye smiled.

"But I forgot to tell you that I had two visits from Marty yesterday."

"What!" Montana exclaimed. "How could you forget that? That Imp never shows up unless something's fixin' to go down."

"See what I mean about crazy males? And that's not all. I, uh —" As close as I was to these women, I still hesitated, and maybe I shouldn't go there. The group scooted their chairs closer. I exhaled, shaking my head and felt Bailey's hand patting my knee.

"Goddess, Tempe." Montana's finger quit its impatient tapping. "Class is about to start. Spill it."

"It seems silly to mention, but every time I turn around, half a dozen times yesterday, I'm either crying, mad or thinking about zapping somebody. It's like the Grandmother of PMSs."

Shannon said, "You poor thing. You've been under a lot of stress."

Bailey squealed, "Oh my God, you're pregnant."

The rest of the SOAPs gave a collective, "Ssshhhh" and after an inquisitive stare or two, the other students resumed their conversations.

I rolled my eyes and they landed on Montana. She gave me a cynical smile, "Happens to the best of 'em."

"Well, in my case there'd have to be a Star in the East."

Everyone laughed, everyone but Aurora whose expression was pensive. Her gaze centered on mine. "It's the quickening," she said quietly.

No one spoke, just looked from her to me and back. Did that mean they agreed, they felt sorry for me, or they were thinking, "She told you so."

Montana said, "It's time, Tempe. I never have understood why you—"

Aurora stopped her with a raised hand. "We'll talk about this later, Montana. Tempe, can you drop by the shop tomorrow?"

"I'll try. I have to go by the Sheriff's Office and fill out a missing person's report on River." I swallowed. "And after I'm done, I want to drop in on Mr. Jackson."

Montana swept her long black hair away from her face. "He'll be back at home harassing you in no time."

"Oh, good." They chuckled.

"Isn't he that retired mail carrier? What was his problem this time?" Bailey asked.

Aurora said matter of factly, "It's the approaching Chaos... What did the sheriff think?"

"He's *dovelo*; he just thinks I'm a kook magnet."

"Oh, I wouldn't say you're a magnet," came the familiar baritone voice. I heard the sighs of the women in the room as we turned to see the broad shouldered form of Jack Lang.

"Ladies," he nodded his head at each of them, hat in his hand. The face that had stopped me in my tracks thirty-six hours ago covered in shaving cream, was now covered with a layer of bronze beard stubble, giving him a rakish, uncivilized look. Adventurous. Dangerous. "What's a 'da velo?'" His gaze focused on me, as the teacher announced the start of class. Five sets of eyes turned toward him and five sets of feet kicked me in the shins in an under-the-table high five.

"So that's Six Packs," Shannon waggled her eyebrows.

Mariah muttered, "Come to mama."

Chapter 19

She had her own version of The Eye.

JACK

The women in the class stared at me, the room going as quiet as the desert at midnight. I looked down at my shirt to see if I'd spilled my coffee, or left my fly open. The tall one, Montana, the EMT, looked like the warrior princess from the TV series, her squinty-eyed focus projecting a warning, "You mess with my friends, you answer to me." It was unsettling.

I did a double take when Tempe introduced me to Bailey. At the DMV, she'd looked like a young Amish girl in her sedate boxy grey top and long jeans skirt, her hair in a tight knot. The young woman in front of me, with her artfully mussed hair, tight black jeans and a hot pink off the shoulder shirt showing a good bit of cleavage, could have been her party twin.

"Sheriff Lang, you may take any of the available computer

stations," the teacher said. "I'll just be a few more minutes getting the video presentation set up."

"Call me Jack," I said, nodding to each of the students in the class. Suddenly, there was a seat available next to Tempe, and I gravitated to it. The woman who'd vacated the seat held out her hand to me.

"I'm Aurora Boreal, I own the boutique downtown. We met at the civic association meeting."

"I remember, Ms. Boreal," I said, returning her firm handshake and getting the urge to tug my hand back when she held it just a tad longer than most people while she studied my face. She had her own version of The Eye. For the first time since boot camp I felt like squirming in my seat.

Tempe said, "Aurora is the. . . President of our group."

"I've heard of your uh, group—the SOAPs, right?" I studied Aurora Boreal. She was dressed in a gypsy-looking outfit of grays and pinks, and looked like the leader of an artists' community. Her hair was streaked black and silver, and dangling from a braid above one ear was a buzzard feather, glinting like a rainbow in the harsh florescent lighting. Around her neck hung an amulet in some kind of studded Celtic design. She didn't strike me as a soap opera lover. "I appreciate your help with my campaign and the voter registration drive."

Aurora nodded, "We were happy to lend our support, Sheriff. It was time for a change. Do you have any leads on the murder at the clubhouse?"

Straight to the point, with a little reminder about who gets things accomplished in the parish? "It's early yet. We're still investigating and interviewing suspects."

Aurora looked at Tempe, then at me. "Tempe had nothing to do with it."

From someone else that comment might have elicited my investigative instincts, but despite their eccentricities, I didn't get the feeling these women were involved. Did they know what Tempe was holding back? I looked at their savvy interested faces. *Definitely.*

I looked at Tempe and said, "She hasn't been charged with anything."

"Yet," Tempe said under her breath. "Aurora, let the—Jack sit down, we're holding up class."

With a look that said she wasn't finished with me yet, Aurora slipped into a chair at the other table, and I sat down on the chair next to Tempe.

"Heard anything from your brother?" I whispered.

"No. Did you get Peggy to make inquiries like you promised?"

"Yes. Nothing yet." I opened my booklet to the first page. "Your friends are quite—"

"Supportive," she supplied before I could choose any other adjectives.

"That wasn't what I was going for. Eclectic? Offbeat?"

"Oh, you haven't seen anything yet." Her smile gave me that edgy feeling for the third time since I'd arrived.

My cell phone rang with the ME's number on the ID. I excused myself to walk out into the hallway. The only class in session the social media class, the rest of the rooms dark. I walked around the corner to the rest rooms so I couldn't be overheard and dialed the Medical Examiner.

Less than two minutes later, I ducked my head back into the classroom and made my apologies. Tempe leaped from her chair and came after me as I walked down the corridor to the double doors leading to the parking lot. I heard her running after me down the sidewalk but ignored her until she called out, "Jack, wait."

I turned at my vehicle, shaking my keys impatiently. "I have to go, Tempe." I unlocked the SUV.

"What is it? Is it River?" She grabbed my arm halting my progress, "Jack, please." Her voice rose in fear, making me feel like a hard-hearted bastard.

"I'm sorry. I can't discuss it with you."

She stood there under the lamplight as I drove away. I wanted to tell her about the call, but I hadn't officially cleared her of any involvement.

The call was from the coroner saying I should get to his office immediately. He sounded shaken.

TEMPE

SOAPs night was always followed by drinks at Bons Amis. Aurora had begged off, however.

I arrived first. The dark haired bartender delivered a drink to a customer a few feet to my right and said, "Tempe, what's shakin', Lass? Was the newspaper right then? You found that body?" The Ireland in his voice was soft but distinct.

"I did, Liam."

Without asking he placed a frosty mug with my favorite tonic water and lime in front of me. If it's news, there are two places you can find it first, Bons Amis and Jane Fortune.

I started to ask him if he'd seen River, but then the customer next to me turned around and smirked at me. It was Fritz.

"Well, if it isn't Tempest," he spat.

Sounded like somebody had received a reprimand from his supervisor.

Fritz is about as unappealing physically as his personality is offensive. His belly overflows his belt to the point that he can barely reach the pedal in his mail truck—or so I've been told. And even in the dimly lit bar you could see the broken veins on his nose and blotches across his cheeks from his excesses. Then there was the mean expression always visible in his beady black eyes. Sometimes I wondered if he was a variant, but *menori* says no. Just the worst kind of human.

"Liam, who let the Toad in? You should cut him off before he makes a bigger fool of himself, or tries to harass one of your customers and gets his ass kicked."

"Oh, yeah?" Fritz' squinty eyes flared as he rose from his stool, "and who's going to kick it? You, little Miss tattle-tale? Couldn't handle me on your own, so you went running to the boss."

"Oh, I can handle it, Fritz, but I wouldn't want to hurt you, so think of it as taking your well being into consideration. If you keep on the way you're going, harassing the women in this town, you're going to wind up hurt." I probably sounded calm —I was working hard at it—but *menori* was stirring the syntaxes of my nervous system and it was taking everything I had to tamp them down.

"You all heard that. She threatened me," he called out to the crowd.

A few of the patrons rolled their eyes, most just ignored him. Liam responded by pulling Fritz's beer out of his hand, upending it over the sink and pouring out the remainder. "Since ye're finished with yer ale, you should leave. That one, 'twas on the house." Liam's smile didn't reach his eyes, and his hand rested on the baseball bat at the end of the counter. Though I didn't think Liam needed a bat.

"You can't throw me out." Fritz turned toward Liam and pointed his thumb at me over his shoulder. "She threatened me."

"That's not what I heard, me boyo," Liam said as his fingers tapped the bat. "Now, are you fer leavin' on your own two feet or bein' carried?"

Fritz looked at me, his lip curled in a snarl. "You haven't heard the last of this, bitch—"

"Now that sounded like a threat, Fritz." I looked at Liam. "Didn't that sound like a threat, Liam?"

"It did, lass. Out, Fritz, and stay out. The Wasted Turtle down by the levee is more your style."

The Wasted Turtle was the dive where the less civilized rednecks went; shootings and knife fights were regular occurrences. A coworker told me she'd been offered a gig singing with the band there, but her husband nixed it. He said there were too many brawls. When she asked one of the band members about it, he'd shrugged it off saying, the fights were "only in the audience."

Coincidentally, it was also the bar where River had been seen leaving on Sunday night and *that* I couldn't reconcile with my brother's lifestyle.

"Better watch it over there, Fritz, turtles are crazy for toads," I said.

This man never listened to reason, thinking himself above the merest rules of conduct, so I wasn't surprised when he turned his back on Liam and grabbed my breast as he got down from his stool.

Pain and rage splintered my control as I saw red. No, I actually saw red. An unfamiliar burgeoning force inside me zinged from my core, through my blood vessels, exploding from each nerve, ending in a shatter of bright red sparks. They shimmered around me. The Toad stiffened as the charge connected. I planted my knee in his groin to cover the real cause of his distress.

With an indelicate wheeze he went to his knees. Liam grabbed him by the elbow and helped him up. "It's no more than you deserve, Fritz." He pushed him through the front door and warned, "Don't come back in m' bar or ye'll be sorry."

Chapter 20

Ah've seen my share of the odd, I have. Fashioned some of me own, if ya' ken.

TEMPE

The mist of red was dissipating by the time Liam returned, concern on his face. "Did he hurt 'ya, dearling?" When he tried to put his hand on my shoulder, I felt the coalescence of energy just before it shot across the bar and latched onto his hand. He jumped back. "What the hel—"

"Shoo—I'm so sorry, Liam. It's this static electricity."

"There's no need ta' lie, Tempe. Ah've seen my share of the odd, I have. Fashioned some of me own, if ya' ken," he said, a reminder to me of his own nature.

Churichauns are distant cousins to the Leprechaun. They are the introverts of the clan, with one distinguishing trait—they're the gatekeepers of the spirits—alcoholic spirits. In the old country, they guarded the wine cellars and casks of whiskey, while their more progressive descendants of the twenty-first century prefer tending bar or working in a wealthy man's wine cellar.

Liam is a Churichaun vampire, bitten back in the eighteenth century by his employer after sampling some of the vamp's rare wine and falling asleep on the job. It's one of the reasons he tends bar. It's a test of his control. And then there's the need to work nights. He doesn't go around after the bar closes and suck neck or anything. The blood thing apparently isn't an issue for him, but light is.

Electricity was the closest I could come to explaining what had just happened. "I wasn't exactly lying, Liam. My frustration toward Fritz put a little extra zip in my zap. Did you...see anything?" Maybe the shimmering red cloud that had obscured my vision hadn't been invisible.

"Like...?" he tilted his head wiggling his fingers in an "out with it" gesture. I recognized Montana's throaty laugh as she and Bailey came through the front door. Liam called, "Bailey, get your flighty arse into an apron. I've been snowed under, waitin' on ya," he winked at Tempe.

Montana nodded her head toward the door. "Hey, Temp. That guy you work with is out there keying your truck. Not that he can do a hell of a lot of damage, but he was on the driver's side—"

I pushed past her through the front doors. Sure enough, Fritz was gouging deep scratches into the side of my mail truck. Thunder rumbled around the parking lot as I raised my hand toward him, "Fritz!" and then he was tumbling ass over knucklehead across the parking lot where he came to rest against a dumpster. As providence, or karma, or supremely bad luck would have it, a familiar green SUV made a sliding stop, sending pebbles flying.

Fritz predictably started whining and pointing fingers at me. "Sheriff, arrest her. She hit me."

I started to argue, to explain that I really didn't go around picking fights and brawling at bars, but Jack Lang looked utterly weary and very irritable. He bent to lend Fritz a hand up but Toady shrugged him off.

What was it with the male population and me the last few days? I must keep that appointment with Aurora tomorrow as much as I dreaded it.

Montana followed me out. "Sheriff, I saw him keying the side of her truck."

Jack Lang arched a brow meaningfully at the passenger side of my truck, where five-years worth of bush, brick, and mailbox scratches had taken its toll.

"The good side," I said, crossing my arms.

"And he assaulted her in the bar," Liam said behind me, where a crowd was streaming out into the parking lot for a firsthand look at the entertainment. "In front of a bar full o' witnesses."

A brief narrowing of the sheriff's eyes was all I saw, but I felt sexual tension grip me, then he turned his glare on Fritz. "What have you got to say for yourself?" The hand on Fritz's shoulder had turned into a twisting fist, and Fritz was standing on his toes, the threat finally starting to sink in. "Well?"

"Ahh, she attacked me... first?"

Wide eyed, Fritz looked into Lang's hard face. Once again,

Jack's focused intensity reminded me of a predator—silent, mesmerizing, deadly.

"Is that right," he said slowly.

Everyone seemed to hold their breath while Fritz just stared, then he shook his head, twice—left, right.

"That's what I thought. Let's see what a night spent in parish accommodations will do for your memory."

"But—but..." Fritz sputtered as the sheriff opened the back door of the cruiser, placed cuffs on his wrists and lowered him onto the back seat, firmly shutting the door on his protestations. He walked over to me.

"We need to talk," he said.

I looked toward his car, "If it's about Fr—"

"Not him." He took my arm and called out, "You folks can go back inside." Montana stayed near the door.

"Go on now," he looked at Montana. Seeing her reluctance, he sighed wearily and explained, "I just need a few minutes of Ms. Pomeroy's time. In private." When Montana crossed her arms and leaned against the front of the building, Jack threw up his hands and swore.

"All right." He turned to me, "Can I trust your friends?"

"With my life," I said. Fear crawled down my spine. "Is it River—" I gripped his arm.

"No. Tempe. There's nothing new on your brother. I need to ask you to account for your whereabouts for the last eight hours."

"Really?" When would this end? I felt like his favorite scapegoat.

"Your friends, too, now that I think about it."

"We've all been in class or here for the last three hours. Before that, I was putting up posters and trying to run my mother down." I looked at Montana, "Not literally, of course."

Montana said, "I was sleeping this afternoon, spent an hour at the women's shelter, then on to class. Bailey and I rode together from there."

"What is it, Jack?" The muscles in his arm were rigid. He pinched the bridge of his nose with the fingertips of those long dexterous fingers.

Finally he said, "I've got good news and bad news. The call I got during class was from the coroner. The good news is the time of death—noonish—pretty much clears you of the murder, as you had a pretty fair alibi at the time."

"Well, I knew I didn't kill him." I expelled a sigh. "And the bad news?"

"The body's missing."

Chapter 21

The way the four women looked at each other then, made my fingers itch.

JACK

"Missing—"

The color that drained from her face was better than a polygraph. It affirmed, if nothing else, that she didn't know anything about the body being stolen from the morgue. She was always in the eye of the storm though, so I had no doubt there was something she still wasn't telling me. My instincts told me that, and they never lied. "I'm afraid so."

"But how can that be?" Montana asked. "Surely someone can't just walk into the morgue, throw a body over his shoulder and walk out. And why would they want to?"

Tempe asked, "Wasn't there a guard? An attendant?"

"There was, but he was on break and didn't notice anything

when he returned. The ME made the discovery when he was preparing to do the autopsy."

"So, they don't know exactly when the body disappeared," Montana said.

I saw the second they realized the implications.

"And without a body..." Tempe looked at me expectantly then her mouth opened in a silent *Oh*... "the bad news..."

"Yeah," Montana smiled, "But bad news for whom?" She looked at me. "If you don't have a body—"

"Just because there's no body, doesn't mean the crime didn't happen. The man deserves justice and I still have leads to follow. Like your brother's involvement, how that vase figures into it all."

"And my brother's disappearance," Tempe said. Montana just looked at me. The arched brow said it all.

"As far as I'm concerned, it's all connected," Jack said. "We just have to figure it out." I wanted Tempe to be innocent of all wrong doing, and it would be a lot less complicated if her brother was innocent as well, but I just couldn't shake the feeling that I was missing something important.

"You've come up with more possibilities than I have," Tempe said, dejected.

"You know where to find me if you think of something. Right now Fritz needs a lift to jail, and I need to get home to my teenager." I didn't bother to request their discretion. It would be in the *Tribune* by daylight.

Then, the door opened, and a slender woman stepped out. Well, what do we have here? My instincts screamed *runner*. Olive complexion with black hair that fell over her shoulders like midnight; she wore black high heels, a black trench coat, and sunglasses—after dark. She looked like Destiny's very own secret agent.

"Oh, excuse me," said Triple O. Seven. She ducked her head and would have escaped back inside, but Tempe stopped her.

"Katerina. Don't go."

She twitched like a nervous cat when Tempe introduced us. "Jack Lang. This is Katerina Blackmoor." Blackmoor. Of course. "Kat, Jack."

Kat waved her small, gloved hand at me.

I held my hand out to her, wanting to see what the skittish creature would do. She contemplated for a split second whether to take it or not, then slipped her slender, black leather clad hand into mine. We'd barely touched before she was retrieving it however.

"I didn't mean to interrupt," Katerina said, looking at Tempe. "I saw everyone follow you outside..."

"It's okay, Kat. Jack was just telling us that the victim's body disappeared from the morgue."

Interesting. Her friend didn't even blink; well, I couldn't see her eyes, but I'd bet she hadn't blinked. I got the impression that nothing much surprised the black-clad refugee.

"It's nice to meet you, Katerina. Are you new to Destiny?" I asked, studying her reaction closely.

"I work nights," Kat offered, presumably to explain why I hadn't seen her around though she avoided a direct answer.

Tempe said, "Kat was looking forward to meeting you at class tonight, but you had to leave."

I'll just bet she was. I'd bet my left nut this woman had been desperate to avoid me. I got that reaction a lot though, so I put it down to eccentricity like the rest of the daytime soap lovers.

I pulled four business cards from my pocket and handed one to each of them. The spy plucked it from me with gloved fingertips and slipped it into the pocket of her trench coat.

"Katerina is an online financial consultant and an archivist for the newspaper," Montana said. It seemed like they were trying to keep me from asking Kat any tough questions.

I smiled at Kat, "Well, I'll be sure to let you know if I find some extra money lying around after buying Jordie's clothes, sports equipment, and paying her tuition." I yawned. "Excuse me."

"Sheriff—Jack," Tempe chewed on her bottom lip. "What do you think happened to the body?"

A bark of frustration escaped before I could contain it. "I have no idea, Tempe. It's like he just woke up and walked away."

The way the four women looked at each other then, made my fingers itch. I was starting to feel like I was being kept out of an insiders loop.

TEMPE

After the sheriff left, we went back inside. Bailey brought our drinks to the table and risked Liam's wrath to sit down. Montana leaned forward across the table keeping her voice as low as possible in the increasingly noisy bar. "What do you think happened to the body?"

"Did the sheriff think you stole it?" Kat asked, her eyes darting around the bar as she fidgeted.

"I don't know. I think he was just crossing us off his list, officially."

Mariah gave Bailey her drink order and said, "He sure is a hunk, don't you think, Tempe? I'll bet he's one of those fitness nuts with zero percent body fat."

Kat said, "He can investigate me anytime."

I nearly choked on my tonic, even though I knew it for a lie. Kat must be feeling more at home with us to even joke about the possibility of someone looking into her past.

"I can vouch for the zero percent after delivering his package yesterday morning. But I didn't know my customer and the sheriff were the same guy until it was too late to make a good impression."

"I dubbed him Six-packs and Shaving Cream," Montana said.

"You mean he was drinking when you met him?" Bailey asked. We all laughed, and Bailey shrugged, returning to the bar.

Montana watched Bailey walk away. "That Bailey is several filaments short of a working light bulb."

We sipped our drinks for a minute. It was getting more difficult to carry on a private conversation with the pool tournament going on over in the corner. Two sets of players surrounded the two tables. I waited until they broke for a new game.

I leaned forward, whispering, "Montana, I don't know how I

forgot this, but the dead man... he was a fae, a variant. I don't know all the subspecies, but isn't there one that smells like rotten eggs?"

"Yep. A Nucklavee," Montana said. "When they are damaged or die they reek of dead fish and sulfur." She pondered her own words a minute, fiddling with her braid. "And wasn't he nude, when you found him?"

I shivered at the memory. The violence of his death still bothered me.

"I haven't seen one of them in a long time." Kat shivered and made a face. "They're disgusting and given their nature, I could wait a lot longer."

I leaned forward. "Montana, what are you thinking?"

Montana said, "If it was a Nucklavee, he could have been playing possum, or in a transition state. And if he wasn't dead, by the time they got ready to do an autopsy on him, he'd have been back to his ugly half ogre looking self."

Kat and I both stared at her.

"You think he just got up and walked out?" Kat asked.

"I guess it's possible..." I shuddered at the memory of his ruined face, "but he sure looked dead to me."

"He wouldn't be the only species that could reanimate as long as his head was still attached," Katerina said.

"Well, if he did, he'd have to grow back most of his head," I said.

"Or not," Montana said.

"Eeeyuk, imagine running into Mr. Nucklavee if that's true.

Change of subject please, oh Goddess of the iron stomach." I took another sip of tonic.

Montana said, "Of course he might have shifted into a less obnoxious form, or even glamoured his way out of there."

"What about River? Isn't there some kind of mindlink between you genie-types?" Kat asked.

My hands made fists under the table. "See, that just makes me feel even worse. I mean, you thought of it, why didn't I?"

"Duh!" said Montana.

"Denial," said Kat.

"I know. I know. I'm going to see Aurora tomorrow. I can't deal with this Paramortal PMS anymore on my own."

Montana laughed. "More like Paramortal puberty, considering the circumstances."

"Peggy's going to ask around at a few bars tonight, but in the morning it will officially be forty-eight hours, and I can go file a report."

Kat checked for listening ears, then asked, "How much does Jack know? About River I mean."

"He knows the amphora is River's, but I'm having a hard time convincing him River is in trouble."

Kat said, "He doesn't know River's a genie?"

"I hope not," said Montana. "He told someone on the police jury when he was thinking about running for sheriff that he was looking for a," both her eyebrows exclamated her next words, "normal small town to raise his daughter. Apparently, he was married to a real psycho and both he and his daughter are in recovery mode."

"So, I heard you met the daughter." Kat looked at Tempe.

"A tactful way to put it." I laughed.

"I hear she's Destiny's hope for a state championship this year," said Shannon.

"I didn't know that. She invited me to her game this weekend though. We should all go," I said.

"I want to go, too," said Bailey, who'd gotten in on the end of the conversation. "Where are we going?" Leaning against our table, she caught the eye of a local bull rider, wound a curl around her finger and batted her eyelashes seductively.

"Basketball game at the high school, Saturday," Montana said.

"Aw, I have to work." Bailey pushed away from the table and headed in the cowboy's direction.

Montana shook her head, "'Mild mannered reporter by day...'"

I watched Bailey put a hand around the cowboy's neck and lean into him. "I think Jack's got her pegged as a 'three faces of Eve' schizophrenic."

Laughing again, Montana said, "He's close."

"Lucky Bailey," said Katerina, eyeing the cowboy. Montana raised her brows at me and winked.

My sudden change of mood must have shown. I've been told I'm not good at hiding what's on my mind. "What's your problem?" she asked.

"I shouldn't be sitting here joking. Having a drink with friends. Thinking about Jack Lang's abs when my brother..." I put my head down on the table, sighing.

"Tell us what we can do, Tempe," Kat said.

"I don't know. If I knew where to look, I'd be looking. I've tried to find his old girlfriend, Paige Whyte. She was a house-keeper at the Red Carpet Inn, but she wasn't there today. I'll try again tomorrow after I file the Missing Persons report. This all just seems so surreal. One day everything's normal, I'm doing my job, running the mail..." I took a sip from my glass and pushed it away.

Montana drummed her fingers on the thick polyurethane tabletop. "I'll contact all the emergency techs and make sure the word gets out in the parish."

"I'd bet my eye teeth someone saw something." Kat was half vamp as well, so that was saying something.

Montana's pager vibrated, and she got up. "Love ya, girls. Try not to worry, Temp."

"Love you too. I don't know what I'd do without you."

Kat put a hand on my shoulder, "Time for me to go, too. I have a stack of articles that have to be archived by Friday. I'll talk to some of the reporters at the paper—see they keep their ears open." I wanted to hug Kat, but I didn't dare. She wasn't comfortable herself yet with the vamp side of her nature.

"Call me if you hear anything," she said.

Bailey was plastered against the cowboy by the men's room. I didn't interrupt to say goodbye.

Chapter 22

"Well, from what I hear, Pomeroy's at it again."

J ACK

The turkey in the jail cell kept me awake, belching and kicking at the bars in his sleep. I called Kirkwood and told him to swing by the judge's office to pick up the warrants and meet me on Washington Street in front of the victim's apartment at eight. Before the day was out, I would have some answers.

I opened the evidence room, going straight to the foot wide cube plugged into the wall. The portable refrigerator had come in handy many times. I unplugged it and carefully transported it to my cruiser, securing the evidence room behind me and unlocking Sleeping Beauty's cell so he could leave when he woke up.

As I drove down the levee road toward Amity, I thought about yesterday's events. When Tempe came to the office later this morning to fill out the report on her brother, I planned to take advantage of her whereabouts. I expected to eliminate her as a suspect today, but she would not enjoy the process. Prior to my 7:00 a.m. appointment with the manager of the clubhouse, I met with Basile to get the search underway.

I stretched a grid out on the reception counter. "I want you to start at this corner and work this way. When the man from DPD gets here in a couple hours, he'll start here." With my finger on a spot on the grid, I asked, "You know what to do with anything you find?"

"Yes, sir." My deputy scanned the paper.

I suspected the manager was not going to be happy.

I was right.

"Are you out of your mind? I can't close the golf course for a week. Oh. My. God. What is that smell?"

Someone needed to remind Giles Fitzhugh—that couldn't be his real name—that he was not the owner of the golf club or the King of Mardi Gras, just a well-dressed peon to the country club set. Not even well-dressed this morning, in LSU sweat pants under an insulated camouflage jacket, the sleeve of which he had covering half his face.

"I'll have you know," his vehemence muffled in camo, "we have a tournament this week and matches scheduled every day, starting at seven tomorrow morning." He pinched his nose between two fingers, cocked one ample hip and poked his finger at my chest. "If we quose for da west of the week, I'll have to caw da bembers. I won't awow it."

The pointed digit came my way again, and he squeaked as I grabbed his finger. I really hate it when someone pokes me with his finger. "You want to stop doing that, Mr. Fitzhugh. I'm sure your members would want to do right by the man who lost his life here," I said, nodding at the floor in front of him.

It was a dirty trick, but the snooty pompous little weasel had pissed me off. He took one look at the blood and other evidence still decorating the hall and ran outside to the nearest bush. I followed him. When he was done, I followed him back inside and described the victim. "Sound familiar?"

"That sounds like Ray, our maintenance man." The way he said the word maintenance implied a class distinction for Giles.

"Did he usually come in on Monday?"

"No. He isn't...wasn't allowed on Sunday or Monday."

"So I guess he got what he deserved." He actually started to agree with me, the mean-spirited stooge. "Are *you* allowed?" I asked.

He didn't get it right away. When he did, he paled. "Well...of course, I'm the manager."

"Did Ray have keys to the clubhouse?" I opened my pad.

"He had a key, but not the code to the alarm. I'm the only one with thos..." His eyes widened, "Except the president of the club. Oh dear, I don't mean to suggest—that is, Ray might have gotten them sometime or other, but as far as I know he didn't know the alarm code."

Though I enjoyed bringing this phony down a notch, I knew he wasn't the culprit. If I didn't miss my guess, he was OCD. Killing someone by bashing his head in wouldn't be his M.O.

Not that he couldn't kill someone; anyone could, given the right motivation.

"What's the president's name?"

He rattled off the name and number.

"What about the locker room? Who had codes to the lockers?"

"We remodeled the locker room and each member in good standing got their pick. First come, first serve."

"Do you keep the list of members and their lockers? Check the locks out by some kind of list?"

"Um, well, I'd have to ask the girl who keeps our files. She goes to St. Mary's High School."

Great. All this posturing and the locks and locker combinations were in the control of a teenager. "Name?" I wrote it down, but I could see there were more holes in the clubhouse security than there were greens on the course.

"Thank you for coming, Mr. Fitzhugh." I held out my hand. "I'll need your key. *And* the codes."

He grumbled under his breath, but delicately dropped the keys into my palm, careful not to touch my skin. "The alarm code will be temporarily changed to protect the evidence."

"One other thing. Do you know River Pomeroy?"

"Never heard of him. Wait! Isn't that woman who broke in a Pomeroy? You know one of our club members filed a complaint against her for theft." This was delivered with an excess of malicious glee. *Interesting.*

"I'm aware of the complaint. So far, there's been nothing to support that claim." Damn it. I shouldn't have responded to Fitz's comment.

"Well, from what I hear, Pomeroy's at it again."

"You're free to leave now, Fitzhugh. We'll let you know when you can reopen."

He stalked out.

Stalked was definitely the wrong word.

Chapter 23

"Yowsa! You got a bigger set than me."

JACK

Kirkwood yawned and rubbed his eyes as I drove up. "What happened to the quiet little crime-free town you promised me, Jack?"

"If you're referring to what I said when I offered you the job, forget it. After five years of custody fights with my ex, no one wants quiet or ordinary more than me." The key the landlord had supplied took some jiggling but we finally got in.

The front room smelled of incense and something I couldn't put my finger on. It was musty but spare, and tiny, the living room just large enough for a small ugly couch, a cheap coffee table and TV. It had the feel of a vacant hotel room.

Ryan spoke as he poked at the telephone books neatly stacked under the phone. "You get the impression he didn't live here?"

I walked over to the kitchen and opened the refrigerator. A pack of off-brand beer, a Styrofoam container of Cool Cats, and what looked like alfalfa sprouts.

"Is that wigglers?" Ryan asked from over my shoulder.

"Yeah, looks like ol' Ray might have been fishing recently. You find anything?"

"There was a desk in the bedroom. I found part of a cell phone bill made out to Ray Meeker." He handed it to me. I was thinking if Ray Meeker was a fisherman, maybe he had been killed somewhere else. Or maybe that accounted for the smell. Nah, didn't seem likely. The smell had been too strong, too strange.

"There wasn't a cell phone on him. Did you find one here? I'd sure like to see who's been calling him."

"Not yet," Ryan said. "Doesn't look like he stayed here. One suit of clothes in the closet, no shorts or socks in the drawers. Nothing but a used razor in the trash can in the bathroom. I bagged it."

I nodded. Kirkwood was a good man. He'd been my wingman in the Navy, but after sinus surgery was told he couldn't fly anything but helicopters and low altitude aircraft. When I won the election, I managed to lure him away from Search and Rescue. See, Ryan was kidding about wanting peace and quiet; it was anyone's guess how long he'd make it in a boring little town like Destiny.

As for me, I'd had more excitement in my personal life than on deployment; enough to last a lifetime. When this case was solved, I could picture myself in an aluminum boat, kicked back, jig pole in hand, a cool cat on my hook...

"All right. Let's make one more pass and move on."

He turned to me, head cocked, eyebrows winging up, "Move on? Where to?"

"Somewhere that's going to get me in a lot of trouble."

"Ohhh, yeah." Ryan grinned.

Was it that obvious?

"You know how it is. War brings men closer than a lot of couples *and* you're broadcasting loud and clear, Laser. Hell, I figured if you weren't interested, I might ask her out myself."

"Well, before you go getting involved with a suspect let's get this case solved," I growled.

Ryan chuckled, "Yeah, that's what I thought."

I never said I was good at subterfuge. "Sweep the bathroom and kitchen, flunkie. I'll double back behind you in the bedroom."

We bagged and tagged what little we gathered. As I locked the front door, I got a call from Peggy. Tempe had just sat down to fill out the Missing Persons report.

I read off some of the most frequent calls on Meeker's phone statement and told her to call me when she knew something. Then Kirkwood and I headed to Harmony.

WHAT TEMPE HAD REFERRED TO AS HER 'VORACIOUS monster' was in reality an elegant, though time worn, plantation home with a classic veranda surrounding the bottom floor. There were two ladders on one side and a sturdy scaffold. Rolls of insulation and stacks of blue roofing tin sat nearby.

"Man, these old places can suck the contents of your wallet and leave it gasping," Kirkwood said.

"My thoughts exactly—but it's got class."

"If you like that old broken down tramp look," Ryan said. "You got a key?"

"Hell, no. We're just going to be here when she gets home. Peggy got the honors."

"*Yowsa!* You got a bigger set than me. You're going to catch it on both ends, Laser." Said the man whose call sign had been *Stones*.

He pulled a breakfast sack out of his car and sipped from a cup of coffee. My head hurt from caffeine deprivation, and my stomach rumbled.

"Give me a break, will 'ya, and hand me that coffee." I held out my hand. I'd taken one sip when I heard tires squealing on asphalt a block away.

"Suck it down, flyboy. It's show time."

HER MARCH TOWARD ME WAS SO DETERMINED, I WOULDN'T have been surprised if she'd taken a swing at me. She was something: the colored strands of her hair flying around, crackling with electricity in the cold air; cheeks flushed with temper. Her eyes, when she glared up into mine, were an emotional hurricane.

"What's this about a warrant, Sheriff?"

She made the word "sheriff" sound like "scumbag". I resisted smiling, as it seemed like a good way to get hurt. "As I told you before, I'm just doing my job."

"Well, just do it then. Here's the key."

Off-guard, I automatically put my hand out. It stung after she slapped the key into it.

"Search all you want. I've searched the last two nights. Now if you don't mind, I have places to go and people to see." She turned, head high, like the Queen dismissing the Guard.

I grabbed her arm. When she turned, I felt the flush to my skin, the hairs standing up like they had in battle, a spontaneous reaction to impending danger. I let go.

"Sorry. You have to stay."

"Really," she said, sarcastically. "*Pour quoi?*"

"Because especially now, I don't want to be sued for stealing something from your house. Honestly, Tempe, I thought you'd be more cooperative."

Her eyes narrowed. "If you'd asked for permission, I'd have opened my door and baked you a cake. But it will be a sizzling hot day in Iceland before I cooperate now. And here I thought you were concerned about my brother. I believed all that crap about getting Peggy to start looking around unofficiall—"

"She did—"

"I even went ahead and filed the report believing you meant to help me find him."

Ryan spoke up, "She did—"

"It's okay, Ryan. Ms. Pomeroy is just a little upset right now." I'll say. I felt the heat of her skin through her jacket and her eyes flickered, hot with anger. I hoped it was anger. She sure seemed to have a way with electricity.

Kirkwood cleared his throat and shifted.

"Deputy Kirkwood is correct. Peggy made the rounds to the surrounding towns. The only bar where your brother was seen was the Wasted Turtle, where the contractor's employee said he saw him. The woman has yet to be identified."

That shut her up. For about two seconds, maybe less. "And you're searching my house for what, exactly?"

"Any possible murder weapon, ties to the victim, clues to your brother's whereabouts. All I have is your word and a statement from this Rutledge guy that River didn't show up on the job Monday."

She started to object.

"I didn't say I don't believe you, but I have to follow procedure. There's been no ransom, no evidence of foul play. He might be layin' up somewhere with this woman. And..."

"And?"

"You might not know your baby brother like you think you do." I thought she was going to blow then. If mad was a planet, she'd have been Mars.

"I want River's amphora back."

"It's still being held as evidence."

Actually, I'd broken my promise to her. It was being tested this very moment. With the body missing, solving the case, finding the killer and maybe her brother, might depend on those backup slides.

I felt a twinge in my midsection when her shoulders slumped. She looked as tired as I felt. Unlocking the front door, she threw the keys on the table in the hallway. "Do your worst; it can't be any more than I did last night. I'm going to make coffee."

She wasn't kidding. The rooms looked like a preschool class had spent the night here. I nodded at Ryan to start in the living room. I headed for the upstairs, her brother's living quarters.

She served us coffee and stayed out of our way. Everything about her was so calm she nearly disappeared into the air around us. She had to be running on empty.

"So, what were you looking for?" I asked.

Her auburn lashes feathered down over pale cheeks as she rested her head against the back of the sofa. "Anything that would give me a clue where River is. His plans, a note—a little black book."

"I take it you didn't find anything." Her lids opened to reveal blue irises. They swallowed me down into their depths and brought back memories of flying across a cloudless winter sky.

"Have you?"

Duhhh, Earth to Jack. The woman is speaking to you, and you're standing here like a horny teenager. "Have I what?"

"Have you found anything? A murder weapon? Blood... anything to point to River as a murderer?"

Accusations. The calm was dissipating like a deceivingly passive electrical line just before the transformer blows. I actually imagined I heard thunder.

"I don't care if you strip my house bare and carry the pieces to the best lab in the country. River didn't kill anyone. Now, I seem to be the only one taking my brother's disappearance seriously." Her voice cracked. "He could be in serious trouble, lying in a ditch somewhere, anything. I have to find him. I took today off for that purpose, and since you're obviously not going to help me..." She took a deep uneven breath.

Here we go again, I thought, as her eyes brimmed. Waterworks. "I will follow up on your brother's disappearance as soon as I get done here, now that you've filed the report." My cell phone rang.

"Yeah, Peggy."

$$\sim$$

TEMPE

I began taking the trash I'd set in piles next to the door last night and loading them in my truck while the sheriff answered his cell. I was tired, frustrated and scared. Really scared. Not for myself, but for River. I wasn't even angry so much about them searching my house, though something in me felt a little betrayed. Well, okay, more than a little, but mostly—it was inconvenient as hell.

Everybody knows the longer someone is missing the less likely you are to find them, and in River's case the reasons were two fold—the time factor in turning up clues to his whereabouts, and the fact that he would die from being away from his amphora for too long. Not to mention that if someone had him, and they knew how to take advantage of his power...

When I entered the kitchen, I heard Lang's voice clearly, "Damn it. Peggy, are you sure?" He rubbed his hand across his neck. His deputy looked from me to Jack, who flipped his phone shut with a snap.

He looked at Ryan, "Peggy did a reverse locator on the numbers."

He skewered me with that cutting stare. "I don't know why I'm surprised. The number most often called was to Alliance." He repeated the phone number. "Ring any bells?"

It was Phoebe's number.

Chapter 24

"What is this, a bong?"

TEMPE

"He called my mother?" My mind stuck on those words in a mire of incredulity, while images exploded like a kaleidoscope, of the man in the clubhouse, my mother the last time I'd seen her. "I-I don't get it. What would he be calling Phoebe for?" My head pounded with confusion.

"I assure you I'll find out." He regarded me suspiciously.

"What? I knew nothing about this." But something niggled at the back of my mind.

Lang noticed. "A man is dead. If you know something, it would save a lot of time…"

"Whose time, Sheriff… yours? What about us? My mother, my brother. It's like a witch hunt." Was there such a thing that applied to Djinn and their families? "And it's all just keeping my energy and yours from finding River. Can't you see that?"

He shook his head disgustedly. "I've asked you to trust me. If your family is innocent of any wrong doing, I'll find the truth."

"If. If. *If. When* you finally figure out we're all innocent of any wrongdoing..." I let him see the fear I was feeling, "It may be too late." I picked up my keys. "Now, help yourself to anything I own, but if you try to stop me from leaving this house, you'll be sorry. That is, if I'm not under arrest." I put as much grit in my voice as I could. The anger and fear I felt was churning *menori* to life. I had to get out of here.

"Hold up," he said. "Ryan, lock up behind me."

He started to put his hand on my elbow, but must have sensed the spinning vortex of emotions bubbling up inside of me, like a tsunami nearing the coastline. An image came unbidden of my mother blowing the windows out of our living room in the middle of an argument with my father. And I hadn't even known she was mad.

He followed me out to my truck as I escaped. "Where are you going?"

"I'm not sure." I wasn't lying. Only burning off this churning energy inside me would keep me from coming apart. I lifted my face to the wind and wondered if I could just raise my arms and let it take me somewhere...anywhere.

"Just... don't do anything stupid. Trust me to get to the bottom of this."

His eyes implored me to do just that, and oh... "I wish I could," I said, climbing into my truck and gunning the engine.

He stood in the street watching as I flew away from Harmony.

~

I DROVE TO ALLIANCE TO TALK TO PHOEBE, TO NO AVAIL. I asked her neighbor watching from his back porch if he'd seen her.

"Not in the last couple days," he said.

I thanked him and drove to the Tricked-Out Tarot to meet a man who dealt in amphoras and demijohns. The vase I'd found at the house was just that, a flower vase with a cork stopper. Dylan had said it wasn't secure enough for a Djinn force.

If I'd known it would be this difficult to find an appropriate genie bottle replacement, I'd have arranged a backup. But Dylan didn't know of one, and promised to find someone to ceremonialize a new one.

The Tricked-out Tarot was a hole in the wall, actually a narrow alley walk between two tall brick buildings; tall in Destiny being three stories. The far end of the alley was dark, but I saw light filtering around the corner and heard what sounded at first like guitar music, but turned out to be ukuleles and *Blue Hawaii*. I expected hula dancers, definitely not the Elvis impersonator who stepped from behind a curtain at the front desk. He eyed me for a moment, then smiled and said, "Tempest Pomeroy. You resemble your mother. Come in. Come in."

Most women hope they can avoid being compared with their mothers. We like to think we've learned from their mistakes and think we will not turn into a duplicate. That particularly applied to Phoebe and me, but I'd heard this comment enough that after the initial irritation I took it in stride. He held the curtain aside while I ducked into the room decorated in red velvet. Tacky didn't begin to describe...

"You mentioned you are looking for a replacement vessel?" Elvis stooped behind the counter and came up with two of the ugliest containers I'd ever seen. One was fat at the bottom and narrow at the spout resembling a teepee—*and* it was orange. The single slender opening at the top where the inhabitant's smoke would exit, or the inhabitant himself, was tiny making me claustrophobic on the future homeowner's behalf. *It wouldn't be my brother.* I guess I should be less "choicey" as Bailey says, considering I was desperate.

The next was twin bottomed, who knew? I couldn't begin to imagine how a genie could make use of the thing. "What is this, a bong?"

Elvis just rolled his eyes and shrugged as if to say "can't blame me for trying" and swapped the ugly mustard colored thing for another—an amphora.

I moved toward it the second it touched the glass counter. A stunning gem-studded blue, it resembled the moonlit sky. I picked it up. The shape and weight of it was perfect. Unfortunately, this amphora was a single entrance model.

"I'm sorry, I didn't get your name...Mr.—?"

"Presley."

Of course. "Mr. Presley. Do you have a flashlight?" I was wasting my time on this bottle—one entrance simply wouldn't do. I know, most Djinn don't bother—they opt for the single entrance and rely on advanced warning systems, like their human masters or familiars, but the one thing River was adamant about was not relying on others for his own security.

All of River's previous bottles had had emergency exits.

I took the flashlight from Elvis and peered into the exquisite piece. The interior was lined in smoky blue and gold velvet, and when I ran my fingers around the inside edge to determine the makeup of the glaze, I felt the tug against my flesh that only the iron infused glaze can produce.

I sighed, handing him back the flashlight. Best not give away my interest.

"I don't know. It's got the basics and it's lovely, but I was looking for one with two door—openings and unless these gems are zirconia, I imagine the cost is more than I can afford."

One thick black eyebrow hiked up under the 'Elvis' lock on his forehead and his lips pursed. I could almost see him adding each tiny gem up in his head. Not good.

Again, he reached under the counter and brought out a straight rod about the height of the bottle. With the flair of an illusionist he made a show of pushing up his sleeves, running two fingers around the length of the rod, a display to illustrate it was clear of any strings or attachments. Then he inserted it straight into the amphora until only an inch of the brass rod remained above the opening. He motioned for me to place my index finger on the end and removed his own. Then he tapped the pad of his index finger against the countertop to demonstrate.

Holding the rod between my thumb and third finger I pressed with my own index finger as shown. Nothing. He said, "Two seconds," placing his hand palm up next to the amphora.

I pressed for two seconds and something tiny flew off the side of the container. Elvis caught it in his hand and opened his palm for me to see. One of the larger gems lay in his hand and when he rotated the amphora I could see a tiny hole in the dark blue exterior and light...

He smiled slyly at my stunned expression. Oops, I was about to give away all my negotiation power.

"How does it work?"

"There is a hidden release under the rug off the center near the couch. He simply toes it up and presses, and voilà—he's out of that little *Heartbreak Hotel*."

"Excellent. Unfortunately, it's still out of my budget."

"Ah," he stroked his chin, the corner of his lip curling in a familiar smile. "I think we can work out some kind of deal, an exchange of services perhaps."

This was going to cost River. But time was of the essence and the midnight blue amphora would be a spectacular upgrade to the old one. It was beautiful, iron infused, and secure. And truth be known, I'd take out a second mortgage if necessary to purchase it for my brother, so after some negotiating I held out my hand.

"Deal."

He swiveled his hips and with that infamous wiggle of hips said, "Thank you. Thank you very much!"

I GOT A CALL FROM MONTANA AFTER SEALING THE DEAL for the new amphora, which was secured in a covered box behind my seat.

"Hi, Montana."

"Hey, Temp. Just thought you'd like to know the last night of class has been postponed until Tuesday—instructor had a conflict. How was your day?"

"I filed the Missing Persons papers and while I was there Peggy informed me that the sheriff had a search warrant for Harmony. Ever since I met that man, it seems like my world has been turned upside down. It's so frustrating. He believes me one minute and the next, he's searching my house. And listen to this. The variant? They found multiple phone calls to Phoebe on his phone bill. What could that mean?"

Montana was silent for a few seconds.

"You there?"

"Thinking. I don't know, Temp. Something's definitely going on around here, like Aurora said, things seem to be building toward the two moon coincidence. Have you seen Aurora yet?"

"I'm on my way. Why?"

"Because I think it's time you explore your potential. You can't put it off any longer."

She was right. For too long I'd downplayed the extraordinary abilities of my mother and father, and tried to think of my brother and myself strictly in human terms, even after River morphed into his genie-hood.

"Tempe, you know I love you, and I didn't see anything wrong with you sticking your head in the sand—don't get your weather radar up when I say that—because it wasn't time. There wasn't anything pushing you until now."

I sighed. "Yes, but what if my knowing, training, practicing sooner meant River wouldn't be in trouble now—"

"I don't believe that, but ask Aurora if you need reassurance."

"Okay."

"Tempe." She paused. "You're not human. You might as well learn to accept it."

"I know." It wasn't a welcome admission.

Chapter 25

"Why do people always tell you to breathe? I breathe all the time."

TEMPE

Aurora met me at the door to her shop. "What's wrong?"

"Nothing." I rammed my fingers through my hair, spun around. "Everything—I don't know." I walked into her back room and she followed, watching me.

"I feel like—" My hands fisted involuntarily. I stretched them out then gripped the counter. "I can't describe it. Like I'm going crazy."

"Sit, Tempe. And breathe." She moved smoothly to the small kitchenette.

I put my head on my folded arms and breathed. It didn't help. "Why do people always tell you to breathe? I breathe all the time."

"Okay, valid point." A cup of steaming herbal tea appeared in front of me as Aurora dragged a stool up to the table. She lifted a strand of my hair and smoothed it behind my ear. When she'd done it the first time, alien as tender demonstrations of affection were from anyone but my brother, I'd jumped like a scared cat.

"Try this—with me. Take a deep slow breath." She closed her eyes and inhaled for about six seconds, her head tilting back slightly. She opened one eye to check on me. "Drop your shoulders. Breathe from here," she said patting her diaphragm. I did. I felt her tap my shoulders, and my eyes opened. "Now slowly, deliberately, let the breath ease out of you."

She made me do it two more times. "Better." She smiled.

I studied this woman who had been friend, substitute mother, sister; and *would* be mentor and teacher if I'd give up my obstinate rejection of my heritage. Though people often described her as elegant and mysterious, a force to be reckoned with, like a regal lioness ready to take down a meal for her young; what I admired was her inner strength, the peace she radiated and especially, the complete mastery over her inner reserves of power and emotion.

Her attire was chosen to have a calming effect on those around her. Today it was the watery blue and aqua silks in various overlapping lengths, under delicate strands of shimmering gemstones that fell to her waist and framed her amulet.

Her azure gaze locked on mine. "You feel like your thoughts and feelings are out of control. You've been able to manage it, push it down before, but suddenly it's like debris in a whirlwind. You feel—"

"Like I'm about to come apart. Isn't that bad?"

She took my hands in hers. They were hot. "It's normal."

I cocked an eyebrow at her. "I hope not."

She laughed. "For someone about to go through her quickening."

"And that's not encouraging."

"How much do you know about the *Vyal K'allanti*?"

Not much. My parents hadn't been around to guide River and me. River took on his genie power when he turned fourteen, but I'd determinedly avoided all discussions of mine, as if that would keep it at bay forever. I'd only made things worse.

"Isn't it the same as the quickening? I know when River's started. He was in the ninth grade."

"That's about right. Most males experience their quickening during puberty. I actually remember when his began. Dylan served as guardian for him until his *Vyal K'allanti* was complete."

I nearly spilled my tea, setting it down with a clank. "How could I not have known that?" Aurora's sleek silver cat curled around my legs, purring as if Aurora had enlisted its help in calming me down. I thought back to that time.

"It was a few months before I turned twenty-one. I'd been working a lot trying to get a career position at the post office —before the new company took over. Phoebe wasn't around much and social services kept butting in and threatening to take River away from us."

"There are few young people who could accomplish as much as you have to keep your family together. Tell me what you remember."

I peered into the cup, thinking back to River's fourteenth birthday. "Phoebe made River a cake for his birthday. I found out later, she had someone else bake it for her but it *was* home made and at least she'd remembered. It was more than she'd done for my birthdays." I winced, looking at Aurora. "Don't get me wrong. I wasn't jealous, just surprised. River had been, too, the shock on his face made me want to cry."

"Dylan was there—he must've been about twenty-seven then." He'd *looked* twenty-seven anyway. "I had wondered because he always seemed to be around... if there was something going on between him and my mother, but later he assured me they were just good friends—he, and Phoebe, and Dutch."

I closed my eyes revisiting that bittersweet time, realizing now that Dylan had essentially filled in for Dutch. Then it hit me.

"Mother knew." She must have recognized the signs of River's emerging power and arranged for Dylan to be there as a guide to protect River, and everyone else, from himself.

"I'm sure she did," Aurora said.

"But that was so out of character," I mused.

"Or maybe things weren't quite as they seemed," Aurora said, cryptically. "What happened at his party?"

"When Phoebe set the cake down, River's eyes got huge. It was this gorgeous, red glazed, strawberry thing—he's crazy about strawberries—four layers with fourteen silver candles on top."

River's eyes had reflected the light from the flames, flickering and bouncing, until he looked at me and I realized the glow, like gold and aqua fired coins, was not a reflection.

"He changed in front of my eyes—his shoulders broadened, his features became angular, chiseled."

Pride, fear, and love warred for first place inside me. The candles flickered furiously and it seemed as if the air was being vacuumed out of the room. Aurora leaned forward. "Then what happened?"

I closed my eyes trying to capture every detail. "River had this look of awe on his face and at first he seemed uncertain. He looked down at his lap, at his hands on the table. He wiggled his fingers like they tingled. Dylan stood up and motioned for River to do the same."

"Instead of pushing his chair back and standing up, River— his upper body expanded like a balloon filled with helium. He levitated above the chair so I could tell the lower half of his body was indistinct, not like smoke but like a white trans-parent fog."

I snorted at the memory. "He looked down at himself and grinned at me, a wide goofy grin, and then he threw back his head and laughed. It was a huge booming laugh, like father's. It startled us all, but River the most. He fell over the chair, down behind the table." Dylan was nearly beside himself with laughter. Then my brother, the newborn Djinni floated up above the chair again, this time with a look that wavered between embarrassment and concentration.

Dylan said, "Very good, River. How do you feel?"

River had this mischievous quirk to his smile, something I'd never seen on him. He wanted to stir something up, make some trouble. "I could swat the world like an annoying fly." He turned to me and thought, "Like I could bring you the moon." *And I'd heard him.*

Phoebe remained silent throughout River's emergence but made eye contact with me. There was such sadness and regret in her eyes that remembering it made the tea in my stomach roil.

Dylan frowned. "Well, maybe one of these days, but right now you have to start small and learn the ropes about granting wishes."

"How do I do that?" He asked Dylan looking down at himself.

Dylan said, "You don't have to try—it comes natural. At this point if you ask for something that's not allowed, nothing will happen. There's a lot that's off limits to you until you are mature enough to handle it."

River looked at the candles on the cake for a long time. His genie self had stabilized into just a fluffier version of his human form, but one I could still see through. Just when I began to think he'd fallen into a trance or something, he gazed at me and I heard him across the mindlink, "I wish I could see dad again."

The laughter stopped. My brother stood stoically, shoulders straight, his gaze locked with my tear filled eyes as a stricken sob escaped my mother. She rose slowly, locking eyes with Dylan.

"That's a dumb wish, your father's gone," our mother said across the link. Pain flickered across River's face and straight into my heart.

Dylan knew something had transpired between us. He said, "You can't make wishes for yourself."

"How about some cake?" River tried to smooth things over by getting up and putting an arm around mother and me, but I couldn't look at her, didn't want to even be as close as the distance across River's now massive body. How could she have been so cruel? That was the last time I communicated with her through the mindlink.

I LOOKED AT AURORA ACROSS THE COUNTER, FELT THE tears trailing down my cheeks, but it was as if they belonged there, as if by wiping them away I would lose the memories.

"That was the first I'd known about what was happening with River, and in a matter of a few minutes he was a full-blown genie. It happened so fast. We didn't know what to expect, other than the fact that Dutch was Djinn, and Phoebe was a Tempestaerie. We assumed we'd follow in their paths, but I have very few memories of Dutch or Phoebe using their talents."

I could see the whole event like it was yesterday. I remembered feeling excited, and a little scared. I hadn't known what to expect. But River had matured in front of me. His solemn eyes met mine and pride swelled inside me. My little brother had grown-up into the being he was supposed to be.

I looked at Aurora. "I think I resented him a little because he'd moved forward and I..." How could I admit this to Aurora? She would be even more disappointed in me.

"You wanted to keep him human with you."

I looked away. "That's horrible. What kind of sister was I to try to hold him back?"

She squeezed my hand. "It was only natural that you resented your mother and father for leaving and didn't want to follow their path. Once he went through the change you felt like he'd left you as well. Am I right?"

I thought about it. "Yes, and when years passed and it didn't happen for me, I started to wonder if I was really...if maybe I was adopted, or if maybe it just fell flat with me, you know, like a dud charge on fireworks. Especially since I was the only one in the family with no talent."

"Power." Aurora corrected. "Or magic. Powerful magic," she reiterated knowing how often I'd resisted the word power. You're not adopted, and you're not a dud."

"There were some good times before Dutch died, but I can't recall them. I have the sense that they were happy before... I guess that's why it hurt so much when she withdrew from us afterward." I spread my hands out and raised my teacup. "That's it. That's all I know. Not much considering how many supernatural beings I've known, but..."

"You've blocked it like you blocked the mindlink. It's all you cared to know," Aurora said, sitting forward over the counter... "until now. You've been closed off for so long that now you must practice being 'open'. Engage with the past, trust in your heritage to take you where you need to go, and to see the truth."

Like a giant wave that churns up everything from the deep— the past, my anxieties and frustrations were brought to the surface and about to crash over me. Was I ready?

Aurora nodded. "Controlling your power doesn't just happen. River probably experienced symptoms other people attributed to hormones, but Phoebe recognized them and knew that his birthday was going to be a trigger for a first event, and it was. That wasn't the end of it though. Dylan spent a couple of years guiding River along, making sure he grew into his Djinni potential, giving him a controlled environment to grow and explore, even providing him with his first amphora. It was as your father wished."

My mind raced. This was news to me. Dear old dad had provided a mentor for River. What about me? I slammed down on that thought at once.

Aurora said, "I was chosen as your mentor when you were ready," she paused. "If you are done with denial and ready to learn how to harness the gift and responsibilities of being a Paramortal, we will begin." She turned toward the kitchenette placing our cups in the sink. Turning around, she leaned back against the sink and crossed her arms. Apparently, she needed my verbal assent.

"So... you mean now?"

A silent, short nod.

I licked my lips. "All right. How much can you teach me tonight?"

Chapter 26

Twilbeck was going to make me crack my molars.

TEMPE

Remember I mentioned humans needing attitude adjustments? Such was Dervil Twilbeck, the trainee I was blessed with Thursday after a late night of instruction by Aurora.

Twilbeck was at least two numbers short of a zip code. How he got through the testing process, I couldn't guess. We hadn't even left the mail center before he suggested leaving the heavy tubs of Ad-mail behind.

While I loaded the truck, Dervil pointed to the mail under his legs and on his lap, between his poochy belly and the steering wheel. "Can't you put this junk somewhere else?"

"Keeping the mail dry is more important than your comfort. And for the record, you are not to so much as toot my horn, unless I tell you to. Keep your hands off the wheel and your feet out of the way of the pedals." I put my face in his and said, "You keep it up and you'll wind up like the ash in that jar hanging from my mirror."

He didn't look frightened.

I must not have done it right.

Aurora had tried to give me pointers on how to *make* the power happen, without words like I'd used Monday morning. She said I should try to "relive" the moment when I created the fire in my palm, to feel it "in my soul". The important thing, she said, was not to let it just happen or even worse take over control, but to reign in the emotions and try to connect with that well inside me from "whence it came". Okay, so those hadn't been her words, but you get the picture.

As practice, I'd sent a message to Marty about someone to initiate the new bottle. He didn't *answer*.

I requested the first packet of mail from the trainee at 9:45, admonishing him to keep the strap around the bundle so the letters didn't fall out. "They allot only a small amount of time at each box, so avoiding issues that cut into your routine is crucial." I quoted the manual's *one-minute-per-box* rule.

"That's a long time," Dervil said, looking at me like I was an idiot.

"Just wait until you have a problem delivery, or you lose mail out the window and have to chase it down. That can eat up those precious minutes."

He waved his hands, "So, if you drop a box of mail, just take it back to the center."

"Where you'd be met at the back door by an inspector who would make you re-case it and deliver it before going home."

He rolled his eyes. "You could throw it in a collection box and let it go back through distribution."

Twilbeck was going to make me crack my molars. His prime directive seemed to be getting out of responsibility. "Then..." *stay calm, Tempe,* "it's a day late to the recipient—and if you get caught, you're gone."

He snorted, crossing his arms. "Look, this isn't breaking down the genetic code or anything. I could do it in my sleep. Why don't you handle it? If I have any questions, I'll ask."

I heard him mimicking me under his breath, "avoid issues that cut into your routine..."

My Tempestaerie thunder rumbled. "Let me ask you something. What made you decide to become a mailman?"

Bushy eyebrows dove toward squinty dark eyes. "Isn't it obvious? The money's great; you're out here in the sunshine, nobody to bother you." He waved his hand at me like some blue-blooded matron motioning her limo driver to 'mosey along' then leaned his head back against the seat and closed his eyes!

Biting back a curse, I decided to take the path of least resistance, since I wasn't getting anywhere. I knew ways to end our relationship, and I'd make it happen.

I ditched him at the diner while I called Montana and Kat to see if they'd heard anything. Kat didn't answer—daylight— and Montana was on a call. I finished my tuna sandwich, walked back into the diner, and found Dervil and Dick sitting with their heads together. *Perfect.* Remembering Sheriff Lang's admonition, I called from the door. "Load up, Twilbeck."

We turned into Enchanted Glen and Twilbeck said, "Show

me where you found the body." He whispered, "I bet there's still blood on the floor."

That did it.

"Do you remember asking me earlier what that little vial contained?" His eyes went to the tiny glass bottle still bouncing from the sudden stop. I pointed to the horsefly on the hump that had been as persistent in his efforts to annoy me as the trainee. As Dervil looked on, I murmured, "Come here, bug."

It was a simple task to use *menori* to move the big fly onto my palm where the mere contact with my skin and its slight charge made him stagger, shiver, and then plop over dramatically onto his back. *Good job, little guy*. This time I didn't imagine my trainee's uncomfortable squirm. It gained me a whole thirty minutes of peace.

It wasn't meant to last.

AT ONE THIRTY I GOT A CALL FROM THE SHONE PET Clinic. A bad feeling coincided with the sky unloading a frog strangler of a downpour.

"Ms. Pomeroy, Dr. Shone was wondering if you could come by and get your dog? He's wreaking havoc over here."

My dog. Now have you heard me mention a dog? "Um, could you describe him?"

A whispered exclamation came across the phone. "A standard red and sable Pomeranian?"

"How did you know he was mine?"

"Well, duh. His collar says, 'I'm Rogue, Tempest Pomeroy's little man'."

I groaned. "Oh, right. I'll be there in five."

Marty had heard me. Why else would the charade have been necessary?

I made a quick three point turn in the street and headed to Shone's Clinic. Dervil woke from his nap. "Hey, where you goin'?"

"We need to take a detour," I said. I parked at the curb and dashed through the rain to the front door. Too bad there were witnesses. I could have split the rain in two and walked in dry as Moses. I'd done really well with that exercise last night.

The Imp was in rare form in the reception room of the clinic as he circled the large center bench in the waiting room hair flying, then took off through an open exam room door into the back and sprang out from behind the receptionist's desk again. Customers and techs ran behind him like a Latin dance chain, and kids came from every direction. A cooing toddler tried to catch him and slipped, landing on his padded rump in a fit of giggles. One vet tech threw a looped cable, attempting to lasso him like a calf in a steer wrestling competition. All those attempts failed.

"Rogue" gnashed his teeth at anyone who got close and managed to pick up some compadres along the way. When I stepped through the front door, his motley pack included a Dachshund, a German Shepherd, a recently groomed Standard Poodle, and an elegant but determined Persian, who gave the impression she was too good for this but having too much fun to quit.

I planted myself in Marty's path on his next pass through the main room and put up my palm, "Rogue, sit."

Marty slid to a halt at my feet, with two of his pals sliding into him from behind, the rest wondering why all the fun had stopped. Their "parents" quickly grabbed each one and took them away while I dealt with the bad boy.

Dr. Shone walked in as I scooped the *Rogue* into my arms. No matter the trauma or excitement, Chris Shone never seemed to rattle. She was blonde, around five-six and pleasantly plump. I'd never seen an animal growl at her. A baby raccoon peaked out from her cleavage. Did I mention she was brave?

"I appreciate you coming so quickly, Tempe. Your... dog seems to have a burr up his hiney."

Having grown up in a Paramortal family, Chris didn't hold me responsible for Marty's actions. "I'm glad you called, Chris." I wanted to hit the little Imp across his "hiney" but I'd probably get strung up in the front lobby, so I settled for looking into Marty's eyes and saying, "Bad, bad dog, Rogue. Shame." The look he gave me lacked remorse and everyone laughed as a sprinkle of pee hit my t-shirt. *That'll teach you to shame me in public*, the haughty fake-dog-look he gave me said.

I left with Rogue in an enclosed carrier to transport him in the bed of my truck. If it weren't for the humans, that would have been entirely unnecessary, but what would I say to the trainee and the customers in Dr. Shone's office to explain riding him in a downpour? So I went along with the charade. Pretending I was taking custody of my "little man", I placed the carrier down on the bed of the truck.

Marty had used the situation to convey a message. He spoke just five words before he poofed that added a chill to my wet clothing.

"It's about wishes and power."

As clues went, that one sucked.

Chapter 27

Do the words "gossip columnist" tell you what I'm thinking?

JACK

I left the parent teacher meeting with Jordie's biology instructor and swung by the DMV to get a picture of Ray Meeker from his record. Tempe's friend was working at one of the windows. Once again, she was dressed like a Quaker out of the 1800s. She pushed black frames up on the bridge of her nose and asked if she could help me.

"It's Bailey Duplessis right? I'm Sheriff Lang. We met at Bons Amis Tuesday night?"

She looked puzzled so I passed the victim's name and license number to her. "I need a DL photo of this man." She pulled up the record and printed the photo out, handing it over. "Is there anything else, Sheriff Lang?"

"No, that'll do it."

Bailey's expression went blank and she directed her smile at the next customer. "Hi, I'm Bailey...."

I slipped the picture back into the folder, thinking my initial assessment of this woman had been correct.

I FOUND THE LITTLE STRIP MALL TWO BLOCKS FROM Phoebe's house brimming with business. I showed Meeker's picture at the bank, the drug store, the Big T gas station and finally hit pay dirt at the Jitney Jungle.

It was some more good news, bad news. Jordie's friend Melissa's mom, the 1-900 psychic and gossip columnist, had been working the weekend before when Meeker came through the line.

Her expression struck me as a little too eager. "It had to be Sunday because I didn't work Saturday. I work at the paper, you know, during the week." She cracked her gum noisily and persisted at scratching her head, which moved her wig a half-inch clockwise with each scratch. I held back a smile.

"What time Sunday?" I noticed a few curious glances from nearby shoppers. "Can we talk somewhere with a little more privacy?" Though now that she was involved... *do the words "gossip columnist" tell you what I'm thinking?*

"Sure, Sheriff Lang." She linked an arm through mine and pulled me to the manager's office. "Ben, can the sheriff and I use the office for just a couple minutes. He needs to debrief me."

Oh, brother. I addressed the manager. "I just have a couple questions for both of you. Mrs. Fortune said this man was in your store Sunday." I handed him the picture of Ray.

Ben leaned forward squinting at the picture. "Yeah," he drawled, "that looks like one of the men with Mrs. Pomeroy."

The gossip cut in, "Not the extinguished looking one." She directed that at Ben. Used to interpreting Fortune's columns, I automatically translated that to "distinguished".

"Phoebe and your guy there—Ray?—they had a hell of a fight in the produce department. She threw an umbrella at him. We couldn't figure out where it came from. I mean it wasn't raining or anything. And there was—" she looked at Ben and lifted her shoulders, "like...exploded fruit everywhere. Ben had to ask them to leave." Ben shrugged his shoulders in silent agreement.

I thanked them and headed to the parking lot when it struck me what they'd said. I tapped on the door of the office where they still stood, no doubt discussing my visit.

"Ben, could you explain what you meant when you said, 'One of the men'?" I asked.

Fortune answered. "The three of them, sometimes four, come in every weekend."

I gazed at her.

The gossip looked at me exasperated. She said very slowly and distinctly, like I was a child or spoke another language. "This isn't the first time Phoebe has visited the store with her accomplices—"

"Accomplices?" I asked. I looked at Ben, who just rolled his eyes and shrugged.

She started again, "The men who accompliced her," Jane swore, nearly yelling, "They go everywhere with her."

Ah, missed that one—the men who "accompany" her.

"No doubt her roommates, or lovers." Her eyes were alight with the potential story.

"Do you have names to go with these... friends?"

They looked at each other. Fortune said, "Phoebe never introduced them." Her head tilted and she looked at me sideways, brows bouncing, "That's kind of strange, don't you think?"

Did I think it was strange that Phoebe Pomeroy didn't introduce her male "friends" to the local gossip? Uh... negative.

I drove straight to Tempe's mother's house. The grass was high, especially for someone with three male roommates. After getting no response at the door, I walked around the house to check for lights. One of the blinds was open on what appeared to be a bedroom, and I saw nothing except a room that looked like it hadn't been lived in.

I headed back toward Destiny. This new information added a whole new dimension to my investigation. And two new nameless suspects.

TEMPE

Phoebe, what are you up to? Can you read me? If you can, we need to talk.

If she'd *answer* I could tell her the sheriff wanted to question her about River and some phone records he found at the victim's apartment. I didn't remember what a mindlink felt like, but surely I could figure out how to receive an incoming message.

Our family link relied on two things—proximity and well

being. Maybe Mother was just out of range, or maybe she'd shut me out as she'd done in the past. But with River missing, her continued absence had me worried as well. No, we had not been close since Dutch died, but I did...love her?

For the first time in a long time, I considered my feelings for her, and not anger or distain. Now they were both missing. And they were all I had. I would drive over to her house again tomorrow if she hadn't returned my call or shown up on my genie radar, and if I didn't find her, I'd fill out another Missing Persons report. My heart skipped a beat.

I detoured to Harmony Plantation to change out of my wet clothes. An old red Ford F-150 sat next to the house.

"Zeus' boney knees!"

The *Un*handyman was here, off his leash and without supervision. You know how some people just really, really, really, really want to make it big as a professional performer or athlete? Well, Freddie is Storm Lake's answer to *Home Improvement*. When you hire Fred, you have to take the breaking with the fixing.

And here he was. On my roof! The liability of it made cold sweat gather between my shoulder blades and nausea threaten.

"Freddie," I called quietly. I didn't want to startle him and have him shoot down the slick tin roof and break his neck.

He didn't look up.

I cleared my throat and tried again. "Freddie, you up there?"

I heard heavy unsteady clomping and Freddie peeked out over the edge of the roof waving. "Hi, Tempest. I know I was supposed to wait for River to call, but I didn't hear from him

Monday or Tuesday like he said, and this roof really needs to be finished before the next rain. There are a couple of new leaks, but don't worry," he held up the roll of silver tape. "I fixed it."

I tilted my head back and studied the darkening sky, every pore sucking in the humidity. What's a little sticky goo compared to a leak? I mean, who would be able to see it but God?

"Thanks, Freddie. I don't know what we'd do without you. I've been too busy to think about the roof leaking. Could I talk to you for a sec?"

"You...betcha." He clambered down the ladder. "Whoa," he said as his wet boots slipped and skidded causing him to miss a couple rungs, but he landed safely. Sauntering over to his truck he grabbed a tub of Orange goop. I'd watched River clean his hands with the stuff hundreds of times, but for Freddie it was a spiritual ritual. I guess if you needed to use it to clean up, then you were doing work that was worthy of notice.

While he worked it between his fingers and under his nails I asked, "When was the last time you talked to River?"

He scrunched his eyebrows together, squeezed one eye shut, tilted his head back. Come on, Fred. "I believe it was Sunday night before his date."

"His date?" I grabbed his arm. "River had a date? Who was it with?" A little urgency crept into my voice, despite my efforts to prevent it.

"He didn't tell me. I assumed it was a date. He said he'd call me Monday about what to do. You know he always calls and tells me, like where to put stuff, and when to meet him, and then we go over his list so I don't screw—er, so I know exactly what he wants me to do, but he didn't show up. I figured he got busy, but since we were supposed to work on the roof and the window this week, I came anyway." His expression changed, becoming concerned. "Is that okay?"

I hesitated knowing how close Freddie was to River. "River didn't show up at his job site Monday morning, Fred. I haven't been able to locate him—"

"He's missing?" Freddie paced. "Call 911. Something must have happened to him. He could have driven off a cliff—"

"Ooo-kay. Let's take a deep breath."

And I meant *we*. His instantaneous reaction made me feel even worse, if that was possible. I put my arm around his shoulder and led him onto the porch. It was full dark now and our breaths were coming out in puffs in the light of the porch. "First of all, there may be one cliff in all of Louisiana, so we can rule that out." Neither of us laughed.

"Aren't you worried?" he asked, eyebrows curled in concern. "I mean it's Thursday, for God's sake."

My eyes burned. "I know, Freddie. I filed a report yesterday morning, and the sheriff is investigating." I hoped. "And our friends are putting out feelers. But no one seems to know the identity of the woman River was with Sunday night at the Wasted Turtle."

"The Wasted Turtle. The Wasted *Turtle*?" Freddie caught me off guard with his vehemence. "River wouldn't have gone to that place on a date, Tempest."

Freddie had a point. If he hadn't gone there on a date, then why? And who was the woman, if she wasn't his date?

"Thanks for fixing the leaks. I'll let you know if I hear from River, and you be sure to call me if you remember anything."

"You...betcha."

I took a Lean Cuisine out of the freezer, and changed clothes while Chef Micro prepared my meal. I ate it without tasting. My cell phone bleeped and I was surprised to hear Jordie Lang's voice on the other end.

"Hey, Jordie. Whatsup?"

"Hi, Tempe." Jordie's voice practically bubbled through the phone. "I'm at practice. You're still coming Saturday aren't you? I mean, with everything that's been going on..." Worry came through clear as spring water.

"I wouldn't miss it."

She shrieked, "Awesome. I needed to know 'cause they're going to let us assign seats for family and friends."

"Well, I hope you have a few extra because you're going to have your own cheering section."

"Really?" She sounded so enthused and...grateful, my heart melted.

"Really. It could be as many as let's see—me, Bailey, Montana, Katerina, Shannon, Chris, Aurora, Liam, Freddie, no, scratch Bailey, but add Mariah—I think that's it."

"Tempe, you're the bomb.com."

"Thanks, kid."

Silence. "Jordie? Was there something else?"

"I was wondering if you know...um, where I might find a part-time job. I'm a really hard worker, but I can't just apply at Gator's Grub or anywhere like Alliance or Hugo where I'd have to drive. And I have to work around my basketball schedule. You have a lot of customers, and Daddy said I should ask people I trust who are in a position to have like, customers and stuff."

I felt breathless just listening to her and smiled. She trusts me. I wondered what her father would say about any suggestions I came up with. "I don't know of anything right off ... "but I'll work on it."

"Thanks so much, Tempe. I gotta go. Don't forget, the game's at 6:30 in the gym, but come any time after two for the Mardi Gras float building and the pep rally. Just tell the guys at the door you're family. See ya."

"Bye," I whispered to the dead line and gulped. *Family.* A warm fuzzy feeling invaded my midsection. I liked Jack Lang's daughter way too much.

Way.

Chapter 28

He was dark and dangerous, and once again I felt the sensual pull.

JACK

A car pulled to the shoulder as I sped by, knowing they'd been about to get a ticket for speeding. Their lucky day. Peggy said, "Okay, here it is...the guy you're supposed to see in Amity is Corporal John Westman. He was home on leave and took his kayak out in the backwater off the parish levee at Spring Bayou."

"Where should I meet him?" I asked, looking at my map. I'd become familiar with most of the roads in Destiny in the last six months, but there were a few elsewhere I had to look up.

"He's at the campground," Peggy said. "Also, Mr. Thorpe called from the lab in Amity. He wants you to call him, says he has some interesting results."

"Patch me through."

"Yes, sir. Hold on."

While I waited for Peggy to get Thorpe, I thought about how I would break the news to Tempe about her brother if the news in Amity wasn't good.

Damn. Sometimes this job sucked like a flooded sewage drain.

"Sheriff? Dan Thorpe here. Got your results, though it won't be what you're hoping for I'm sure. The only fingerprints on the vase were Ms. Pomeroy's, but it was not the murder weapon. The vase itself is quite unique. It's some kind of Chinese artifact worth a fortune and really, really—really old. My advice is don't touch it unless you're insured with Lloyds of London."

So Tempe hadn't been exaggerating about the vase being old. And Thorpe's findings confirmed I still didn't have a weapon. Amity's Medical Examiner filled me in on the problems he was having with the samples.

As I continued toward Amity, I thought some more about possible motives. Tempe might have had motive if Meeker had been keeping her from getting to the valuable heirloom. Or, if she suspected he had something to do with River's disappearance. Or, if the guy was blackmailing the family over... what?

Then there was Phoebe and her roomies, cohorts, lovers, whatever. Phoebe had been seen arguing with the victim the afternoon prior to his death. Maybe they had some kind of lover's spat. I needed more information about the other two men. If the victim had something to do with River's disappearance, Tempe's mother might have confronted him. When was the last time that she'd been seen? Sunday evening?

And we must not forget the brother. Yeah, yeah, even Peggy sang his praises. Of course, if River had killed the guy, he'd have taken his fancy vase. Unless he didn't know it was there. Maybe he couldn't smell it like his sister. I barked out a laugh remembering her lie. I hadn't found anything that incriminated either him or her.

So unless I thought Tempe and her brother were in this together, I had to get over to her side and really start looking for her brother before she got herself into more trouble. *If* he wasn't in the backwater at Spring Bayou. And if he was—I wasn't looking forward to giving Tempe that news.

There were a lot of odd and yet-to-be-explained events involving Tempe, but they didn't add up to murder. So for now, she was off the hook. River and Phoebe Pomeroy were another story, but I'd wait until I had more evidence. There was also the matter of the official report on River. I had a responsibility to look into River's disappearance.

TEMPE

A big, pricey looking Harley sat in the intersection two blocks from Harmony. Its driver, dressed in shiny black leather, turned his dark-visored helmet toward me as I approached then looked away. After nine years of running the mail, my attention to oddities—was infallible. The motorcycle rider was not from around here. And it's a cold night for a ride, I thought as my cell bleeped again.

It was Kat. She sounded strange. "Tempe, one of the reporters called and said there was a...look, don't jump the gun yet, okay?"

Suddenly I couldn't hear anything except blood rushing in my ears. "I'm listening," I whispered.

"Some guy camping down in Amity found a dead body."

THE MOTORCYCLE RIDER FLEW CLEAN OUT OF MY HEAD. I coasted to a stop, my hands gripping my stomach. I leaned my forehead on the wheel as tears welled.

"I said, don't jump the gun." She waited then perhaps thinking I'd hung up, said, "Tempe, are you there?"

Knuckling moisture from my cheeks, I took a deep breath as Kat waited on the other end of the line. I let it out. "What else?"

"They don't even know if it's a male or female. A call was dispatched to the sheriff's office since it happened outside the town of Amity."

"That's all they know?" I was starting to panic.

"That's it, and none of the reporters can get anywhere near the scene because the S.O. has the roads blocked off."

"I'm familiar with Sheriff Lang's tactics." He'd probably added to them after dealing with me at the golf course. "Thanks, Katerina. I'll see what I can find out."

So here I was again, sending a message to the one person I could always count on. I sent a text, and at seven-thirty I got a response, "Pepper, meet you later at BB's." *When* exactly had he started calling me by those pet names?

Sometimes sweet, always intense and sexy, I'd thought he was as into our relationship as I was. But I'd turned the corner—literally—one morning and there he'd been, bestowing all that sexiness on Ms.103 Sweet Briar Court.

I'd thought about that moment many times, in fact, every day I turned *that* corner and drove past *that* house. He hadn't reacted like a man caught in the act of cheating. And Ms. Sweet Briar, damn, what was her name? Well, who cares? She'd started taking her mail in a drawer at the central office. She hadn't seemed embarrassed either, or at all shamed that she'd been caught with the object of my affection. At the time, I'd been too hurt and shocked myself to see anything other than what it had looked like on the surface. Now, I wondered.

Dylan apologized, but didn't ask me to give him another chance, leaving me with the appalling, embarrassing feeling that he'd wanted out but hadn't had the guts to just tell me. He'd said he just wasn't meant for a monogamous relationship.

That hurt because I'd allowed myself to think I might have a normal life, like everyone else, including romance. Looking back, I'd have to say my parent's relationship prepared me for failure. I hadn't been surprised by Dylan's betrayal. It just seemed that romance wasn't for me.

Women loved Dylan. Men hated him. Actually, that wasn't true. His coworkers admired and respected him. His job as a PI called for strict discipline, integrity, and a certain detachment from personal relationships.

"Listen to me, making excuses for him." I pulled into the parking lot at BB's lounge and shut the truck off, sitting there for a second to compose myself. Tonight would only be the second time I'd been in Dylan's presence since the breakup, two years ago. And if I hadn't been desperate for news of River, we wouldn't be here now. As always rain stirred my emotions, putting me in a mood.

I walked through the open door hearing the conversations at tables and the clink of glasses behind the bar. I ordered a tonic, then after thinking about the evening ahead, the meeting with Dylan, and the impending news from Amity, I ordered a shot of tequila, and downed it feeling the burn and the satisfactory warmth, and knowing I'd regret it.

I sensed Dylan's potent aura before I heard the heels of his boots thunk against the hardwood floor, then his shadow fell across me. With a slight tilt of my head I saw black hair wet with rain combed away from his beautifully dangerous face, his lips a mere breath from mine, so close I could see each stubbled hair on his cheek; the eyes I knew to be a rich forest green, were obsidian, wild.

Blast those pesky pheromones! Instead of remembering why we'd split, my body was begging me to jump him, the memories of our limbs entwined in a hot morning caress making it nearly impossible to maintain a facade of irritation.

"Dylan." I pushed the glass away.

His lips crooked up at the corner and he relaxed, flopping onto the nearest barstool. He looked me over, refrained from commenting on my messy appearance. "You look stressed. I was going to buy you a drink, but it looks like you've had one." His brow arched at the sight of the shot glass.

I returned his perusal, raking over the black duster where moisture steamed off that big hard body. The only obvious break in color was the shiny gold badge on the black id wallet visible between the leather lapels. He was dark and danger-ous, and once again I felt the sensual pull. I rubbed my fore-head, willing those thoughts away.

"What did you want to talk to me about, Persephone?"

"That's it! Just once, could you call me by my friggin' name?" I pushed off the stool and turned on him, fisting clumps of my hair.

He sat back, looked at me closely. "Talk to me. What's going on," he said.

"I need a favor, Inspector."

He slid off his stool, motioning the bartender away with a look. "I think you've had enough."

I turned on him, "Who died and made you the keeper of me?" And then I remembered what I'd learned, and a sob escaped my throat. I turned away. *Get a grip*. I signaled the bartender to bring me a water, and felt Dylan's hand squeeze my shoulder gently. I didn't mean to let him, but it felt so...comforting.

"Bad day?" His voice was a calming purr. "Bad week," he corrected. He could be so sweet. I hated that I remembered that about him, too. "I'm sorry I was late. I've been on a job in Baton Rouge." He stroked a length of my hair behind my ear.

I could have easily allowed him to shoulder my troubles. Fix everything. No, that was tequila thinking. I didn't need the betraying bastard to fix anything for me. "I've changed my mind. I don't need you."

I think he winced, but my vision was suspect.

"Come on, you need to call it a day." He got up towering over me.

I slid off the stool, swaying just a smidgen. I was sure he didn't notice, but then his hand settled on my hip steering me between the other stools and patrons into the fresh rain-washed night. I tripped on the uneven walkway of the porch and felt his hand on my elbow.

He said, "Tempe," and turned me toward him. "Damn," he muttered, looking off.

"Ah, so you do know my name," I said.

"Look, I need to talk to you. Privately."

I guess the dark night with only a few people coming and going from the parking lot wasn't private enough. He led me around the side of the building. The comforting song of the rain frogs started up again as I propped myself against the outside wall. He placed both hands on either side of my head.

"This may not be the best time, but I need to say this." His flippant manner was gone, replaced by frank sincerity. Whether he was deciding to continue or just weighing his words, I waited. He sounded different, almost humble. Huh.

"When I was on that job in Baton Rouge, I realized that I couldn't let something happen before I got the chance to tell you..." he let out a deep breath. "...about what happened two years ago, I didn't mean to hurt you. There were—are reasons why..."

I guess what he saw on my face he took for forgiveness, instead of shock. "Oh, hell." His lips touched mine in a kiss reminiscent of those nights by the fire, touches drenched in desire, his body like hot steel...I groaned.

There was comfort in his kiss, and in the long overdue apology. The last few days had been a nightmare, with memories and revelations coming at me faster than I could assimilate them. Then my conversation with Aurora resurfaced. I flattened my hands on his chest. "Dylan, no."

I heard boots hit the porch and pushed harder.

"Well, damn. Looks like I've come at a bad time."

Chapter 29

Don't turn that black squadron commander look on me.

TEMPE

I froze, recognizing Jack Lang's voice. Dylan simply lifted his head, but stayed where he was. Sheltering me from embarrassment, or using our embrace as some kind of territorial declaration?

I broke away from him and turned. Jack's face was hidden in the shadows. "Here I was thinking you might be worried about your brother, and I find you on a date with Diablo.

Diablo? A date? I frowned. "I've been trying to call you."

His lip curled up in a sarcastic smile. "Yeah, I can see you were real worried."

"Please, just tell me that body—" I choked.

"It was a female victim," he said, apparently realizing that I was on the verge of losing it. I sagged against Dylan, then, realized how that looked and shook him off. I bent over with my hands on my knees and heaved with relief.

"But I have other news you might find interesting."

"What?" Dylan didn't lose a beat.

I stood up. Jack looked at me. "I'm surprised you didn't recognize the man at the clubhouse. Apparently he lives in Alliance."

"So?"

"With your mother."

My mouth gaped open.

"The clubhouse records listed your mother's address as his permanent address, not the apartment."

"But that doesn't make any sense. I've never seen that man."

"That's not all, I found two people at the grocery store in Alliance who remember your mother from Sunday." He paused, watching me, like I was going to run away or something. As if I could. There didn't seem to be any end to this nightmare.

"She was with three men, in whose company she's been seen every weekend. And on Sunday afternoon last, your mother and Mr. Meeker got into a heated discussion in the produce department during which she threw an umbrella and some melons at him."

"I—" He was waiting for me to say something, but my senses had flipped to off like a circuit breaker.

"You don't have anything to say, when I tell you your mother has three lovers, one of whom you found dead in the clubhouse the day after she had a fight with him?"

"Phoebe couldn't have been involved with him; he was…uh… African American." I struggled not to roll my eyes at the lame explanation. But what could I say? It wasn't his race that was an issue, but his species. I scratched my head looking at the floor. "I know that sounds terribly un-PC…"

Jack looked off, looked at Dylan then back at me, his gaze inscrutable. "Don't go anywhere. I have some questions for you in the morning, when you sober up. You might want to get some help for that drinking problem."

That did it. "Don't turn that black squadron commander look on me. What do you mean, sober up? I'm sober enough to tell you what I think of your investigating abilities, Sheriff." That's telling him, I thought as I spun around… and tripped. I would have fallen off the porch if Dylan hadn't caught me around the waist and hauled me against him.

"Yeah," said the sheriff. "I assume you won't be driving home," but he was looking at Dylan.

Dylan shook his head. "I'll make sure she gets home."

I sensed the testosterone in the air. They reminded me of two Rottweilers fighting over a poodle. But I was no poodle.

"*I'll* make sure *I* get home. And you know where to find me at six-thirty in the morning if you have questions for me." I jerked free of Dylan's grip and gave all my concentration over to looking normal as I stomped carefully back into the bar.

I'd only had one drink. All I had to do was wait until it wore off. I thought about the sheriff's report. Mother always had a man around. But three? It was time Phoebe and I had a serious talk.

∾

You'd think someone would be at Phoebe's at two o'clock in the morning, especially if she was supposed to have roommates, but the place was empty. I had decided to use *menori* to get in if I couldn't find a key, but Mother was as unimaginative as ever in her choice of hiding places. As if no one would ever think to lift the rubber mat to check for a spare. It gives a whole new meaning to the word *welcome*.

The door opened into the kitchen. This was not the house River and I grew up in, so it conjured no sentimental feelings or memories. Phoebe rarely cooked so as expected, there were no aromas lingering in the air. I opened the refrigerator and peered inside. Empty. I walked through the hallway to the living room. "Anyone here? Mother?"

The living room was spotless, with the exception of a man's cane leaning against the couch. I sent *menori* on a search of the rest of the rooms. No humans present. Now I was just curious about what clues I could find to Phoebe's whereabouts or the identity of her "friends".

The first bedroom held no personal items, and the double bed was simply covered in an old chenille bedspread. The next bedroom was the largest and obviously Phoebe's. A few pieces of her clothing still hung in the closet. A mirrored tray held candles and a translucent gazing ball perched in the palm of a ceramic water sprite, as well as a beautiful hand blown bottle of liquid. When I looked closer, I could see a kaleidoscope of movement, storm clouds, swirling winds, the expanding plume of a haboob. I blinked. I'd never seen anything like it. It was...weather in a bottle. I studied it for a minute longer, fascinated. There was something familiar about the swirling concoction, but I couldn't put my finger on it.

This room was the only one in the house that looked occupied. Phoebe's side of the bed was recognizable by a set of her earrings in a shallow dish. I finished a scan of the room, finding a set of men's slippers on the other side of the bed. The spread had been pulled back, but my little aura reading talent was telling me this house felt abandoned, which was what I'd sensed from the minute I'd walked into the kitchen.

So if that was true, why was the key still under the mat? And most importantly, why would Phoebe have left the items on the dresser behind for anyone to find?

As an afterthought, I looked on the wall behind the door and was shocked to find a picture of Phoebe, River and me. River was showing his new front teeth, and I was crossing my eyes at him. I felt a clutch in my stomach, and dread. Finally, I put a name to the emotion—fear. I was afraid to remember. I'd pushed the memories back for so long. Had they become skewed in my head from hurt and anger? I took a deep breath.

Since my meeting with Aurora, I was making a conscious effort to fight the fear, to allow those memories to reform, and see the truth. Next to my mother an image materialized. I knew before it was fully formed, it was Daddy. The bronze skinned giant with his red gold hair and copper coin eyes, had one arm around my mother, the other around River and me. That day came back to me now.

I'd been a happy seven-year-old when the picture was snapped on one of our family picnics. My hair had still been red. Just red. On a humid spring afternoon our parents had taken us to Lightning Bayou, where they tried to outsmart each other in a stormy battle of elements.

At one point, Mother, holding River in her arms, rolled Daddy down a grassy slope, with a dust devil that soared into the clouds. He landed in the mucky swamp water, with a splash, his voice booming, "You weather witch, top this!"

River giggled hilariously as animal cracker shaped hailstones bounced around us. Daddy winked at River, and cocked an eyebrow at mother, looking triumphant, thinking he'd won. Mother just smiled, took both of our hands in hers, and changed into an umbrella.

Daddy's laughter thundered like the great hall of echoes. If the locals noticed, they probably just thought it was a pop-up thundershower.

My heart ached now thinking about the way he'd looked at Phoebe. Intense pride and love blazed from his eyes, and I'd followed his gaze to mother's to find a crafty yet sweet smile, which had been all for him.

I'd forgotten how happy they were before Dutch died. Why had she withdrawn from us, as if we no longer mattered?

My father's image faded until all I saw was background again. I rummaged through Phoebe's closet for a tote bag, finding a plastic green sack, into which I loaded the mirrored tray and its contents. I found a scratch pad in the kitchen by the phone and wrote, *Phoebe, or whoever is living here with my mother, please call me.* I wrote my cell phone and signed it, *Tempe.* At least if she returned, she'd know I had the items from her bedroom.

I sank into the kitchen chair in the dark, overwhelmed by a feeling of loss. My brother was missing, and my mother wasn't just incommunicado, she was gone as well. Was it voluntary, or was she a victim of whatever had happened to my brother?

Any other time the tap on the kitchen door would have made

me jump, but I just didn't have the energy. It eased open, and I heard the clump of heavy boots on the kitchen linoleum.

"What the hell are you doing here in the middle of the night?"

JACK

The room was dark, but the meager light from the window illuminated my quarry at the kitchen table with her head in her hands. "What the hell are you doing here in the middle of the night?"

I winced as my question came out more harshly than I'd intended. When I went back to BBs the bartender said Tempe had paced the floor of the bar drinking coffee for an hour, then asked for the truck keys McGuinness had tossed him. Without a word, she walked out the door and drove off.

I'd tracked her down to tell her I was sorry for the way I reacted at the bar when I discovered her with the PI. I was beginning to suspect jealousy might be at play.

She looked up from the table, light reflecting on the silent tears coursing down her cheeks. Oh, man. I couldn't help feeling that my actions might have put a cap on her day. She'd been shocked at my announcement earlier, but instead of leaning on either me or the inspector, she'd told us where to go and set out on her own to get answers. If only I'd stuck to the plan I'd made on the way back from Amity...

I'd been worried about the body being River's and how I would deliver that news. Instead of giving her the good news like I intended and telling her I planned to step up my investigation into River's disappearance—after finding her in a lip lock with McGuinness—I'd blown a fuse and kicked her when she was down. I felt like a jerk.

The woman got to me. She got on my last nerve most of the time but it was usually preceded by a jolt like the one from my F-18's afterburners. The Tempe I was used to, with her feistiness and weird little "talents" didn't resemble this Tempe, who seemed to have run out of *feist*.

My fingers itched to touch her, so I balled my hands into fists to keep from reaching out to comfort her. "Are you all right?" I glanced toward the hallway. "What happened?" Maybe she discovered her mother lying in one of those rooms, or her brother. Why did she look so sad?

Flashes from the outside lights flickered across her eyes when she looked up, making them appear lit from within.

"Stay here." With my hand on my Glock, I searched the house, noting the slippers next to the bed and the cane in the living room. Finding nothing but an empty house, I was curious what had brought on such a reaction from her. I heard water running in the kitchen.

I looked behind the bedroom door and found a picture of Tempe, her mother and River. She must have been around eight, her eyes bright with laughter. She was tickling her brother and making a face, her red hair draped around his face. There was an odd expression on Phoebe Pomeroy's face. As if she was smiling at someone next to her but no one was there.

I heard water running in the kitchen, closed the door and walked back down the hallway. The light was on, and Tempe stood at the sink drinking water out of a Styrofoam cup. I put my hand on the refrigerator door, and for the first time since I'd arrived, Tempe spoke. "It's empty." She blew out a sigh placing the cup on the counter, leaning her hip against it.

"It looks like no one's been here in days, possibly longer," I said, worried about her frame of mind. I walked over to her, and this time I gave in to the impulse to comfort her, placing my hands on her upper arms and rubbing as if I could flush the chill from her heart.

Did she fall toward me, or had I embraced her? All I knew was I felt comforted as well with her head resting against me. She felt real and solid. She'd scared me with her lack of fire. This was not my Tempe. I sucked in a breath.

So, there it was. I was starting to feel possessive towards her. Especially since it no longer compromised my job or my principles. "Tempe." I held her at a distance so I could tip her chin up.

I never noticed how beautiful her irises were, the flecks like flying snow lit in the beam of headlights, sparkling gold and silver; they were alive with every emotion stirring inside her, which was encouraging.

"I'm sorry." I watched those expressive eyes widen as I bent toward her.

Chapter 30

He kissed me like he was starving.

TEMPE

Cocooned in Jack's embrace after feeling like I'd never be warm again, my heart soared with hope. His heart thumped against my cheek as I breathed out against his chest, reassured for once that we weren't at cross purposes.

"I'm sorry." The words rumbled up from his chest as he tilted my face up to his. He was so handsome. This close, I could see the laugh lines and the crease in his cheek that became a dimple when he smiled, which wasn't often enough.

My eyes widened as those silver green eyes softened and his face came closer. His lips touched mine in a comforting kiss, at first. Then the spark ignited and brought me alive. I threaded my hands through his hair and tugged his head down, yearning for more.

He moaned and took the kiss deeper, his tongue coaxing the seam of my lips as I opened for him. He kissed me like he was starving, devouring my mouth, holding me so tightly I could feel the steely muscles of his biceps. I drank him in, inhaling his scent, tasting his exquisite flavor. His lower body pressed against me once, then the hard ridge of desire, which had drawn an answering clench within me was withdrawn. The kiss ended. A small whimper escaped.

He chuckled. "Feeling better?" One hand rested gently on my shoulder, the other stroked my hair as he studied me.

"Is that how you lift the spirits of all damsels in distress?" I asked.

"Nope. This was a first." His rueful expression confirmed it.

"So what were you sorry about?" I looked down at his belt buckle noting that his interest hadn't waned. "Kissing me?"

He made a choked laugh. "Is that what that kiss felt like to you?" He pressed against me again before putting some space between us. He sighed, and ran a hand through his hair. "I... oh hell, Tempe. I didn't mean to strike out at you earlier. The ironic thing is I wanted to be the one to tell you the good news about what I found in Amity—"

"Instead you hit me with the bad news about Phoebe," I said.

"I wish we could do the whole evening over, forget about that whole scene at BBs." He squinted at me, "Especially the part about you kissing McGuinness."

I felt the flush rise on my face. "Well, not that you have any right to tell me who I can kiss..." His eyes flared again. I smiled, "But there really isn't anything between Dylan and me anymore. He was apologizing, and I was in a vulnerable state."

"Uh-huh. So did I take advantage of you just now? If so..."

"Please don't say it." I rolled my head back and looked at the ceiling and wondered once again—with everything that had been going on with the male population lately, both human and fae—how I could trust this moment, or my emotions to be based on anything but the craziness of my impending change.

"Why don't you tell me why you were sitting in this empty house, in the dark, looking so lost." Jack said.

Without being able to explain to this human about the connections between Paramortals, and my family in particular, I had to rely on something he could understand.

I looked through the window over the sink across the backyard to the road that led out of town. "I can't feel them. Have you ever felt so far away from someone you loved that..." I couldn't say it. What if giving voice to it brought about the very result I feared?

He said, "That you can't feel their presence. It's like they're—"

I turned and gripped his arm. "Don't say it." I squeezed my eyes shut.

Strong arms wrapped around me, one hand stroking my hair, as he spoke softly, "When I was on duty overseas, I remember wondering if Jordie was okay, if something had happened to her. I didn't talk to her for months and couldn't feel her... existence. *Feeling* that, fearing it, even saying it won't make it so, Tempe. We are going to find them."

"It's..." *We are going to find them*. Did he mean it? The truth behind his words hit me. "You believe me," I said, relief bringing on more tears.

"Yes. That's what I intended to tell you last night. Even though I can't say I believe everything you've told me. You're holding something back."

I bit my tongue and subtly switched subjects. "I'm going to go home and get a couple hours sleep before work."

"All right." He looked around the barren kitchen, adjusted his belt. "Jordie says you've been arm-twisting your friends to come to the game tomorrow."

I smiled. "It didn't get that far. She's a big hit with everyone who meets her."

"She's more excited than I've seen her since...well, ever." He grinned. "And for that..." he reached for me.

One thoroughly toe curling kiss later, he was gone. As soon as I uncurled those toes, I followed, locking the door and taking the extra key with me.

TEMPE

Friday turned out to be a light mail day, but before I left for the route, Richard brought me a complaint. "Mrs. Wisner called. He read the note, 'The mail person on Wednesday did not come to the door. They left the pink slip in her mailbox instead.'"

I knew that sub. If she didn't get out, there was only one reason—a bad dog. She would have honked a half dozen times and sat in the driveway until she figured the residents weren't home, or they were ignoring her. It happens.

So now I had to explain, yet again, that a customer's beloved "harmless" pet was a problem. I'd heard the arguments a zillion times.

"My dog doesn't bite."

"Oh, he's not serious, he's just barking."

"You're afraid of a little dog like that?"

"But he's just a puppy."

Or the infamous, "He just wants to play."

I'd been bitten by friendly dogs, mad dogs, playful dogs, and puppies—intentionally and unintentionally. But the result is the same. If we report a dog bite, we're fired. Is it any wonder few are willing to take the risk? And we take the heat from both ends because we're expected to deliver the mail anyway.

I honked and the woman stepped out onto her front porch. I felt stupid explaining why the other carrier hadn't gotten out when the canine actor playing possum at her feet never even barked. With one sarcastic lift of her eyebrow and a glance down at her "harmless" dog, she said disgustedly, "Whatever," and walked back inside, unconvinced.

Some situations are a *lose-lose*.

THE BELL ABOVE THE DOOR TO AURORA'S SHOP JINGLED AS I pushed it open.

"I'm back here, Tempe."

I don't know how she did that, but it's always weird. I walked around the wall into the rear portion of the shop where Aurora stood surrounded by boxes. "Wow, what a mess," I said. "Can I help?"

"Didn't you have plans this afternoon?"

"I'm waiting to hear from Dylan regarding River's amphora, to do the ceremonial initiation."

"Tempe, why didn't you say something? Call Dylan and tell him to find another Djinn and meet us at La Grand Morte at 11:00 tonight. Bring the new bottle."

"Big Mort? What about Lightning Bayou? It's bigger, plenty of water, lots of gators and other sacrificial candidates."

"That's the point, dear." She smiled while she continued to unpack, "We need a dead lake."

"Oh." I didn't know what ceremonializing a bottle involved, but I figured it probably meant a spell or two...and blood... and who knew? Apparently, everybody but me.

Aurora stopped her unpacking and tilted her head. Waiting.

"Oh, right. I'll call Dylan."

I walked outside. Dylan seemed to know exactly what Aurora had in mind and promised to be there promptly at eleven.

When I reentered her workroom, Aurora was head down into a large box of dress bags. "Help me with these, will you?" The slithery plastic held oodles of frothy ball gowns in an array of colors and sizes. There must have been forty of them. Some were sheer filmy chiffon and others heavy with multi colored sequins and rhinestones. I held hangers for her while she unfolded and priced each one. I then moved each one to the appropriate section on the rack. I could do this. There were Cinderella-styled ball gowns, figure hugging knits, flowing silk A-lines, and ornate fit and flares, according to her. I learned more about fancy dresses in thirty minutes than I ever could have imagined.

My eye caught on a dress hanging on the steaming rack. It was the color of a winter thunderstorm. Its heart shaped bodice and waistline were covered in rhinestones that reflected like diamonds. To say I wasn't a girly girl...well, we've been there, but this dress made me want to be.

"Beautiful isn't it?" said Aurora from over my shoulder.

"For sure, but I'd never have the occasion to wear something like that. What's next?"

"After we get these gowns up, I have candles, and look at these wonderful blown glass earrings."

There were decanters, the thingies that sit down over candles, sequined shoes, and a box full of jewelry.

"My last shipment of Mardi Gras masks and gowns is due tomorrow. I'll probably be here Sunday trying to get everything priced and displayed before Monday. Next week will be crazy leading up to the Grand Ball, not to mention the upcoming proms."

She was playing right into my hands. "I might have the perfect solution for you."

Aurora poured us each a cup of tea and leaned against the counter. "Tell me."

"Have either Montana or Kat mentioned the basketball game tomorrow? Jack's daughter is the star player, and I promised her a bunch of us would be there. I sorta volunteered you as well."

"So it's 'Jack' now?" She laughed at my poor attempt to keep a straight face. "Anyway, the daughter, Jordan? I read the sports column about her in the *Destiny Tribune*."

Now that was an image. My otherworldly mentor, Aurora Boreal, pouring over the sports section.

"Jordie says this is a huge game for them, and she apparently doesn't have a lot of friends. She invited us to come for the Mardi Gras float decorating at 2:00 and stay for the pep rally before the game."

"Sounds like fun. I'll look forward to it. But I'm not sure what time I'll get there, since there's a Mardi Gras ball tomorrow night, and I'll probably have last minute customers. I can bring some special beads and trinkets I've been holding on to. Now tell me about this perfect solution."

I squirmed. "Oh that." She cocked her head patiently. "Seems Jordie's looking for a part-time job after school. But it has to work around her practice schedule and her father's..."

"Suspicious nature?" Aurora smiled. "If I like this girl, I'll definitely hire her. I need some late afternoon help, and a popular teenage athlete would be good for business."

"You may as well write her name on your schedule, because she's a jewel."

She reached over and took my hands in hers, her expression turning serious. "What else is on your mind? Your aura is a bit gray."

"Really?"

"No, silly. That's your bailiwick. But I can tell you're a bit down. What is it?"

I sighed. "Jack—" I started to tell her what he'd told me about Phoebe, then blurted out, "kissed me."

Her eyes and mouth turned up in delight. "What brought that on?"

I bounced up, pacing to the door and back. "Okay, that's the point. I'm asking myself the same thing. I mean, was he feeling sorry for me, or did he finally give in to this attraction I've felt since I first saw him?"

"Why would he feel sorry for you? I'm pretty sure he's felt more than a little irritated with you since you met."

"This is true." So I told her about meeting Dylan, about his apology, and finally about Phoebe's connection to the victim and her supposed "lovers".

"Poppycock!" pronounced Aurora, her eyes flaring with indignation.

"Well, I searched her house. There was a man's set of slippers by the bed and a cane in the living room."

"Don't jump to conclusions."

I paused, tapping my fingertips on the counter, thinking back over the condition of the house.

"What is it?" Aurora asked.

"I don't know. There was something wrong about the house. The whole place looked like it had been cleaned out to rent but..."

Aurora finished off her tea and set the cup in the sink. Sounding somewhat distracted, she asked, "Do you want to try the mindlink?"

I chuffed, "I'd have more success posting on social media, and you know how adept I am at Squawker and Snapchat." My sarcasm was met with a hug.

"We're going to find them, Tempe."

"Funny. That's exactly what Jack said to me."

"Well then. Believe it."

"How much longer does River have, Aurora? Can he last until the full moon, or is it the Coincidence?"

"The time of the lunar full moon is mathematically predictable, based on a millennia of observations and modern technological reporting. It's a matter of gravity, orbit and distance from the earth. The full moon begins next Friday and will provide the strongest boost to your family frequency. If you're going to connect with River that would be your best opportunity, until the Coincidence."

Seven days 'til the full moon, I thought. Maybe we'd get a break before then.

Aurora went on, "The full Para-moon or Coincidence isn't as certain. It happens infrequently. The last one was four hundred years ago. Its coincidence with the lunar moon is based on magic, not science, so until the time is closer and I can do an astral seeding, I can't give you a more accurate guess than sometime before the lunar full moon begins its descent. After next weekend, possibly Fat Tuesday."

"Is that what you've been calling 'Chaos'?"

"Actually, Chaos refers to the twenty-four hour period when the full moons coincide, and all Paramortals lose their power until the next moonrise."

"*Zeus' darkest hour!* This is serious."

"Yes, well, we'll worry about that after we find River."

In other words, we had to find him before the Para-moon when all hell would break loose. I couldn't help but wonder how Jack would respond when a bunch of variants and other unfriendly creatures had twenty-four hours to create havoc on the streets of Destiny.

Chapter 31

"Is this where the party's goin' d-down?"

T<small>EMPE</small>

La Grand Morte was indeed dead. The ancient swamp had been barren for so long that the trees had petrified in their stumpy stages. The bed was cracked from lack of moisture, some of the chalky grey crevices curled up along the edges, and many were pulverized into a powder. Each step Dylan took along the bank created a tiny puff of matter I was pretty sure I didn't want to inhale. There was a lot to making a beautiful gemstoned antique into a viable genie bottle.

Dylan threw a military style duffle down at Aurora's feet. "Careful, Dylan," Aurora scolded. "Buzzard's knees, but you can be such a man sometimes. Tempe, please bring the new amphora over here and help Dylan carefully unpack the contents of this bag. I'll set up the base for the ceremony."

She gathered several items from the bag and the new

amphora and walked out into the center of the flat lifeless swamp, her feet not kicking up the first bit of dust.

"Did you find a Djinni?" I asked Dylan.

"Uh-huh." He unpacked three more items and followed Aurora across the lake.

"Wait—"

"Is this where the party's goin' d-down?" asked a young familiar voice behind me.

I whirled to find Andy Rush standing hands in his pockets, looking out across the old swamp toward Dylan and Aurora.

Of course. Andy was the newest Djinni, and a good choice because he was already connected to River through their training sessions.

Aurora motioned for us to cross over to where she and Dylan had been busy setting up a small altar. "Hurry on over, Andy."

Aurora placed candles at five points on the perimeter circle Dylan had marked with salt. After Andy and I entered the circle, he closed it with the remaining salt.

"Hand me the other herbs and minerals from the bag please, Tempe."

I recognized the wolf-bane, mugwort, Job's Tears, and Cinquefoil. "What are these?" I held the brown pieces of root in one hand and what looked like twigs in the other.

Dylan said, "The one in your left hand is High John the Conqueror, and the 'twigs' ironically sometimes called that, are devil's shoestring. It provides power, while the High John helps with healing. And this little package..." he pulled a mesh bag from his pocket "...will purify River's new home."

He bent over to pick up five small stones from the pack. "And these little jewels are boji stones for protection."

"You two stop gabbing and help me finish setting up before we run out of time," Aurora said.

I didn't know we had a time limit. "Midnight?"

Aurora smiled, placing a large clear crystal in the center. "Yes. Andy has a curfew. Andy, stand over there at the South side of the circle where you can hold your arms over those two points. Tempe, over here at the head, and Dylan and I will stand opposite here. We're one week from the full Quickening Moon and our Para-moon. We'll pay homage to them as well. Tempe, please light the candles."

I looked around for matches.

Dylan cleared his throat, and Aurora raised an eyebrow. "As a Tempestaerie, please."

I swallowed. It was a defining moment, here in the night with two Paramortal pros. They didn't cajole, or intimidate, or push me to do what I was supposed to be able to do. They simply expected it to be done. *Immediately*.

So I extended my hand and brought fire from that well of *Qi'menori* inside me. Like a Zippo in the shape of a finger, my flame blossomed briefly then burned steadily as I lit the five candles representing earth, air, water, fire and spirit. I took my place at the top of the five-pointed star.

There was a bright three quarter moon surrounded by a halo and the stars were so bright and distinct, they seemed pluckable. Pleiades was clearly visible. I loved its nickname—the seven little sisters. It kind of reminded me of the SOAPs.

We held hands. "Damn, Tempe," Dylan said. "Put the flame

out first." He licked his palm where the fire had left a burn mark. The mark disappeared.

"Sorry." I extinguished the flame and took his hand and Aurora's.

> "On Freya's night of Venus, goddess of love and happiness. Under the seven sisters of Pleaides —Maia, Alcyone, Asterope, Taygeta, Celaeno, Merope and Elektra,"

I was counting in my head and lost track. Would that affect the spell? Regardless, Aurora went on...

> "On the approach of the Quickening Full Moon,
>
> I call upon the power of Earth to the North.
>
> Hail and Welcome.
>
> I call upon the power of Air to the East.
>
> Hail and Welcome.
>
> I call upon the power of Fire to the South.
>
> Hail and Welcome.
>
> I call upon the power of Water to the West.
>
> Hail and Welcome.
>
> I call upon the powers of our Spirit guides to join us in this circle for the purpose of protection for two of our own."

I'd never been to one of these ceremonies before, but I felt the connection to the elements Aurora implored. Especially the elements that ruled Tempestaeries like me and Phoebe, air and water. As she called to them, my blood seemed to flow

227

much faster through my veins, and I saw the detail in the landscape around us.

Where the dead swamp had seemed just a flat expanse of grey gumbo, I could suddenly make out the pattern of tiny roots in the surface, and small fissures around the dead stumps in the distance, thirty or forty yards away. She continued.

"Sister, Brother, Djinni kin,

Mentor, guardian, apprentice within

The circle protects, distributes the power

For all supplicants at the appointed hour

That hour we know not but we pray it is soon

For the one endangered to be found by Full Moon"

Aurora lit another white candle and the scent of sage rose with smoke from the small tray in front of her. She dribbled salt around the midnight blue amphora, and placed ladies' stones at three points on the circle.

"With salt and flame and herbs and metals dear

We purge malevolent spirits

From the hearth of River's amphora

And call on the three ladies to protect this hearth

Until our Djinn's son, River comes home."

She held out her hand. Dylan placed four small cylindrical tubes in her palm. Lighting the herbs in the wide pan near the amphora, she threw the tubes into it. They exploded, sending sparklers and three plumes of light into the air.

"Fair Ladies forgive the inaccuracy of the color.

Fourth of July fireworks were all I could find."

There was a vibration beneath our feet, and Aurora said, "Stand firm, everyone." The amphora rocked from side to side, moving faster until it was clearly vibrating on its base like a child's top.

Andy blanched and said, "Whoa," as a dark smoky shape exited the top of the navy container, followed by several smaller slender shapes, offspring? Ugh, house cleaning. The three stones glowed red like charcoal briquettes and the shapes dissipated. Another popped out of the *back door* and was zapped out of existence.

Now I knew why Marty had been terrified of River's amphora. There had been spirits still left in it that might have enslaved him. The devil's in the details...

Aurora took my hand again and held it up.

"For the Tempestaerie here

Father Sun and Mars provide protection

Mercury speed healing,

Mental acuity and communication."

She uncovered a circlet made of vines and placed it on my head, returning to her place.

"We ask for clear answers to find the 'son' and

Light surround father, mother, brother.

Bring clarity to the connections within the family bond"

What did that mean? It was all some kind of rhyming astral puzzle, and I didn't know enough to figure it out. I looked over at Dylan who winked at me and grinned. We both looked at Andy who was getting tired of holding his arms out at the forty-five degree angle.

"Bless the young apprentice and the 'son'

In whose place he stands,

Make swift and sure discovery of that one

So the evil can be banned.

As new life permeates the ground under our feet,

We demand old evil here make a final retreat."

For the first time, I noticed tiny sprigs of grass bursting forth from the dead earth. Then as quickly, small springs of water spurted from the cracks and ran across the ground. The years-dead limbs on stumps seemed to inhale and began to extend, twigs becoming thin branches that thickened and turned into limbs as the stumps rose out of the wet muck.

Five inches of water now lapped at the edge of the circle, as if we stood in a glass enclosed cylinder. Aurora lifted her hands and we all followed her lead.

"To the Eastern guardians of the Air,

If you cannot stay, thank you and farewell.

To the Western guardians of the Water,

If you cannot stay, thank you and farewell.

To the Northern guardians of the Earth,

If you cannot stay, thank you and farewell.

To the Southern guardians of the Fire,

If you cannot stay, thank you and farewell.

I bind the Spirit guides of the Paramortal nations to

follow, lead and protect those present in the pursuit and elimination of ones intent on harming River Pomeroy

Blessed Be."

Dylan chimed in, "Blessed Be."

I was too late, so I just stood there waiting to see what came next. Hopefully, we'd get out of this cylinder surrounded by growing waves of water before we drowned.

"You have so little faith, Tempest," said Dylan who kicked the salt line barrier. I gasped expecting the water to pour into our space. I went for River's bottle and the lids, but Aurora beat me to it. She took her time, pulled a leather tote from under the altar and set it on top as Dylan put the candles out and loaded the supplies into his duffle bag.

"Place the amphora, with the lids removed, into the bag and strap it in. Set the rocks around the base and cover it with the cloth inside, then surround it with the High John, Job's Tears and Wolf-bane until you get it to River.

She helped me place the items as she described, then flipped her hand in the air and the straps came alive, tucking themselves into buckles and securing the bag for transport.

I stared, dumbfounded realizing there much I didn't know about Aurora, or Dylan for that matter. And probably a lot more.

She shrugged. "Now, shouldn't we get out of here while we can?"

Andy turned and leaped out into the rising water, high-stepping and splashing as he ran toward the bank. "I need to have a talk with that kid," Dylan muttered. He looked at me and swung his arm out in a courtly gesture. "After you."

"Thanks. I think."

I prepared to make a run for it, but Aurora placed a restraining hand on my arm and said something in a strange language. In a matter of seconds the circle of dry ground under our feet transported us to the bank, but the area between each of us was filling in with the fast rising water.

"Hurry up now or you'll make my spell irrelevant," Aurora admonished.

We each stepped over onto the bank. I looked back. The Big Dead was no more. It was now brimming with lush trees, with water splashing against the bank and the sound of birds arriving to nest in the freshly reborn cypress and oak.

"It's wonderful," I said quietly.

Dylan said, "You can always tell when a spell is done well, the excess pours out into the surrounding environment bringing healing and protection with its overabundance. Good job, A."

"Thank you, Dylan." I could tell when the moonlight shown on Aurora's face that she was pleased with the compliment.

"So, you don't get a chance to do a ceremonial spell often, huh? As far as I could tell, with my limited experience," *duh, none,* "it was a doozie."

"Let's hope it was enough." She looked at Dylan, then me. "I don't get the chance nearly as often as I used to, but I suspect that might be changing. Come along. I still have stock to price, and you promised to help."

Oh, that. Good thing I was off on Saturday. It promised to be a late night.

I looked back at La Grand Morte, which was no longer *morte*. It would have to have a new name. I would have liked to be around the first time someone saw its new abundance.

"I christen you La Belle Copia." *Lovely abundance.* I smiled and followed Aurora.

Chapter 32

"I just heard her w-w-wishing."

TEMPE

I dreamed of a dozen moons racing toward the Earth like asteroids...not enough time, no way to slow them down and my brother suspended in between. I was there, too, trying to use my mediocre wind power to keep them from smashing him. Tossing the sheets aside, I got up and slipped into some kick arounds.

Since I couldn't sleep, I'd do some work on the house until time to go to the school. Freddie had left the yard in a jumble of supplies and trash. I figured the physical activity would help clear my mind, maybe give me some new direction to go in. I organized roofing materials, collected trash, and used a metal detector to run over the area to collect nails and tacks. When I thought of how my roof looked from the air I winced. That was just one more thing River would have to fix...

I stopped in the middle of the yard as helplessness surged through me again. And with that thought came the memory of Jack's strong arms and low soothing voice. In a few hours, I'd see him again without the suspicion that had been present before. I set the trash bag aside. It could wait until Sunday.

THREE COTTON TRAILERS SAT READY FOR THE FINISHING touches to their Mardi Gras decorations, surrounded by a dozen teenagers and a few adults. Boys hammered, girls strung decorations, and a group played pickup games in the parking lot. A few of the girls simply sat on the bleachers, tanning and trying to look *hot*

Andy approached me when I arrived, shaking his arms like a swimmer loosening up for a big race, hopping from one foot to the other. "Miss Tempe, any news about River?"

"Not yet, Andy."

The boy swung away from me, cursing under his breath, his hand gripping the back of his neck. Drugs? Please not.

"Is there a problem?"

"Uh, yes...m-ma'am," he said. "I, uh, d-d-don't know wh-what t' do."

I took his arm and led him over to one of the temporary bleachers. I suspected Andy's problem was a mixture of hormones and his blossoming Djinn nature. River had expressly forbidden Andy to use any of his powers unless he was with him.

"Tell me what's happened." He seemed to have an easier time

talking if I didn't look at him, so I pretended to be checking out the activities around us, and waited.

"W-well Missie, that is, M-midge Gaines goes to my s-sixth period English c-c-lass...and, uh, I heard her mention that she wished Mr. C-crr-enshaw would lose all the tests because she was p-p-pretty sure she was going to get an F. I didn't mean to do it, Miss Tempe, but..."

"What did you do, Andy? Exactly." Wishes were a tricky part of a Djinn's life. I thought again of what Marty had said. '*It's about wishes and power.*'

"Andy—"

"I z-z..zapped the English test—all of th-th..them. Phhht... gone." Then his lips turned up in a mischievous smile. He wasn't sorry; he was just worried about the consequences.

Oh, boy. Wait until River heard about this. Andy would probably be on probation, or lock down, or whatever River did to rebellious Djinn newbies to make them understand their responsibilities. "What I want to know, is how did this girl know about your abilities?"

"She d-doesn't. I just heard her w-w-wishing."

"What do you mean, you heard her wishing?"

"I heard w-what was in her m-mind." This time he did not look at me. Or smile.

"*Zeus' inbred offspring!* Andy..." I lowered my voice. Puberty and genie abilities were a dangerous mix. I remembered, though River had always taken his responsibilities seriously. I said, in as fierce a whisper as I could, "You cannot go around granting wishes willy-nilly, not even when they're spoken, but especially...tell me this was the first time. No, the only time,"

I corrected. I nailed him with a smokin' hot glare, and he yelped. *Don't mess with me kid. I may not be a Djinni but I've got some moves.*

He jerked, eyes wide. He'd heard me. Apparently last night's demonstration of the powerful magic older Paramortals possessed didn't impress him. Or it had, but in the opposite way.

"I'm afraid you're in for some discipline, Andy. For now, I'm warning you. These abilities are not a toy. And there are dire consequences to treating them as such."

Andy ducked his head, and nodded, but I was pretty sure he was already planning on circumventing the rules. He reminded me a bit of Dervil right then, which made me glad he was someone else's responsibility.

I FOUND AURORA AND MONTANA ATTACHING PURPLE AND green crepe paper to the sides of the downtown development float.

Montana looked bored, Aurora aggravated.

"Montana, quit pulling that down and hold it where I told you to." She turned to me. "Good thing you're here. Would you mind..." She caught Montana unawares and tugged the string from her hands.

Relieved, Montana jumped down from the float giving Tempe an eye roll, "Aurora acts like we're in a blue ribbon competition, or decorating for a real New Orleans parade. I'm going to get a Dr. Pepper. You guys want something?" She took our drink orders and escaped to the concession stand.

"I don't know why she came," Aurora said, blowing long strands of silver out of her eyes. "She's worse than those teens sitting on the bleachers, twitchy. She needs to hammer something."

"Well, she's willing at least."

"Oh, Bailey called and said she'd be here, but late. She got lucky—"

"Again," we said in unison.

We worked for a couple hours, managing to put Montana to work banging a hammer, using her warrior goddessness for something practical.

As game time approached the crowd grew. Bailey finally showed, and energized by her recent conquest, showed a fair aptitude for float decorating.

"You're very good at this, Bailey," Aurora said.

"I love doing this kind of stuff. Liam lets me decorate the bar for Christmas and New Years—Oh. My..." Bailey's eyes turned into piercing beams of gold. We all turned to see what had gotten her attention. A bronzed figure in knee length shorts and blue *Destiny's Finest* t-shirt glided across the parking lot toward us.

As if he'd cast a spell on every female in sight, heads turned, and bodies froze as he approached. The air had turned to clear plastic sludge, and the only being able to glide through it was assistant coach, Jack Lang. His stride was all long limbs and easy confident grace.

"Hmmm," breathed Aurora.

"Yeah," said Bailey. "That is one fine human specimen."

"Rock my world." Montana said. "Tempe, ante up or set him free. The adoring are drooling and taking numbers."

The world must have resumed its spinning, but I still found myself unable to add my own thoughts as he stopped directly in front of me. This close I read the fine print on his shirt, *Road to the Finals*

"Ladies." He glanced over at the float and back at me. "The float looks good." I was suddenly conscious of staying up all night, not taking time this morning to dress more fashionably, much less put on makeup.

"Um…" seemed to be my best attempt at conversation.

I was aware only of the heat building between us, a shimmering electric current flooding my blood and fairly lifting me off the ground. Then I felt Aurora's spell spiral around my ankle and tug me back to earth. I stared at her suddenly realizing that my body had involuntarily begun to levitate. In public!

Jack saw my panicked expression and put a hand on my shoulder, "Are you ok—" His eyelids floated down to half-mast.

Oh, yeah.

Aurora's voice cut through my haze. "Sheriff, you came along at just the right time. Montana's not quite tall enough to reach that corner. Would you mind?"

He turned slowly toward Aurora, and she gave me a get your head together look. I tried. Really, I was stirred and shaken to the core, with memories of that last kiss awakening my dormant sexual drive. It was different from what I'd felt for Dylan, deeper and very hard to ignore.

"Hey, Tempe." Jordie's voice sounded above the din of workers. "I can't believe you all came."

She walked over to us, then uncharacteristically she was watching her feet, fiddling with her hair. I hugged her and whispered in her ear, "Just be yourself, honey," and felt her relax.

I released her and asked, "Have you met Aurora?"

Aurora smiled and stepped forward. "I'm so happy to meet you, Jordan. Tempe tells me you're looking for a part time job, and by coincidence I'm looking for a part time employee, preferably a student. Why don't you come by the boutique on Monday after school? That is if you don't have practice."

"Oh, yes, ma'am, I mean, no ma'am, I don't have practice and I—Monday's perfect," the girl enthused. "I'll see you Monday." She jumped up and down and ran off toward the gym, then turned around and ran back to us. "Thanks, again, Ms. Boreal." She raced off through the crowd.

Jack spoke to Aurora, "I appreciate your offer. I'm just not sure she needs to be working."

He looked in the direction his daughter had gone. Then, he looked at me, "But I figure you ladies know something about teenage girls, and I think I'm outnumbered in this department, so I'm going to allow it for now. Until her athletics or her grades suffer."

Leave it to a man to be as concerned about sports as he was grades.

Aurora said, "Jack, I can work around her schedule nicely, and I really could use a hand a few afternoons a week. It'll be good for both of us." She patted his hand, "And for Daddy, too." She resumed her float trimming.

Jack tacked trim to the last corner.

"So, did you need to talk to me?" I asked him.

He looked over his shoulder at me as he tapped the decorations in place. "I have to get over to the team now, but I was wondering if we could meet somewhere later and..." he winked, "compare notes."

Four sets of eyes met mine. Three of them accompanied by nosy smiles. SOAPs never got the concept of minding their own business.

"The kids are going to Breaux's after the game. You could ride with me and we could talk."

"What about Jordie?"

"She's riding with Melissa."

We agreed to meet at his cruiser after the game, and he left for his pre-game meeting. The view as he walked away was pretty nice, too.

Just before the game started, Liam and Kat showed up. Even Bailey's cowboy made an appearance. Apparently Jack's parents had driven down to New Orleans for the weekend. Delighted to have a full family cheering section Jordie waved at us enthusiastically. The game was an exciting matchup with one of the top teams in the state. Jordie scored the most points on either team in the first half. As the other team made a hard defensive push to keep the Destiny Wildcats from scoring, their point guard went down, untouched, grabbing her thigh and writhing in pain.

The crowd surged to their feet in concern for the teenager. Montana jogged down to the court to offer her expertise. Tense moments followed as coaches and players knelt nearby praying for the downed player. While the medics readied her for transport, I looked across the floor and met the guilty eyes of Andy Rush. The little miscreant had transformed someone's wishes into reality. Again.

Chapter 33

"Ride with me," he said, his voice seductive and low.

Tempe

This time I punched in the speed dial of someone I figured Andy wouldn't ignore. While Dylan's phone rang, I kept an eye on the teen as he raced down the bleachers and out the side door of the gym.

"You can run, kid..." Hiding from Dylan wouldn't be easy, though an out of control teenage Djinni could probably come up with some creative evasion tactics. I attempted to follow the boy, but lost sight of him in the crowd of concerned spectators.

"Aren't you supposed to be at a basketball game?" Dylan asked.

"I am and there's something I need you to take care of."

"What?" Now this was the real Dylan, a man of few words.

"It's Andy. He's been reading minds and granting unspoken wishes."

"Where is he?" he growled.

After siccing Dylan on Andy, I went back to the game, which had resumed, but half-heartedly as news reached the gym... the opposing team's star player had broken her leg. Still, after the Wildcats' win, the team and their excited fans planned to celebrate at Breaux's Pizza after the game.

Jack approached as I waited outside. The weather had cleared and we watched teenagers load into vehicles and squeal out of the parking lot. Being teens, they probably thought Coach Lang would give them a pass tonight, but they'd be disappointed if their actions endangered anyone. Then they'd meet Jack "Laser" Lang, hard-nosed commander. I'd have to ask him how he got that call sign. It fit.

I studied him as he walked toward me. He had showered and changed and he towered over me in his jeans, insulated jacket and flannel trooper's hat.

"Ride with me," he said, his voice seductive and low.

"I could follow you, if you'd like." Follow you anywhere...

"No, this will give us a chance to talk."

He was right of course, but the more I thought of being surrounded by his scent, hemmed in with his imposing aura, the more my Tempestaerie protons yipped like happy coyotes, anticipating the rush. Still, I was more nervous than I'd been on any first date. The tension of lawman vs. suspect was gone, but it had been replaced by a thrilling desire, the desire to engulf him with all of my nature. Though I wasn't sure what that meant, I was damn sure it would scare us both.

We were silent for a mile until he slowed the cruiser and pulled over at the park turnaround. A quick flip of his light sent a car full of necking teenagers scurrying for a different location, but not before one of them shouted, "*Allriiight*, go for it, Coach."

He chuckled. "I don't remember ever being that carefree."

"I never was," I admitted, immediately regretting it.

"It seems like I'm always apologizing to you, but I *am* sorry we got off on the wrong foot. I was just doing my job. You have to admit, it looked pretty suspicious. You were at the center of everything; you still are for that matter. But as a victim, not a perpetrator."

"I am not a victim," I declared.

He considered that for a minute. "And you don't like relying on someone else for help."

I didn't reply, but really looked at him; at the almost dimples in his smooth cheeks, his wet bronze hair combed away from his face. My eyes travelled down the strong column of his throat where the ridge below hinted at the well-defined muscles of his chest. The memory of that splendid set of pectorals had the blood rushing in my ears like thunder.

"Ahm," he shifted in his seat and my eyes shot back to his.

He pushed his seat back and stretched his legs as far as the space would allow. Then he spread his jacket across the console. My eyes widened.

"Come 'ere," he said, patting the jacket.

I smiled at him as I unfastened my seat belt and crawled toward him. It felt odd and yet, freeing to act on my feelings for him, spontaneously. He slipped his hands under my arms and lifted me across, surprising me by just snuggling me against him. I rested my hand on his where he stroked my stomach.

"Just relax a sec," he said.

Friday morning Jack had surprised me with his tenderness. Now, wrapped once again in his arms, I felt the tension ease and my muscles relax.

"I wanted to tell you what I've found out so far." He rubbed my back slowly as I stiffened. "It's not bad news, just an update. I got some interesting feedback from a lab tech over in Amity, where I took some fluid and hair samples, and your amphora." I pulled back, scowling up at him.

"Don't look at me like that. It's safe."

"Ah, well it doesn't matter now. Keep it as long as necessary. Wait, what do you mean fluid samples? The body was stolen." Or regenerated. Or evaporated or whatever Nucklavees did when they died, I thought.

"Yes, but I took the backup slides to an associate who called me yesterday with his preliminary report. He found no blood on the vase which means we can confirm it wasn't the weapon, and no fingerprints but yours, so no leads about who took it. He said he's having trouble with the DNA tests."

I'll bet he is. I said, "Isn't that a tad illegal?"

He snorted, "No more than somebody stealing the body. Because I didn't go through channels, that evidence wouldn't be admissible, but I'd take the trade-off if we can find the murderer, *and* your brother."

I snuggled against him, sighing. "You really do believe me."

"I do."

"I hear a *but* at the end of that sentence."

He hugged me tighter. "I just hope you can trust me with those secrets of yours before long."

Yeah, I couldn't wait for that to happen...

"There was something else. The fingerprint slides of the victim were essentially blank, not even a trace of sweat."

He saw my puzzled look.

"The human body produces sweat, which is what makes the print 'stick'. Thorpe said if I indeed collected the victim's prints, somehow, they were not on the slides."

"Really!" Was it guilt making me wonder if he doubted my surprise was genuine? I decided it was. "What do you make of that?"

His face moved away from mine and he stared down at me for a second, eyes narrowed. Satisfied he said, "Well, all I can figure is that somehow the samples got contaminated before or after I got them to him. It wasn't like they were in a perfect environment. But the blood told him one thing. The man was already dying. He said the way the cells were 'breaking down' the body is probably totally decomposed by now; *and* there was a high concentration of iron in his system."

I perked up, knowing what that meant. Whether or not he knew what happened to River, Ray Meeker had had his hands on River's amphora. The ancient Chinese Dingware was painted on the inside with iron infused paint. Iron killed fae, but it didn't affect Djinn, which was why my father had always insisted on that particular glazing for the family digs. It inherently eliminated a lot of threats.

"So you think he stole the amphora, and when he wasn't feeling so hot, hid it in one of the lockers? Why would he even bring it to work with him? And what was he doing there on Monday? Oh—"

"Yes, I think he was meeting the killer, perhaps to sell the amphora, and something went wrong."

"But the alarm was still going when you got there after me, wasn't it?"

His body stiffened slightly against mine. "Very good, for an amateur. I'll have to rethink that angle."

"You said you were going to get a sketch from the guy who saw River..."

"I've arranged for him to meet with the sketch artist in Baton Rouge. I have to wait until he has a day off, though. I also put more men out canvasing the area for leads." He squeezed me and rubbed his cheek against my hair. It was a sweet gesture that made my heart lurch.

"I wanted to tell you earlier, but we had too much company. I used the key you gave me to your mother's house and had it processed for fingerprints and other evidence. I was going to wait until you filled out a report on her, but I get the impression from you that time is of the essence."

I tensed at first, glad that I wasn't facing him when he gave me that bit of news. But I realized he hadn't waited because he knew I wouldn't want the delay to keep us from finding Phoebe and River. "Thank you, Jack." I was curious to know what they'd find in those fingerprints. For all I knew Tempestaeries didn't have sweaty fingerprints either.

"Unfortunately, the place was even cleaner than it looked.

These guys, whoever they are, know what they're doing. It's like some spy operation."

We sat in the dark for several minutes, neither of us speaking in the ensuing silence. Then he brushed my hair from my face, tangling it in his fingers. He shifted me so he could see my face as his warm lips trailed across my cheek, my jaw, while his hand inched up to the buttons of my blouse. Fingers stole into the cup of my bra and across my nipple. I gasped.

He tilted my head so he could kiss the pulse at my throat. "I want you, Tempest Pomeroy. I have since the second I opened my door and found you ogling me so lasciviously."

He tweaked my nipple between his fingers. When all I did was make a begging mewling whimper, he crushed my mouth under his.

Once again I flew...the sensations like a blast from a gale force wind, shattering my carefully built barriers like windows in a New Orleans high rise. One minute I was staring into heated silver eyes, and the next there was black shining water coming at me. I was flying along the surface, like a racer with no finish line in sight. Blue sky whirled above me, then my body was crushed under an unseen ton of weight.

There was the high shrill sound of...of...I can't place the sound. An image rises against the night—a silver dragon, flames spewing from its mouth. The water blows up behind me, blasting out of the depths of midnight.

Like a roller coaster up—up I go spinning toward the deep blue horizon, dropping all at once toward the earth, my stomach lurching, ears popping and I am bound with iron chains, my body smooshed under hundreds of pounds... The weight is lifted and I'm falling...falling...

cheeks press into my teeth making it hard to speak...silver wings flapping! Creating the sound of thunder...

"WHOA," I GASPED. MY EYES FLEW OPEN TO MEET JACK'S. I put my hand to my forehead, "What was that?"

"What was what?" he asked, his eyes sparkling in the moonlight.

I breathed out waiting for my heartbeat to return to normal. "It's weird, sometimes when we touch, there's..." I shifted to look at him. His hand slid out of my blouse, and he frowned. I took his hand and chuckled.

"It's not a bad thing. It's just that I see, like, deep blue water passing me by so fast, and a twirling sky, and I feel like I'm on a roller coaster doing loop-d-loops. It's beautiful and dizzying, and just plain weird."

He grinned. "Do you feel like you're racing through the night sky or see yourself flying inches above the ocean at supersonic speed? Hear a sonic boom?"

My mouth dropped open, and I nodded. "You saw it too?"

"Not exactly." He laughed. "Sounds like you were taking a ride along with me on a night flight. Was it good for you?"

Chapter 34

It looked like a dog and acted like a dog, and possibly even smelled like a dog. *Not.*

TEMPE

I threw my arms around his neck and kissed him. With only a small *oomph,* his hands cupped my butt tugging me closer so that I felt his arousal. When air met my skin, and he cupped my breast again, I froze. *What was I thinking?* That's the problem, I wasn't. It was too soon. I wanted him desperately, and hopefully it would happen, but not yet. Not until he was able to accept the real me, and the real Destiny. "Jack."

He took my moan as assent and latched onto my breast with the hot cavern of his mouth. "Oh, Jack..." My breath hitched as he drew away.

A lock of his hair had fallen over his forehead, his eyes were liquid silver in the moonlight, like some otherworldly creature. I'd torn the button on his shirt, and there was lipstick on his face.

He used his fingers to comb his hair back and smiled. "I didn't mean to attack you—"

"I think it was the other way around." I laid my fingers on his lips, "No regrets. Later, okay?"

"And in a better location," he said, looking around at our cramped position in the cruiser.

"Oh, I don't know. It would have been my first time in a police cruiser," I said.

His brows lifted. "Well, I don't want your first time with me to be in a car." Was he worried that I would hold that against him?

I sobered. "I need to find my family, Jack. I know it seems like I'm all over the place emotionally. I'm not, normally..."

"Sweetheart, I'm not rushing you. Not on purpose anyway. As far as finding River and Phoebe goes, I told you, I'm going to keep the pressure on. This lake really comes together when you need them. I've got volunteers from as far away as Rome and Amity putting out flyers and checking vacant houses.

"Let's head over to Breaux's. I'm hungry." He winked, "But I'll settle for pizza."

My phone vibrated with a text at the same time Jack's rang.

"It's Aurora," I said.

He nodded and put his phone to his ear. "Aurora, Jack. What's up?"

Jack stopped smiling within seconds. He cranked the engine

and spun around in the small gravel turnout, heading back toward town. "I'll be there in a few minutes."

My eyebrows rose when he flipped on the emergency lights. As we passed under the streetlight I saw the worry in his eyes and the hard set of his jaw. "What is it, Jack?"

"Jordie's sick. Aurora took her home. She said her fever is already 103."

By the time we turned onto Crystal Lane, Jack's tension was palpable.

I'd tried to think of something to say to reassure him, but I know how I'd felt when River was sick. Nothing could keep me from worrying. That didn't happen until he was feeling better, and I was certain he was going to live. Death always enters your mind, when they're sick and helpless, especially when you've seen bad things happen; experienced death or loss. You're always afraid it will revisit.

I admitted this to myself, even as I understood Jack's fear. "She's going to be okay, Jack." I said with fervor and prayed it would be true.

He nodded as we drove across the manicured grass and into his driveway. Aurora was waiting on us at the door. "That was quick."

In the hallway he brushed by Aurora, asking, "Is it just fever? Has she thrown up or anything?"

We both tried to keep up with Papa Bear, who was eating up the distance to Jordie's bedroom as if a squad of terrorists were on his six. Aurora said, "Her tummy isn't upset. It seems to be just fever and a rash. Maybe she brushed up against something she's allergic to."

We got to Jordie's bedroom door just in time to see Jack throw his hat on the chair in the corner of the room and kneel by the bed. He bent over Jordie and, kissing her forehead, said, "Baby, Daddy's here."

A little moan came from under the covers about the same time as a low growl from the other side of the bed. Jack looked over his shoulder at us and moved his finger to his lips. As he reached for his gun, Aurora said, "Jack, don't. I thought Jordie might enjoy the comfort of my big Beffie." She called to the animal. "Beffie, up."

A giant gray spotted dog, which looked like a cross between a Great Dane and a Catahoula Cur, rose over the other side of Jordie's bed. His intelligent, soulful eyes looked from Aurora to Jack and me, then back to Jordie. He whined as he nuzzled her through the covers.

Jack looked at the dog and replaced the strap on his gun. "Hey, boy. You been looking after my baby girl?"

He reached out his closed fist, and the dog wagged its tail and licked his skin. "Good boy."

He breathed out and turned to Aurora, removing his coat and tossing it on top of his hat. "She hasn't been sick in years. How high was her temperature last time you took it?" He sat on the side of the bed stroking Jordie's hair, I suspected more out of a need to comfort himself, the need to do something to combat the helplessness.

"It was 103.2 right after I called you. Which has only been ten minutes I think. She said she could take aspirin, so I gave her two."

"It hasn't had time to work then," he murmured. Beffie whined again and looked at Jack. "What's he want?" Jack asked.

"I think he wants to crawl up on the bed with Jordie. She coaxed him up there before but I made him get down."

Jack patted the blanket beside Jordie. "You want to crawl up here, man? Come on then."

The big dog jumped gracefully and landed gently on the bed, stretching out beside Jordie. In her sleep, she poked a slender arm out of the cover and draped it across his back. His head angled up so that he could lick her chin a couple of times, then he breathed out a contented sigh.

"They certainly seem to have bonded quickly. You say this is your dog?" Jack asked watching his daughter and the big dog together.

"Actually, he needs a new home. His old owner moved on and left him here. I've been kind of his caretaker in the meantime."

"Hmm. You mentioned a rash?" Jack asked.

"Yes, on her hip. I decided not to treat it or put lotion on it until later. It may go away on its own."

"Possibly," Jack said. "I'll keep an eye on her tonight and if the fever gets much higher, I'll run her to the emergency room."

"You might give Montana a call if you get worried," I suggested.

"Okay, do I have her number?"

I gave it to him.

"Now that you're here, I'll get going. Call me, though, if I can do anything else." Aurora said.

Jack rose and took her hands in his big ones. "Aurora, thank you." Those three words spoken with so much sincerity made the normally pragmatic Aurora smile warmly.

"I'm glad I was able to help. I'll see you tomorrow morning, Tempe, if you can still help me at the shop."

"Absolutely." I'd do whatever pricing and tagging she needed as long as I could work it around looking for Paige.

I walked Aurora out. On my way back to the bedroom, I took a detour through the dining room to get a chair. I bumped it into the doorframe, and Jack looked up from his post by the bed. "Here, let me get that for you." He got up and swung the chair one-handed into the center of the room across from him where we could both view his teenager.

"Why don't I get us a cup of coffee and make you a sandwich?" I asked.

Jack stared at Jordie. He sighed, "Coffee would be good, but I'm not hungry."

Hmm, that's what a sick child will do for you, I thought. Make you forget you were starving just twenty minutes ago. I went to the kitchen and started rummaging around for filters and figuring out how to use his coffee pot.

I'd recognized the grey spotted dog. Aurora had spoken correctly when she said it needed a new home. The beast wasn't really a dog. Oh, it looked like a dog and acted like a dog, and possibly even smelled like a dog. *Not.* It was in fact a Befanas, a creature be-spelled to protect a certain household. And Aurora had hooked him up with the Langs.

The question was why.

Chapter 35

Her hate nearly pierced the wall of rain I'd constructed.

TEMPE

Jordie's temperature dropped a couple degrees and we moved into the living room where our conversation wouldn't awaken her.

We sat down on the couch and he rubbed the back of my neck absently. "Did you do the decorating?" I asked softly. The autumn tones were warm and made the atmosphere as comfortable as Jack's soft olive overstuffed sectional.

"My mom and dad found the house for us and she furnished it." He rolled his head to the back of the couch. "I know what you're doing."

"Me?" I laughed, "I was—"

"You were distracting me." His eyes had warmed to the color

of moss. Mesmerized, I stared at his lips as they descended toward mine.

He pulled me to him, deliberately giving me time to pull away. His eyes flicked closed and he dragged his bottom lip across mine. He urged my lips open and the kiss became a flurry of passion. I ran my fingers through his hair as his tongue tangled with mine. The man could kiss. My hands explored the strong muscles of his back until a quiet, *"ahem"* interrupted. Jack's hand stalled on my breast, and discreetly eased back to my waist.

He looked over my shoulder at Jordie, who'd just come out of her bedroom. "How are you feeling, sweetheart?" he asked the girl, holding me still. I knew if it hadn't been for a certain *incriminating presence* between us he would have leaped off the couch to check on her.

He didn't seem embarrassed. He didn't jerk away, or stumble over his words. I relaxed against him. The last two weeks had taken a toll on me. Anxiety, revelations, lack of sleep, the job —had all been stressful. I tilted my head back toward Jordie.

"I heard a commotion—" she grinned. My face heated, but I didn't move away. "I'm going back to bed." Before she closed the door she said, "Carry on, father."

Jack laughed long and hard, probably as much from relief as mirth. He let me go and wiped his eyes, he looked at me, "That girl is always surprising me."

His eyes shown with so much love and pride that I gulped, tamping down the anguish I felt at the loss of that relationship between me and my own father. "That *young lady*," I corrected, "is so lucky to have you."

For that, I got a ferocious hug and a kiss that left me wishing I hadn't stopped him earlier.

As I'd told Aurora Sunday morning when we priced gifts and masks and gowns and shoes and an untold mass of other stuff—retail was definitely not my calling—number one on my list was locating River's old college girlfriend.

Paige is a minor, make that negligible Tempestarie, meaning her hair gets frizzy when rain hits the city limits. She works for Aladdin's Rub, a housekeeping service with both commercial and private customers, and at the Red Carpet Inn in Alliance part-time.

I called Aladdin's Rub first. Her boss said she'd be returning around two. I looked at my watch. Thirty minutes. I might as well get something to eat while I waited. I dug a pack of stale peanut butter crackers and a too-ripe banana out of my lunchbox from Thursday and parked behind a big live oak at the edge of the lot. I didn't want to miss Paige, or give her boss a chance to warn her.

Twenty minutes later she drove into the parking lot in one of those square shaped cars. Ugly but extremely practical I guessed for carrying mops, rugs, vacuum cleaners and whatever other cleaning supplies she needed.

She was bending over the back seat when I approached. "Paige?"

She whirled around, a startled look on her face. "Sheeit, Tempe, you scared me to death. What do you mean sneaking up on a person like that?"

I hadn't been sneaking. "Sorry, Paige, I just wanted to talk to you for a minute."

She smoothed her hair back with nervous energy. "Oh? About what?"

She seemed a little wary of me. We hadn't really gotten along when she was dating River in college, but River had never said why he broke it off with her.

"About my brother," I said, monitoring her reaction.

"River? What about him?"

Was it my imagination, or did she stiffen at the mention of his name? "Have you seen him lately?" Damn, I'd meant to ask that a different way so I could judge whether she was lying or not.

"No, why?" *Zeus' primed fist!* It was like pulling teeth getting answers from her. Was this why River broke up with her? Was she the jealous type, or just suspicious by nature?

"I haven't heard from him since Sunday—"

She snorted and shook her head. "Tempe, River's a big ole boy, and you are not his mother. That's part of the reason we broke up."

Really.

"I got tired of being constantly compared to you."

I was the one startled now. Both by the venom in her comment, and that she was jealous of me. Granted, I was more of a motherly sister—I'd had to be, but I'd never tried to tell River what to do in his relationships.

"Gee, Paige, why don't you tell me what you really think of

me? Better yet, just answer the question, and I'll leave. When was the last time you saw River?"

She glared at me, arms crossed, foot tapping. "I haven't seen him since we broke up two years ago." Then she tempered her response, almost as an after thought, "I hope you find him, but stay away from my jobs." She slammed the back door and grabbed her purse.

"Right. And Paige?" As she turned toward me, I said, "They give anger management classes at the outpatient clinic."

The gesture she made was not one of agreement.

The gesture I made created a perfectly square thundershower directly over her head, complete with thunder. As rain saturated her hair and clothes, she just stood there glaring at me. Her hate nearly pierced the wall of rain I'd constructed.

"Just sayin..." I closed my hand leaving her once again standing in sunshine. The training thing was working. I fist pumped, *Yes*.

I turned and squeaked to a stop when Jack stepped out of his cruiser and strode over to me.

TEMPE

"Did you see that?" Jack asked as Paige pulled a jacket from the car, and scurried off toward the building.

"What? So you had the same idea." While he scratched his head and tried to make sense of what he'd seen, I created a distraction. "She says she hasn't seen River in two years."

"You don't believe her."

"I'm not sure if it's because I dislike her so much or what, but no, I don't."

"She's not blonde..." Jack reminded me.

"And we both know how easily that's remedied."

"True."

"How's Jordie?" I asked. Jack looked tired, as if he'd slept little in addition to the stress of the murder investigation.

"She's better, except she's got this strange rash on her back and thighs. Her fever is going down, and hopefully she'll be ready to go back to school by morning."

"I'm so glad." My hand went for his forearm and I felt the steady thrum of energy beneath my hand.

"The funny thing is that big dog Aurora brought has slept right next to her all night, and though he hasn't threatened any of us, I get the feeling he'd be a forbidding protective presence. I felt better having him in the house."

I'd asked Aurora about Beffie. Somehow she'd managed to change the subject. She knew that I knew Beffie was no ordinary dog, and there was a reason she'd placed it in Jack's home. Obviously, she wasn't ready to explain, and when Aurora slammed the lid down on a subject, it was both a mark of how important it was and how strong an immovable object she could be.

JACK

It must have been the mention of the vision Tempe had when I kissed her that made me run back over some of the things that had happened since the day I met her; the weirdness surrounding the scene at the clubhouse. Her actions, which had made her seem guilty; the half truths, omissions, absurd explanations and the outright lies she'd told me.

And still here I was, on her side, believing her, practically attaching myself to her like a lapdog. I didn't like the image, but ever since that dog had crawled up onto the bed and curled up next to Jordie, I couldn't get the thought out of my mind that I needed to stick close to Tempe. That something was going to bust loose, and I was not going to be the same.

Personally? Professionally? I didn't know, but I didn't seem to have any choice in the matter. *That's not true.* We always have choices. So...mine was to watch Tempe's six.

She was impulsive, loyal, hotheaded, and fierce. There was no telling what might happen when we found River. I'd been reluctant to be completely honest with her, like I usually am in similar situations because...

Damn. I scrubbed my face, trying to wipe away the fatigue and worry. On the heels of the nerve-wracking fear of losing Jordie last night, now I was experiencing a more insistent kind of worry for Tempe. About how she would cope if we didn't succeed in finding River alive. How it would affect our relationship.

And there it was again. I wanted a relationship with Tempest Pomeroy. I cared about her, even with all the craziness, her little "talents", and the outrageous fib she told about being able to smell River's bottle in another room when the overwhelming stink of the body made that impossible.

I remembered her devastation when I'd found her at Phoebe's, felt the ache right now when I remembered her breaking down in my arms. Last week when I'd first met her, I'd thought she was a nut case; and now, when I knew her, and still wasn't convinced she wasn't at least a little crazy, I could no longer walk away.

"I'm screwed."

My phone vibrated, and I saw Jordie's name on the screen. "Hey, sweetie. How are you feeling?"

"I'm okay. Just wanted to remind you to stop for some dog food for Beffie." She sounded tired, but much improved. The dog hadn't left her side, and he never seemed to drink or eat. Jordie was certainly enamored with him. Whatever helped her feel better was okay by me.

"He seems like a well trained dog. I wonder why his owner didn't want him."

"He says it's because he's here to take care of us," Jordie said.

I laughed, "He told you that did he?"

She paused. "I guess I dreamed it. But he seems like he's been with us forever doesn't he?"

"If you say so, sweetheart. I'll run by Dollar Town and be home as soon as I put out more flyers."

TEMPE

Jack called Monday to tell me that several members of the civilian watch volunteered to take some flyers over to Hugo and Amity.

"You think he could be in Hugo?" I asked. Hugo was on the northern side of Storm Lake, about sixteen miles from Destiny, and on the other side of Alliance where Phoebe lived.

"We don't know where he is, Tempe. What if he hit his head and has amnesia and wound up somewhere where no one knows him? Or, he might have been kidnapped and no longer in Destiny. We're covering all the bases. We already put the report on NCIC."

"Wow, when you get on board, you go all out."

He breathed heavily into the phone, I thought a sound of frustration. "I didn't mean that the way it sounded, Jack. Do I wish you'd believed me that first day in the clubhouse? Absolutely, but to be honest, you about had me convinced I was guilty. I don't know how I could have expected you to see what was going on when I didn't know myself."

I'm still not sure, *and* I'm still holding back. And how is he going to react when he finds out we're rescuing a genie? Or that the dead victim, wasn't a victim, wasn't dead, and most all, wasn't human? Whew! I didn't want to think about it, because the truth about my family and Destiny's other world was not going to register in the safe zone on Jack's "normal" meter.

"Look—shoulda, woulda, and coulda won't do any good at this point. Let's deal with what is and find River," he said.

He was right about looking back... what if I'd called River's cell phone as soon as I'd noticed his amphora missing? Should I have risked getting in trouble at work and gone looking for him? Absolutely. Would it have made a difference? I didn't know.

"I think most of this had played out by the time you got to work Monday morning," Jack said as if reading my mind.

"I know. I just—" wish, I'd started to say. Wishes is what usually brought the Djinn in my family trouble.

"How's Jordie today?" I asked as I drove out of the mail center parking lot.

"Except for the fact that she wanted to stay home with her new pal... perfect. Like she was never sick. I just dropped her off at work." There was silence on the other end for a moment. Before it could get more awkward, I said, "Okay, well—"

"Wait. I'm about to take a coffee break. Can I buy you one?"

It sounded like he had more on his mind than just coffee.

"The UPak-It, in ten," he said. "Gotta catch this, see you there."

I hadn't heard any beeps or radio calls on his end, but decided I'd meet him anyway. I was as curious as a cat with five new mouse toys.

Chapter 36

The man was a rock. Nothing rattled him. Still, he was a human *rock.*

TEMPE

TEMPE

Jack handed me the cup of black coffee I'd requested. He'd parked on the side of the building, and it seemed I was the only one brave enough to park next to a cop car. We leaned against the truck. "God, I love this coffee," he said. "The UPak-It does it just like we made it in service. You'd leave the ops room at 4 a.m., fly out on a sortie, and when you got back that afternoon, it would be just right."

Jack's coffee smelled like rotted sewage and looked like drilling mud. I made a face, "I prefer it dark, but not aged like the swill you're drinking."

I sipped mine while he stood against the car, tapping the roof with his finger. I figured eventually he'd get around to the

267

reason we were standing outside the convenience store, the objects of quite a few curious glances.

"I, uh...wanted to ask you something." In the brief time I'd known Jack Lang, I'd never seen him nervous.

"Sure."

"I'm not good at this. It's actually a first for me."

"You've got my curiosity peaked."

He spoke in a rush. "Would you like to go to the Grand Ball with me next Saturday? It's not normally my thing, but I was thinking..." his voice trailed off.

"Yes?" I stalled, dragging it out because I couldn't believe what I'd just heard. It was like being asked to the prom. Which had never happened to me, or a dance, or a party. I'd better stop thinking about it, or I'd wonder why he was asking me... me, Tempe, to the Grand Ball!

"I'd really like to see you all dressed up." That surprised me. He placed his hands on my shoulders, "And then I'd like to peel your clothes off one layer at a time." That didn't. My blood heated and my breath hitched on the next intake.

"Um, Houston, we have a problem." I looked down, waving my arms. "This is as close to dressy as I have in my closet."

His chin lifted and he looked away, "I, uh, took care of that. I hope you're not offended. You can still say no, but I was hoping you'd agree. When I was in Aurora's back room, I saw a dress, and when I thought about you in it..." he saw my expression change... "No, wait."

I really wasn't okay just the way I was. He had to dress me up to make me look better.

"That's not what I meant, Sweetheart. As awesome as you are in shorts and ankle work boots and no makeup, I can only imagine you'd be the most beautiful woman at that ball all decked out."

My jaw dropped. "Wow, you're good. Does that silver tongue get twisted up very often?"

He looked serious and...hurt. "You should know me well enough to know when I'm serious, even if expressing it is new to me. Having a semi-normal person to care about in my life..."

"Huh, you'd better shut up while you're ahead." I put my arms around his neck and smiled up at him. "When you can't say what you mean, or you think you've screwed up, just kiss me. You do that really well."

His mouth covered mine softly, thoughtfully, at first, and then he proved he was an expert at expressing himself with a kiss. His tongue swept into my mouth, dueling with mine, and I lost all track of where we were until a truck coasted by and some teenagers whooped.

"Hey, isn't that the girl's basketball coach?" and someone whistled and yelled, "Way to go, Sheriff."

He placed his chin against my forehead. I could feel the thrum of his heart beating in unison with mine.

"So, about Saturday." I said. "I've got this thing."

He leaned back looking down at me, the warmth in his eyes dimming. "Look—"

"It's got to do with River."

I couldn't say, *I have it on good authority that there will be a Para-*

moon this weekend. I know you never heard of it, but that's because you've never heard of Paramortals, and I can't tell you because you not only wouldn't want to take Cinderella to the ball, but you'd probably run freaking screaming if you even got a glimpse of me in Tempestaerie mode.

I settled for, "I have a feeling if we don't find my brother by next weekend, it'll be too late."

His gaze softened once again, and he took my hand. "And I have one—call it a policeman's instinct—that says we're going to find him by then." He wrapped his arms around me, and I snuggled into his warm strength. The man was a rock. Nothing rattled him.

Still, he was a human rock.

"I've never been asked to a dance before," I said. I desperately wanted to go.

He must have seen the longing on my face because he said, "I won't go without you. The Mardi Gras ball is just an excuse to see you in that dress. If things don't work out for us Saturday —we'll make it another time, soon."

He walked me to my truck. He leaned toward me, and my eyes drifted shut, expecting another of those mind-numbing kisses but he tilted his head, looking off. "What's that noise?"

I didn't hear anything.

"Is your truck running?" he asked, releasing me and walking to the back of my truck.

"No," I said, curious. And then I heard it. "Er, Jack, it's nothing—" I flushed.

"Well, it's something. Sounds like it's coming from inside your trash bag."

"Uh, yeah, it is." My face colored. "Just some... things I bagged up the other night when I was house-cleaning." And frustrated, I thought. I crossed my fingers that he would let it go.

He didn't. He grinned at me, lifting the bag to his ear, pretending to try to deduce the evidence. Then his eyes glinted, holding a burning promise. "You might want to save those batteries. Toss everything else." He set the bag down next to us in the pickup bed, still vibrating.

"You won't be needing it."

TEMPE

Still giddy from Jack's invitation, I had to share it with somebody, so I called Montana. I kept my eyes on the wet road as I waited for her to answer. Clouds had rolled in and the highway was dark with only a single headlight in my rear view mirror. The driver probably wouldn't try to pass with the intermittent rain making the road slick.

"Tempe, what are you doing?" came Montana's voice.

"Guess what?" I teased.

"I don't know, but from the sound of your voice, it was un... expected," she said. Then it dawned on me.

"You knew. That Jack asked me to the ball this weekend." I said. "Who else knows?"

She chuckled. "Just me. And Aurora, of course. And maybe Katerina, and Shannon."

"Everybody?" I asked experiencing a bit of a letdown that I couldn't share my excitement.

"Not Bailey. We were afraid she'd mess up and you'd find out before Jack could surprise you. You were surprised and pleased, I hope. And you're going?"

"Yes, yes, and...I'm not sure."

"Tempe," Montana groaned. "You're hopeless."

"I want to go. Really. Montana, I've never been asked to a dance or ball. This is a first. Of course I want to go, especially..." *Just come out and say it.* "Especially with Jack."

"Then what's the frickin' problem?"

"The ball is Saturday. Aurora said our best chance to connect with River is going to be during the full moon which begins next Thursday night."

"I see. So how did that go over with the good sheriff?" Montana asked.

I smiled thinking of our conversation. "He understood. He —" it looked like the vehicle behind me was finally going to pass as I slowed at the turnoff to Harmony. I kept my eyes averted slightly so his headlight didn't blind me.

"Tempe?"

The motorcycle roared past as I turned. "I'm here. Guess I was holding up traffic. Let's just say Jack isn't taking no for an answer."

"Good." There was a pause on the line and then Montana said, "Tempe, we'll find River. Have you thought about how you're going to balance the pretend life that Jack sees, with your burgeoning new life?"

"It's all I've thought about most of my life, Montana. If Jack finds out and leaves me, it's no more than I've expected all along. I don't have a choice though, do I?"

We both knew it was the truth.

Chapter 37

Over the centuries I'd learned to ignore the pain.

Dylan

It had been a week, and Lang wasn't getting anywhere solving the murder or finding River. As a law officer myself, I was sure he was frustrated, but he didn't realize that many of the clues he was aware of were misleading because of what he didn't know. I called Tempe Tuesday as she was leaving UMC and told her to meet me at the clubhouse at dark.

Ever since our moment at the bar, I'd been nagged by guilt. I had my reasons for the things I'd done—good reasons— reasons I couldn't share with anyone. But rationalizing or explaining didn't keep me from feeling lower than a sewer rat when she looked at me with her big stormy eyes. It was like a kick to the gut to realize it hadn't been false, that I'd come to really care about her. And now Lang was in the picture. I wasn't entirely sure I liked him.

There was truth in what I'd told Lang though. I am a true friend of the family and whatever I could do to help Tempe find River, I would do. I figured I was much better equipped to track the minutia of creature evidence left behind at the clubhouse. I should have thought about it before the scrubbing the manager had ordered despite Lang's orders, but it wouldn't keep me from finding what I needed.

Before she arrived I used the time to sniff around the grounds of the clubhouse. Because of my nature, even after the recent precipitation, I was able to pick up more trace evidence than the sheriff could have.

I wondered if he'd seen the length of flattened grass and the deep nonhuman footprints just the other side of the starting tees. And I was sure he would have been unable to catch the scent of the variant who'd dropped his guard momentarily on the sidewalk near the locker room exit.

I used the alarm code I'd gotten from the club manager, who had not been too happy at yet another violation of his facility. That man threw out a lot of empty threats and strutted around like a banty rooster. He couldn't be good for business.

The change isn't something I go through if there's any possibility of exposure to humans, so I threw out a web of invisibility which shimmered like haunted house mirrors, creating a camouflage affect, much like that of a stealth bomber. Then, I became Finrir. It happened in the blink of an eye but it didn't feel like it. Time always seemed to drag in those milliseconds my bones and organs were shifting, breaking and reforming. Over the centuries I'd learned to ignore the pain.

On all fours, I licked the surface of the floor, tasting the foul bleach and industrial cleaner. The sheriff was good at his job but he didn't have the advantages of olfactory perfection, senses so acute they were, well, inhuman. I mentally catalogued the traces of the non-human DNA—two variants, including the victim. Not enough evidence to identify the variant's nature. My guess would be something incorporeal, a possession of some kind.

Nucklavee did fit that scenario. They were very rare. And if he'd been involved with Phoebe, it wasn't for romance. Their motives were totally self-serving. I was surprised, though. Ray, Sam and Nigel had been checked out and given the highest recommendation. So most likely, Ray the victim, wasn't the real Ray Meeker, Phoebe's guardian companion.

I stood up, but couldn't straighten. The room's seven-foot doorways were not tall enough for me to walk through. So I ducked through the door leading to the locker room, stopping just inside to allow my superior senses to sift through the cleaning chemicals to the minute traces left behind by the killer.

I opened my mouth to collect dormant or leftover particles from the air in the room, my tongue sifting and sorting them like a living centrifuge. I allowed those senses to lead me around the room, by the bar, the exit door, the entertainment center and finally in front of the locker where the strongest spores remained...

"Dylan! What are you doing?"

I dropped the invisibility cloak, since it didn't do any good with Tempe anyway, and changed back to human form.

"Checking to see if there was any trace evidence left after the cleaning."

"Did you discover anything?"

"I believe the victim was a Nucklavee, but I don't think he was really Ray Meeker."

I heard a vehicle pull up outside and within seconds, the sheriff entered through the doorway. He looked at me over Tempe's shoulder. How much had he heard?

"After you two explain what you're doing here, you can tell me what a nuckle v is, and what you meant by that comment."

She jumped nervously, maybe guiltily, as Lang transferred his gaze to her. I felt a stab of jealousy when I saw the flash of heat coming from him and the flush that rose on Tempe's face. The nerves along my back bristled. I fought for control over my Finrir who wanted to tear Jack Lang to pieces.

TEMPE

Jack looked mad, but I couldn't tell if he was mad because he thought we'd once again trespassed on his crime scene and were "sniffing" around—if he only knew—or because he walked in on Dylan and me alone...again... especially after last night.

Zeus' stars! A thought struck me out of the blue. What if he started thinking the reason I didn't want to go to the ball was because I had lingering feelings for Dylan. Misunderstandings and assumptions have a way of putting relationships in Splitsville.

"Jack, you startled me." I wanted to turn him away from any of those ideas.

"Tempe had nothing to do with this, Lang. I got the key from the manager. Looks like he ignored your orders not to have the place cleaned. I asked her to meet me here. I'm looking into a related UMC incident, which was in progress before this happened. If you like, I can fill out an official request but usually, the inspectors work closely with local law enforcement."

Jack had a first class bullshit meter and paid no attention whatsoever to Dylan's words, except where his laser focus had remained since he entered. "What's a nuck..nukl—" he scratched his head trying to remember what he'd heard.

"Nucklavee," Dylan said glancing at me with a let-me-handle-this look. "A Nucklavee is a small group—" *Well, yeah, as in rare faerie,* I thought. "—of professional thieves and con-artists. If this man has been involved with Tempe's mother then he's up to no good." I stared at Dylan, wondering at his ability to create alternate truths on the fly.

Jack's expression didn't change a wit. It was as if he'd made up his mind when he saw us not to believe anything we said. He studied both of us in that still, predatory way he had. I was getting a bad feeling. He had something on his mind.

"Dylan is just trying to help us connect the dots," I said.

His sardonic smile should have been a warning, but I still wasn't prepared. "Oh, right." Jack said, looking straight at Dylan. "And is your dead father on one of those dots?"

Dylan's hand tightened on my shoulder. I frowned, put off by Jack's insensitive words. "What about him? What has my father's death got to do with this?"

I was sick of him giving, then withdrawing support, blind-siding me just when I thought I could trust him. Was it some kind of interrogation tactic used by law enforcement to trick the truth out of suspects? Dylan shifted uncomfortably. At the time, I mistook it for worry on my behalf.

Those piercing silver eyes turned toward me. "His death has nothing to do with this."

I grabbed my hair and growled in frustration. "Then—"

His narrowed eyes met mine. "Because he's not dead."

Chapter 38

When I finally grasped the truth, I felt the rip in my soul.

JACK

When Peggy had given me the news that Dutch Pomeroy was alive, I'd been surprised, and a million questions had bombarded me; but Tempe looked like she'd been hit by a lightning strike out of the clear blue sky. More interesting even to me was what Peggy had relayed after that. "I forget that you weren't here then, Jack. Everyone around here knows that Tempe woke up the day after she found out her father was dead to those bright streaks in her hair." I ached for her, as I imagined what it would have been like for Jordie to hear her daddy wasn't coming home, ever again.

Tempe's skin was translucent; she swayed like a fragile willow on the verge of collapse and reached for the counter, something solid to hang on to. This woman always rolled with the punches, and there had been a lot of them. I hoped this one didn't send her over the edge.

McGuinness on the other hand was grinding his teeth and sending me laser missiles from eyes suddenly black and deadly. What? I was just the messenger. Oh, yeah, he had his own secrets.

Finally a whisper of a question escaped her, "What do you mean he's not dead?"

She glanced at the inspector who didn't return her look, then back at me. She was slowly coming to her senses, like a fighter from a knockout punch. A tear escaped from her flooded eyes and spilled down her devastated features. I could only imagine what she was feeling, having built her life around the belief that the father Peggy said she'd been rarely seen without was dead, and now to find out *that* was a lie.

I hadn't wanted to believe Tempe knew about her father, and was a good enough liar to keep it from me. But that would have been better than the anguish and hurt she was experiencing now, and the betrayal that would be exposed in the minutes to come. *Don't shoot the messenger, Sweetheart.*

I was still getting the scary looks from Dylan, but now they were mixed with what looked like concern—for Tempe? Or the relationship he hoped to resume? She might have thought it was over between them, but I got the sense that McGuinness was still interested.

I cleared my throat and slapped my hat against my leg. This whole investigation had been like a cancer with feelers going out from the tumor at the center. The problem was I had been missing important information.

Thinking all along that Tempe had been at the center, when all the while we'd each been tending to our respective responsibilities—me, to the investigation of the murder—and Tempe in her worry over her brother.

At each stage of the investigation, I'd learned more about Tempe, about what she'd been through to keep her brother with her, about her loyalty to her friends, the strained relationship with her mother. I'd seen the longing in her eyes when she talked about her father's "death". Her vibrant hair was proof of the shock she'd received and what it meant to her.

Now I wondered if everything didn't boil down to *why* her father had faked his demise. And if she hadn't known about her father, then there was something else she was hiding. What was it?

I felt a wave of rage wash through me as I thought about what her parents had put her through. I hated that I was about to add to that pain. Our budding relationship was liable to hit the skids once I explained, but I owed it to her. "The other day, I gave Peggy instructions to dig into your family background."

She tilted her head and burned me with a glare. "That was—"

"Before I knew your brother had gone missing."

Her shoulders relaxed a bit and she nodded, waiting for the rest.

"If it hadn't been for a security leak a few days ago we might never have known. This morning Peggy got a wire from an official at a high-max prison where your father has spent the last nineteen years."

Tempe swayed again and I grabbed a chair from the dining room. She waved me away, "Go on." She rubbed her temples as if the words weren't making sense. Dylan put a hand on her shoulder.

I grit my teeth and continued, "Apparently, when he was working in the Mideast, he ran high stakes cons from Dubai to Kiev and stole from some powerful people, until it came crashing down. He pled guilty, but the authorities said unless he turned over the numbers for the offshore accounts, he'd rot behind bars."

She exhaled the breath she'd been holding while I related the details. "Where is he now?"

"Well, that's kind of interesting. He was released the day after your brother was there. Sunday—which was just prior to the murder of your mother's alleged lover, her disappearance, and that of your brother."

"What—" she turned a bright shade of pink. "What are you saying? That he had something to do with the murder? With my brother's disappearance?"

I scratched my head, trying to ignore what I saw in her eyes. I softened my words, "I don't know, Tempe. The timing is just so damning." And what kind of scum keeps his family in the dark, letting them think he's dead, hmm? "It makes sense," *in a sick kind of way*.

"About as much sense as me being a murderer, Jack," she said, hands on her hips and color blooming in her cheeks.

I winced. As gently as I could, I asked, "Did you miss the part about your brother visiting him last Sunday?"

She turned away, her head shaking furiously. Then her shoulders went stiff and she spun around transferring her glare to McGuinness. She'd figured it out. A tiny sliver of satisfaction poked me in the heart, but found itself lodged next to the resident empathy as she made one step toward Dylan and swung her knee up, nailing him in the groin, before either of us could react.

Not that I would have stopped her.

He went to his knees, the groan that escaped making me sympathize, but not much. "Tempe, let me—"

"You!" She grabbed the bright strands of her hair, twisting it with her fingers. "I can't believe it. What was your game in all this?" She paced back and forth.

I just stood by like a spectator and waited to see what secrets would be unveiled. Maybe now she'd confide in me.

TEMPE

I couldn't believe Dylan could do this to me...to my family. We'd been lovers, friends—at least I'd thought so. It made me sick that I'd fallen for that false sincerity, and thinking of his apology and that kiss... *Arrgh*. I turned back toward him. My vision blurred for a minute. What was the likelihood that River and Dylan were the only ones who had known about Dutch? Did Aurora know?

Something didn't ring true. Dutch gambling? It wasn't that he couldn't have done what Jack said. But *why*? He was an old, powerful Djinni. He had merely to wish a billion dollars into an offshore account, or into Jack's trunk for that matter, and it was *there*, no-no or not. Could it have been boredom? Did he need some kind of diversion because my mother was such a flake?

I felt the stir of electrical forces race to my nerve endings.

Dylan straightened, his expression closed off, while I came to the most shocking conclusion of all. Suddenly, his dark eyes held compassion and understanding.

"She knew." When I finally grasped the truth, I felt the rip in my soul. A choked sob was torn from my chest. "Phoebe knew." I turned away from them, my heart sinking into a deep valley of confusion.

Dylan made no attempt to affirm or deny my conclusion. I paced again, trying to make sense of my life, the people I loved—the order of things tumbling around me. Everything I thought I knew for sure had been upended and stomped into the Louisiana gumbo.

Menori responded to my distress, revving my molecular engine, stirring the elements to a dangerous tipping point. I heard my own heartbeat race, thumping in my ears, drowning out the sounds around me. I panted as if I'd just completed a sprint, then it simply... stopped, like a pot of boiling water removed from the heat. I made my way to the chair and sank down on rubbery knees. My head dropped into my palms.

I seemed to be the only one who'd been left out of the loop. Why? How long had this been going on? When did River find out? What did all of this have to do with his disappearance? Now what?

I sighed and lifted my head to look at Dylan. I felt Jack on the periphery but all my concentration was on this new knowledge. I asked the question, "What now?"

"Now it begins, Tempest."

Finally, my name.

What I saw in his eyes was disconcerting... kindness,

triumph, relief? How long had it been since I'd heard my *real* name come across his lips, *before* that night at BBs. "You didn't use one of those ridiculous 'P' names..." I half muttered.

"There's no longer any need," he said cryptically.

Chapter 39

※☜☞※

Offspring. That was an archaic way to put it.

JACK

I threw up my hand. "Wait, wait!" There was a whole level of communication going on between Dylan and Tempe I wasn't privy to. They didn't even act like I was there. *That* was about to end.

Okay, so my theory about Tempe's father being responsible for the murder, or being connected to Phoebe and River Pomeroy's abrupt vacations didn't seem to work for them, but why couldn't they see the connection?

"What am I missing?" Both of them turned to me, surprised. "Yeah, still here."

I addressed Tempe first, "I get the feeling that you don't see your father for the scumbag he was. All of the problems you and your mother and brother had, the financial hardships, the discord, were caused by your father running off, faking his death and ending up in prison, unable and unwilling to be a part of the family, or support it. He sounds like a pretty self-centered bastard at the very least and a criminal to boot."

She just stood there with her hand on her hip like I was more irritating than her *friend*, McGuinness. I turned to him.

"Why are you aiding and abetting Dutch Pomeroy, keeping Tempe in the dark, and pretending not to know what's going on? If Dutch's location hadn't been leaked, I might never have found out. I could bring you up on obstruction charges you know."

Dylan cursed. "You sound like one of Tempe's supervisors, Lang, 'All I know is what I read in the *Destiny Tribune*'. It's time you tried to think outside your comfort zone. If you were the cop I pegged you for, you'd pay attention to your instincts, think beyond what you 'see' with your eyes. Why do you think Dutch's location got leaked now? Because you had Peggy search?"

He rolled his eyes and snorted derisively. "Right. Like that hasn't been done a hundred times since his apparent 'death'. The same goes for the report you got on the gambling problem. Why didn't that show up on some interagency report before now? Shouldn't there have been some activity in oh, say, the last nineteen years? You really think you're that talented?"

He pointed to his own head. "Think, man."

THE POINTS HE RAISED CAUGHT ME OFF GUARD. I PRIDED myself on having an open mind, but it had been difficult in this town, ever since... well, ever since I'd met Tempest Pomeroy. Had my attraction to her skewed my instincts somehow? Something had bothered me about the reason Dutch went to the prison. "Why were you involved?"

The PI breathed in a harsh sigh and glanced cautiously at Tempe. "I was chosen as kind of a godfather and mentor for River and Te—and Aurora, for Tempe."

Tempe's head swiveled quickly toward him. Her narrowed eyes hid a wealth of emotion. She seemed about to blow.

Dylan? A mentor? I'd have to ask him about how that worked. The creep. Was he supposed to be mentoring her when he was sleeping with her?

"Dutch and Phoebe have... enemies," he said. "He went underground, so to speak, 'off the grid' to protect his offspring and Phoebe."

Offspring. That was an archaic way to put it. "I don't understand. What kind of enemies? Gambling associates?"

"Gambling is a human failing. That was not an issue for Dutch. It was all a cover."

A *human failing*, he'd said. I thought I was a pretty sharp detective, but I couldn't figure out where he was going with these odd phrases.

Tempe faced Dylan, "Aurora knew all of this?"

Dylan had the decency to at least look contrite. "I'm sorry, Tempe. It was all for your protection and River's."

I butted in, "What about the relationship you had with Tempe a couple years ago?"

Tempe's eyes focused hard on Dylan. "Yeah, what about that?"

"It's not that I didn't care, Tempe. I did."

"It was all a lie."

Tempe's voice was small, but I wouldn't have made the mistake of calling it weak. It felt like the air leaving the atmosphere before a hurricane. "The truth—now, Dylan." Her voice vibrated with fury.

McGuinness held up a hand. "My breaking up with you, making it look like I was involved, it was cruel, but nothing else was working—"

Was this guy callous or what? I'd met men like him. He'd cheated and let her catch him because she wouldn't leave their relationship? Tempe's words about trust came home to me; plenty of her closest family and friends had lied, or at least kept the truth from her. They'd controlled and influenced the last nineteen years of her life. I had to give her credit. I'd be venting my rage on the closest target.

"—I did it to try to force you into your... maturity," this with a glance at *me*.

What? He was expecting support from me? I almost laughed in his face, but just shook my head. He was too much. A liar, manipulator, and then to throw more excuses at her... I had to hear his answer if only for the entertainment.

"What the hell did that mean, you ass? Her maturity?"

They both turned toward me. Dylan said, "Her *Vyal K'allanti*, the quickening."

Huh?

JACK

"Huh?" My gray matter had turned to cotton, and I had a sudden premonition that I should stop him from speaking, that there was more I wasn't ready for, but apparently it didn't matter.

"All of this because I wouldn't accept my gift?" Tempe asked him.

"What gift?" I asked, again feeling extraneous.

Dylan's black brow arched. "Are you sure you want to know?"

Why the hell not? "Go ahead, hit me."

Here comes the secret, I thought, just as I was slammed back against the wall by a sudden icy wind, and had to spread my legs to stay upright. I looked toward the front door, or tried to. The force of the wind kept me pressed against the rack of clubs and shirts, the shelves digging into my back. Tempe's hair was whipping around her head like debris in a vortex.

Frozen in place, I watched as she raised her fist and brought it down, as if backhanding some invisible surface. Thunder shook the foundation, and clubs fell narrowly missing my head. *Thunder? Nah.*

Her eyes flared when they met mine. There, I saw not only her anger and frustration, but an explosion of light particles like a meteor shower moving from her pupils to the edges of her irises. She extended her fist; uncurled her fingers. Brilliant white fire sizzled there, snapping and hissing, reflecting in those otherworldly eyes.

"What the—"

She flipped her palm over and aimed a wood scorching white-hot blade in my direction. The trail of charred hardwood halted between my trembling legs. But she wasn't done. Eyes transfixed on mine, she raised her arm toward the ceiling.

I'm not that slow. I ducked, but it wasn't a fire bolt this time. Fat droplets of water fell around me like the early seconds of a hard thundershower, then came a deluge. My first thought was the sprinkler system, but that didn't explain the *thunderclouds* floating just below the ceiling or the *hailstones* bouncing off the floor.

Indoors. It was hailing...*indoors*.

Visible beyond the French doors, through the water pouring off the brim of my hat, were the sun-baked greens at the back of the clubhouse.

Tempe and Dylan stood beyond, untouched by the stormy weather in the room. Was I imagining this or was this her gift —that she was able to make me *think* I was in the middle of a thunderstorm?

The force pressing me against the wall eased. I looked down at the uniform clinging to my body, my pants and shoes. They were soaked through. "Tempe..." I started forward as soon as I was able to move. That got me another declarative strike, this one aimed strategically higher.

"Enough!" I growled.

The pressure against my body and the...elements subsided. I couldn't name them rain or thunder because I was inside an enclosed building, and it just...wasn't...possible. Where was the thunder and lightning and the wind now?

Looking at Tempe and Dylan on the other side of the room in their dry clothing, one might believe it hadn't happened. That is, if one could explain the sodden rugs, beads of water on counters, and the smell of ozone rising from the inch of golf ball sized hail littering the floor among the actual golf balls.

SILENCE PREVAILED FOR SEVERAL LONG SECONDS, WITH Dylan and Tempe both looking like two battle ready warriors awaiting the next move from their opponent, me.

Well, I'd asked for it. Of course, having no idea in hell what I was asking, I couldn't help but think Tempe had taken her mad out on me. Why not McGuinness? The obvious answer was that I was the one with the learning curve, so I'd pulled the short straw. It struck me then that I should be running for the hills. Why wasn't I?

I removed my hat, tilted it and held it at arm's length, so the rest of the water could run off onto the already soaked floor. I pretended a calm I didn't feel having learned years ago never to let junior officers, perps or, in McGuinness' case, rivals sense any weakness. With him, it could be fatal. Swiping a hand over my face, I blew out a long breath and placed the hat back on my head. Crossing my arms I leaned against the wall.

"I guess you'd better start at the beginning."

Chapter 40

"You might want to sit down."

Tempe

The beginning? Which beginning? Jack *thought* he wanted to know everything, and yet he kept looking at me like I'd grown a fork in the middle of my forehead. That would probably have been more palatable than what he'd seen—or what was to come.

"Was that the extent of your 'gift'?" he asked. "A little mini shower when you get mad?" His eyes widened. "It was you! You... rained on Paige in the parking lot." He scratched his head. "I'm sounding crazy even to myself."

Dylan cut in, "For the details..." He looked Jack over, probably wondering how our sheriff who fancied all things normal had so easily accepted my bolt-throwing exhibition. "You might want to sit down."

I looked at the long stainless handle on the door and almost laughed out loud. We were about to sit down in the same chairs Jack had handcuffed me to just over a week ago. And the three letter sign on that restroom door held even more significance now.

"Let's start here." Dylan pointed at the wet foyer. "What do you remember about the day you found the body?"

Jack looked surprised. He'd obviously expected Dylan to go right to the information regarding my parents. But he didn't miss a stroke, reaching into his jacket for that little notebook. Finding it soaked, he merely blinked and returned it to his pocket.

"The victim was nude, the body temp was cooler than it should have been. He'd suffered blunt force trauma to the face and smelled like dead fish and rotten eggs."

"All evidence that you were in the presence of a Nucklavee," Dylan said, matter of factly.

"The con-man? According to whom?" Jack asked.

Dylan shrugged. "There's kind of an unwritten book on people of power."

"People of power?" Jack frowned at Dylan, then glanced at me. I shrugged. "What do you mean power?" he asked Dylan.

"Hold that question, S-Man." Dylan was enjoying himself a little too much. "We were talking about the Nucklavee. Nucklavees are mean creatures who can...slip into someone else's place. When they are about to die, they smell like rotting fish and sulfur. Unless you take the Nucklavee's head off, it can regenerate."

Jack blinked, mumbling, "Take... its... head off."

Dylan raised one black brow, pretending concern. "Are you okay, Jack? You're starting to sound like a parrot."

I sighed and punched him in the arm. "Dylan, get on with it." I wanted him to get to the end of the story, the part about Phoebe and Dutch. I wanted to know why Aurora had lied to me.

"You're telling me that the guy..." His eyes darted to me then back to Dylan. "...the victim Tempe found in the foyer wasn't..." his voice trailed off.

"Human." Dylan grinned, steepled his fingers casually, and leaned back in his chair, the front legs kicking up. "He wasn't a zombie, exactly, but he did come back to life—if that's what you want to call what they do—in the ME's autopsy room, and walk out. I assume someone fingerprinted him. That would verify what I've just told you."

Jack rubbed his chin, his eyes moving around the room as he remembered the details of the case, the night the body disappeared, and what the ME had told him about the fingerprints. I saw that suspicious look in his eye as he rocked back in his chair and settled his gaze on me. "Did you know?"

"Not until later. Well, I knew he was a variant of some kind," I said.

He made a face and rolled his eyes to the ceiling.

Dylan said, "Variant is a word for creatures like him who are..." He tilted his head and nodded at Jack. "We'll go with your description, bad 'people of power'."

Jack squeezed his eyes shut for a few seconds then opened them. "So who killed him?"

Dylan looked off. "We're not sure. The Ray who was working in the clubhouse was in fact one of the three bodyguards who arrived this year to keep an eye on the Pomeroys. Something happened to the real Ray; the Nucklavee probably killed him. The iron in his blood tells us he *handled* the amphora, so he *was* involved with what happened to River. My guess, he had a falling out with whoever is holding him."

"You're sure River's been kidnapped and didn't just leave like Phoebe and her other bodyguards?"

Jack was starting to catch up quickly, I thought, oddly proud. "You're handling this rather well, Jack," I said.

He frowned at me, a shocky look in his eyes. "Yeah, well, I liked you better when you weren't tossing electricity at my privates."

That hurt. And I noticed he hadn't called it lightning.

JACK

My mind was so far out in left field, I wasn't sure if I'd make it back to shortstop much less home base. Either they were both crazy, or my mind had gone AWOL. I couldn't believe I was still standing here having what seemed like a normal discussion about extremely un-normal events. *All part of the psychosis, Lang.*

"I'm going to pretend this is all an illusion, like an episode on Syfy." I squeezed my eyes shut hoping when I opened them we'd be standing in my office discussing the weather. *No, not the weather.* My eyes flew open. Tempe and the PI just waited, I assumed for a sign I wasn't going to run screaming from the clubhouse. I couldn't guarantee *anything* yet.

"I have a question."

"Just one?" Dylan smirked.

I ignored him. "I still don't get why this Nuckle vay wanted River's antique vase."

Tempe sighed. "I'm afraid... I misled you, Jack. The amphora isn't River's favorite collectible. He, um... lives in it." Without blinking she followed that with, "He's a genie."

My mouth fell open but no words came out. I listened for signs that I wasn't in some alternate universe. But phrases like "take its head off" and "zombie" and "not human" bounced around in that cotton, none of it taking hold. And now the "g" word. No.

"No." I gulped several breaths and threw my hands in the air. "Nope, can't do it. You two are nuts. You've given me no proof, shown me *nothing* but some special effects and magic tricks—"

Dylan looked at Tempe. She crooked an eyebrow. My eyes narrowed.

There was a sudden blur of movement, a deep growl, and then I was staring up—way up into the face of a shaggy wolf or *bear*-like creature with a long snout and massive head.

"Oh, f-f—wh... s-sa-sasquatch?"

"He's Finrir, Jack," someone said from outside the cotton as the beast moved toward me. Tempe?

Its *paw* came up, and I ducked away from the long claws as a mouth as big as a trashcan opened to reveal many, many razor edged teeth. I jerked back and slammed against the wall. Clubs rained down around me.

The thing was as big around as a grizzly and at least eight feet tall. It stalked me, opening its cavernous jaws. My feet slipped on the wet floor and I went down, my head bouncing off of something. All I saw were those slavering teeth and odd intelligent eyes before everything went black.

Chapter 41

He'll probably want to leave now

Tempe

"Dylan, look what you've done." I knelt at Jack's side and touched the knot on his head where he'd struck the corner of the display. "Was that really necessary?" I asked. "He'll probably want to leave and find a *really* normal place to live now. A town with only humans." I said, more to myself than Dylan.

I'd only recently realized how much Jack meant to me after learning to trust again. What would he do now that he'd seen a bit of Destiny's and my true nature? Would the relationship that had blossomed between us wither and die? Would he take Jordie and run as far as he could get from us?

Dylan shifted back into his human form. "Maybe not. He said he wanted answers. When he wakes up, we'll tell him everything he wants to know, if he's not too chicken to hear the whole truth." He stood with his hands at his sides, looking down at Jack's prone form. I didn't like Dylan's aura. It resembled a volcano in the middle of an eruption, fiery red and charcoal gray. "Tempe, if he's not on board, he's a problem."

I flinched at the threat behind Dylan's words and faced him. "You will not let anything happen to Jack." Unspoken was something he wasn't used to hearing from me, a personal threat. Where had the courage—or stupidity—to threaten this powerful Finrir come from? His head came up sharply and those dark man-lined eyes narrowed. For a few seconds, we locked eyes.

JACK

My head hurt like hell. I was trying to regain my wits when I heard voices. "Dylan, look what you've done." I watched through slitted lids as she stepped toward me. I concentrated on not moving as she knelt at my side. She laid her hand against the lump where the shelf hit me. "—that really necessary?" she said. "He'll probably want to leave and find a *really* normal place to live now. A town with only humans."

Most likely. It was all I could do not to flinch as Dylan shifted back into his Diablo form. "You know as well as I do a place like that doesn't exist." *What?* I'd hoped Destiny was an exception but apparently not. I'd handled a lot of surprises in my life but this... it was like something straight out of the movies. He hadn't tried to kill me though. *Yet.* My fingers eased over the grip on my gun that was hidden under my jacket, not that bullets could do any good against this beast.

He frowned down at Tempe. "He said he wanted answers."

"Uh, that was before..." She kept her hand on my skin. It was soothing but I didn't let on I was awake. Call it *recon* or avoidance, I didn't want to talk to her yet. I had a lot to process and there'd been so many lies. Though what would I have done if I'd known about the craziness, about *her*?

Dylan said, "When he wakes up, we'll tell him everything he wants to know, if he's not too chicken to hear the whole truth."

Chicken, huh? He stood over me, only his hands in my vision. "If he's not on board, Tempe, he's a problem." *Whoa.* Maybe this was where he killed me. I reminded myself that my status here had just changed along with my circumstances. I didn't doubt that Dylan could take me out. But then Tempe surprised me.

She drove to her feet and got in his face. "You will *not* let anything happen to Jack." A growl sounded in Dylan's throat and pressure stopped my ears up as if the barometer had taken a sudden dive. I got the feeling he wasn't used to being threatened and she'd done it—to protect me. For a few seconds, they had a stare-off and I halfway expected a bear/stormwitch mini-war to commence but then he backed off, verbally at least. She must have bigger bolts in her bag of weather tricks than I'd seen.

"There's no time to coddle him," Dylan said. "We have plans to make."

This guy just kept pissing me off. I may not understand what was going on exactly but coddling isn't in my DNA. The inspector and I were going to have a conversation.

"You heard me," Tempe said. Dylan seemed to realize Tempe was prepared to do battle over this, over me. "Besides," she continued, "Aurora said we'll need our mortal friends during the Para-moon. I have to believe Jack will come around, especially after he's had a chance to regroup and realize that

Paramortals are actually just like him—defenders of the weak —not monsters. Just... not mortal."

Not monsters, eh? What did she mean by Paramortal and what was a Para-Moon? The Destiny dictionary was obviously different than Webster's. Maybe I should get a copy. *Damn,* I was losing it. *Concentrate.*

Tempe sighed, "I still can't believe it—Dutch, alive. Why didn't he come out of hiding earlier to help me find River?" Her voice cracked when she said, "Every one of you were in on this."

"I'm sorry—"

"Sorry doesn't cut it, Dylan. I want to see Aurora. Of all people to lie to me." She stooped once more by my side. Her fingers touched my neck to check my pulse, then after hesitating briefly, she rose and walked to the door.

"I'll call you after I've talked to your sheriff," Dylan said.

The door opened and Tempe said, "You better ask him if he's my anything." Then she called out, "I'm going now, Jack," and the door slammed. A chuckle sounded above me and I pushed off the floor squeezing the "rain" out of my hair with my hands, slapping my sopping hat against my wet pants leg.

Dylan leaned against the opposite wall, unsurprised. "Playing possum?" He looked like Diablo now, just a man, albeit a dangerously intense one. I wondered if some of that aura of danger came from the *monster* inside him.

I didn't want to believe what I'd learned today. This town wasn't what I'd expected—understatement—but it was the first place Jordie and I had been able to even think of calling home since I'd left for the service. I couldn't accept or reject what I'd seen until I got the facts but I realized now there'd been things happening in Destiny for months, small things that hadn't made sense. I crossed my arms and looked at Dylan. "So, talk."

TEMPE

I was sure Jack had been pretending, his pulse halting under my fingertips when I touched him. He'd been listening to every word, waiting for me to leave, and while I was relieved, I understood why. He was horrified at seeing the freak I'd become in front of his eyes, not to mention Dylan's Finrir. But that was just the tip of the iceberg. *Zeus,* I hope I was right about him.

I got in my truck, but before I even started the engine, my phone rang. It was Dylan. "Jack's fine. I told him if he was just going to wallow, he might as well leave. We don't have time for his pity party."

I smiled. Knowing Jack and his pride, that had probably been the perfect thing to say. I heard him curse in the background. Dylan said in a low voice, "Don't worry, I'll make him see reason." He must have read my mind because he added, "I won't hurt him." Jack said something else and Dylan growled, "Unless he does something stupid."

I gave a heavy sigh as I cranked my truck. "What about Dutch?"

A pause, then Dylan said, "What about him?"

"When will I see him?" I couldn't keep the anger out of my voice.

"When he's ready, Tempest."

We'd see about that. I was going to get some answers, but

more importantly, we had to find River before his life ebbed away. Surely, my father could help.

At the end of the driveway, perched atop the clubhouse mailbox, sat Marty. I drew to a stop, my window level with the box, and rolled it down. As if he'd never had a problem with my truck—the little diva—he took hold of the top of the door and swung in, dropping lightly onto the seat.

I pushed the accelerator and drove out of the subdivision. The truck swayed and bucked, but Marty floated on air, unaffected by the truck's movement. He tilted his head back against the doorframe, studying me as I drove, an odd feeling let me tell you, being under the microscope by a thousand-year-old mini-demon. Okay, so he's not actually a demon, but with his pointy tail, skin like a wrinkled mushroom, bright amber eyes and sharp teeth, he'd pass for one.

"I've been remiss in my duties. The family would be very upset with me if I let something happen to you," he said.

I gawked. Since when had Marty become a member of the family? He hung around River a lot… "What?"

He cocked his head and the skin above his eye wrinkled. "I've been serving your family for a very long time, Tempest."

Now, all of a sudden, everyone was calling me by my full name. What was *up* with that? All I'd gotten from Dylan was that cryptic, *It's not necessary anymore*.

I pulled into the driveway of an abandoned house and parked, leaving the engine running. Exasperated, I turned to the Imp. "What are you getting at, Marty?"

He uncrossed his legs, climbed up onto the back of the seat, wrinkly butt in the air, and retrieved a package from the mail tub. Seating himself on the square box, he placed his hands on his knees and leaned forward. *Let's get serious,* his posture said. "You need me to make sure you stay out of trouble."

Hel*loo. Pot—kettle!* I couldn't dismiss what he said though. This ugly little creature might be a bit on the unpredictable side, but he did have resources. He'd already unearthed one clue, and his connection to River and Dutch had to be an asset.

His little wrinkled snout turned up. "I'm not ugly. That hurts my feelings, Tempest."

You can read my mind, I thought toward him with all my strength. Marty just tilted his head. I focused my eyes on his. He stared innocently back at me—a word that doesn't apply to Imps.

Shrugging, I said, "I guess we could give the *familiar* thing a try."

He stuck his arm out. A human sized hand morphed out of his pointy paw like some *elasto* cartoon character's. I guess that meant we had to shake on it. Then, flipping the hand over, he spat into the center.

Eeeuw! Imp spit. I looked Marty over closely. His loose flappy skin was the color and texture of wet Louisiana gumbo, giving him an unpalatable veneer. "I have two stipulations." His hand shrank back a bit.

I said, "This is only temporary, until we find River." He nodded. "And, you have to have a new look."

"What's wrong with my 'look'?" He posed, twisting back and forth, the other hand on his hip. Finally, he stilled. "What do you have in mind?"

"You decide, but it has to be something that doesn't call

attention to you or look odd to humans." I thought about it. "You could just be Rogue. Now git, I'm busy."

He poked his hand at me again. I looked down at that nasty looking wad in his palm, thought of River, and took the rubbery appendage in mine, only to find my hand captured and held as he met my eyes. "Everything is going to be okay, Tempest."

Tears sprang up, and I blinked. I wanted to smart off to this tiny unexpected source of compassion, but his sincere expression made that impossible. He seemed so sure. I closed my eyes allowing hope to rise up. I cleared my throat and asked, "How do you know?"

He squeezed my hand. "Trust me, Tempe. Over the centuries, we've been through tougher challenges than this. Against overwhelming odds, we've faced fae wars, Para-moons, and evil you can't imagine. You and River, even your lover, are but infants in our Paramortal world. There are always changes, but remember, much remains the same."

He winked and poofed away before I could ask what he meant by "even your lover". Who was he referring to? Dylan and I were no longer lovers and Jack... Maybe the Imp *could* see the future. I hoped so.

I continued downtown to Aurora Borealis. I had things to discuss with Aurora. Things like—why I'd been left in the dark for starters. Things like—why she had let me believe the worst about my parents. My heart leaked tears at the agony I'd felt over my father's death, at my mother's withdrawal. I was going to have to reconcile twenty years of pain, disappointment and false reality with the truth... that my parents had distanced themselves from us to keep us safe.

There were only four days left until the beginning of the full lunar moon cycle, when we might be better able to contact my brother's weakening force and according to Dylan, we had plans to make. What plans exactly?

Dylan was right about one thing. While Jack had come to Destiny looking for a *normal*, ordinary town to raise Jordie, someplace like Mayberry, I'd had a major case of denial, *pretending* to be normal.

But Destiny isn't Mayberry. It's more like... Middle Earth. I finally understood what Aurora had been telling me for weeks. My future and that of my family might depend on embracing my birthright and accepting the past.

Jack had a lot to accept as well. He'd told Dylan he wanted to know everything. He'd also promised me we'd find River. I can't help but wonder *if* he stays, and if we find River alive and well, will he still want to take me to the Mardi Gras ball?

Menori isn't holding her considerable breath 'cause there's a *lot* of *everything*.

THE PARAMORTALS ARE IN FOR A WILD RIDE ON THEIR journey to their destiny. Ready for next Paramortals book? Get Cry Me a River at your favorite ebookstore now.

But before you go. . .
Join Livia's spam-free newsletter for new releases, special offers, and exclusive giveaways.
Click here to JOIN
For more information:
www.liviaquinn.com

Livia moved from D.C. to Louisiana where the weather and culture of the region inspired her writing, including her storm faerie, Tempest, *and* her contemporary romance series. She's stored up fodder from her jobs as mail lady, salesperson, plant manager, business owner and professional singer to share with readers. Think of her as her characters' biographer! On the bayou, she is protected from the alligators and bears by her husband and feisty Pomeranian, Dusty.

The no drama way to follow me and get my updates is to visit my Livia Quinn Writes blog

If you'd like you may sign up for my occasional **newsletter** to get new release alerts and receive exclusive offers OR visit my blog to get updates and interact with me the no drama way..

As they say in one of my favorite places. . .

Caide Mile Failte', A hundred thousand welcomes.
Livia

Get in touch, stay up to date
Livia Quinn Writes
liviaquinn.com
liviaquinn@liviaquinn.com

Please Support our troops! It's not a cliché that we owe our veterans our very freedom. Many of our soldiers return with Post Traumatic Stress Syndrome (PTSD), Traumatic Brain Injury (TBI), debilitating injuries and illnesses. Trauma affects the *whole family*.

Veterans Crisis Line call 800-273-8255, press #1

Urgent: Vet needing shelter? Call 1(877) 4AID-VET

Suicide: If you or a loved one has contemplated suicide, call or go online to: http://www.stopsoldiersuicide.org

Women Veterans Health

Military Sexual Assault https://safehelpline.org 877-995-5247

Drug Rehab addiction help https://drugrehab.com

Mesothelioma Mesothelioma Navy "Most veterans suffering from a service-related asbestos disease never bother to file a VA Disability Compensation and/or Pension Claim; either because they don't think they are eligible, or simply assume the VA will deny them. "

Volunteer or Donate to help a vet

American Legion (help applying for benefits)

Vet to Vet assistance (a fellow vet helps you w/ info) https://nvf.org/veterans-request-assistance/